Financial Mafia, Broken Trust.

Tommy O'Neill

Chapter 1

Sean scanned the meeting room; it was an unusual gathering of senior staff members. Landec the head of Marketing, or colouring in department as Sean liked to think of them, was projecting the usual noisy and ebullient character, so familiar from the many smug corporate video messages that Sean had forced himself to sit through. Sean couldn't help thinking that being so permanently cheerful and full of energy must be very exhausting.

Mr personality was currently waving his arms around in an animated fashion in front of the very concerned looking Heads of Risk and Operations. Of more interest to Sean was a group centred on the hulking and very tanned form of the Finance Director Trevor Reid.

Mr Reid as he liked to be called by the staff, had come to the bank with a wealth of investment banking experience in eastern Europe and America. Or at least that's what his profile on the corporate website said. Sean couldn't help thinking that a lot of this experience might have been confined to long corporate lunches, if the ample bulk straining the buttons of his expensively tailored Saville row suit was anything to go by.

The Finance Director was currently talking in a low rumble with a tall, slim, hatchet faced individual dressed in a well fitted, very expensive looking grey suit. The final character in the physically mismatched trio was the diminutive figure of Magda Harte the Chair of the bank's board.

From the few occasions that he had met her, Sean had formed the opinion that she was a kind individual not particularly concerned with details. Strange considering the position she held within the bank. The previous chairman had been a much more challenging individual who had asked many difficult questions of both executive directors and senior management.

The small, elegant woman dressed in her petite expensively tailored double breasted suit had made her fortune in the IT industry. She had held board level positions in several multinational IT service organisations, before becoming chief executive of an IT security company with offices in Florida and London. Her appointment to the board had made complete sense, after all modern finance depended on its IT systems.

In the far corner of the room the balding and overweight figure of the IT director Richard Head, was wilting under the withering gaze of the scowling figure of John Covington. An impressive figure slightly shorter than Sean's six-foot two, dressed in a smart looking prince of wales suit, he was CEO for Credit Finance Bank the company for which they all worked. A man with a dominating presence and from what Sean could tell, a man totally ruthless in pursuit of his plans for the bank.

John Covington had joined the bank two years previously as chief executive and where once the pace of change in the bank had been positively glacial, he had put the banks change process into overdrive.

With a breath-taking turn of speed, he had replaced the Finance Director with the current incumbent. Removed the IT Director and replaced her with Richard Head and been instrumental in persuading the board to appoint Magda Harte as the new Chair of the board.

Having put his stamp on the senior team within the bank, he had encouraged the board to look to new markets. This resulted in the bank opening several branches in Eastern Europe, in Prague, Krakow and Bratislava. Much to Sean's amazement this had been a tremendous success with a major influx of new accounts coming from all three branches.

Sean was intrigued by the current situation on a couple of fronts. Firstly, why were senior members of the board for the bank standing in meeting room one in the bank's primary data centre in Sussex. These people would have been more at home meeting comfortably in the board room in their shiny glass tower in docklands.

The current location an anonymous, windowless, low rise building, situated in the middle of an industrial estate, was a building designed to protect the equipment that the bank had housed in it. A lot of money had been spent on cooling, power protection and security. Virtually nothing had been spent on the human comforts that the banks management would be used to.

Secondly why on earth had he been invited to this meeting. Sean had been involved in meetings with many of the individuals present this morning. His contribution to those meetings tended to be ten minute pre-planned presentations on the work being done to secure the banks systems.

Today's invitation, or rather the demand to attend that he had received, had come totally out of the blue. He had been amazed when 60 minutes earlier whilst having breakfast, he had received an email directly from the CEO's mobile requesting his presence at this meeting.

He had absolutely no idea why the chief executive, thought it necessary to have him at this meeting. Sean had attended many meetings at which John Covington had been present. At those meeting the CEO had done a sterling job of reminding Sean of his insignificance, making no attempt to make even the most minor of conversations. This lack of regard rankled with Sean who valued the contributions made by every member of his own team and made sure they knew it, whatever their level.

After leaving University in Belfast with a good degree in Information Technology Sean had joined the RAF as a Communications and Electronics Engineering officer. His commanding officer, or "God" as he was affectionately referred to, knew the first names of all the men and women under his command. He made sure that everyone no matter how low their rank, knew how important they were to the smooth running of operations.

Sean had joined the bank five years previously and had found a similar people centric environment under the previous chief executive, Bill Weaver. With the changes at the top since the appointment of John Covington, things had taken a turn for the worse.

Office politics which had previously been a thing of myth and legend, was now riff within the bank. People worked to their own agendas and were only too happy to dump on anyone who got in their way. What had previously been a fantastic working environment had become a toxic swamp of internecine conflict.

So it was that Sean felt uncomfortable and out of place amongst this expensively suited and booted collection of the great and the good. In his current attire of Chinos and open necked printed floral shirt he had a feeling that reminded him of his sister's wedding.

His sister Aisling had got married in Cornwall to her husband Jack. The wedding service had taken place at the Lusty Glaze beach wedding venue. It had been a glorious sunny day and the men had all worn Hawaiian shirts and flipflops and the women had all been comfortably dressed in floating summer dresses. Sean had turned up in his usual blue 3-piece wedding suit and brown brogues.

To say it had been an uncomfortable day was something of an understatement. Sean had been sweating like a Russian athlete at a blood test due to his high-quality woollen three piece. All the other guests seem to think that his attire signified that he had some sort of control over the running of the venue. This resulted in him having to listen to complaints about slow bar service from the more inebriated wedding guests, or comments on the beautiful location from doe eyed would-be brides. At least today, Sean was under rather than over dressed, but that didn't make him feel any more comfortable about the current situation.

As the last few stragglers entered the room and the door closed with a satisfying metallic clunk curiosity replaced Sean's discomfort. There was one notable absence from the current gathering. Ceri Gillis the Chief information security officer for the bank, she was nowhere to be seen or heard.

When it came to all things Security Ceri was the in Sean's opinion a bit of a show pony. She would canter through meetings skimming the surface of the work being carried out by Sean and his team. Shinning a bright rose-tinted search light on what a wonderful job she did in keeping the unruly Security team on the straight and narrow.

So why was she not here amongst this current collection of the great and the good? Sean didn't have long to ponder that question as the John Covington moved to the head of the meeting table and asked if everyone could please take a seat.

Chapter 2

Sean watched as the chief executive drew himself to his full height and cleared his throat before starting to speak in a firm and authoritative voice.

'Ladies and gentlemen, you have all been invited here today because of some very disturbing news that the board became aware of yesterday evening.'

He then surveyed the room, to assure himself that everyone's attention was focussed on him, before continuing.

'We believe that Ceri Gillis the banks Chief Information Security Officer has been kidnapped.'

He paused to allow the sounds of consternation which had just broken out around the table to subside before continuing.

He informed the now mesmerized audience that the bank had been contacted the previous afternoon by the metropolitan police. Apparently, they had been called to a disturbance at Ceri's home by a concerned neighbour.

The same neighbour had told the police where Ceri worked and so on finding the house had been ransacked and no sign of Ceri, they had contacted the bank.

Lowering his voice and speaking softly John Covington continued with the story.

'At that point we had no reason to resume that anything more sinister than a burglary had occurred. We informed the police that Ceri was on leave and provided them with her mobile telephone number.'

As Sean looked around the table, he could see that John Covington had the rapt attention of everyone apart from Trevor Reid, Magda Harte and the hatchet faced individual, who's name he didn't yet know.

They were obviously well aware of what everyone else was now hearing for the first time. The two men were sitting back in their chairs, arms behind their heads, with eyes focussed on what must have been completely fascinating ceiling tiles. Magda Harte by contrast sat bolt upright with hands tightly clenched and a look of deep concern on her face as she tried to burn a hole through the table with her eyes.

'Unfortunately, yesterday evening things took a rather more sinister turn, when I received an email from a group calling itself Hidden Cobra. This email stated that they had taken Ceri hostage and demanded the payment of ten thousand bitcoin for her release.'

The chief executive paused, before continuing in a more dramatic voice.

 'For those of you who don't know 10000 bitcoins at the current rate is equivalent to two hundred million pounds sterling.'

There was a gasp of incredulity, followed by complete silence around the table as the audience absorbed the news. There were a lot of startled looks on the faces of some, in Sean's view they had just realised that their choice of career in banking had suddenly turned them into potential kidnap victims.

As John Covington took his seat, Magda Harte looked around the concerned faces at the table and spoke softly in a conciliatory tone.

'You can all be assured that the board will make all reasonable efforts to resolve this situation and ensure the safety of Ms Gillis.'

Sean took his job as IT Security Manager very seriously and was well aware of cybercrime groups targeting financial services. So, the name Hidden Cobra, or the Lazarus group as they were more popularly known rang a very loud bell. But there were two things with the current situation that Sean found troubling and difficult to get his head around.

Firstly, Sean simply couldn't understand how on earth the kidnappers thought that the odious Ceri Gillis could be worth the amount of money they were demanding.

Secondly and more importantly, it didn't make sense that a gang who successfully operated behind the curtain of anonymity provided by the internet, had suddenly decided that physical kidnap and ransom was a good idea.

This same group had brought the NHS in the UK to its knees with its WannaCry ransomware attack. They had also successfully stolen hundreds of millions of dollars from banks mainly in South America and Asia using carefully crafted malware.

As far as Sean could remember, the last idiots to think that kidnapping bank staff for financial gain was a good idea, were Republican terrorists in Northern Ireland. Sean had been at University in Belfast back in 2004 when a Tiger Kidnap had netted the IRA £26 Million from the Belfast headquarters of a local Bank.

So why had Hidden Cobra, a group with a high level of sophistication and Cyber capability decided to revert to the crude techniques used by non-Cyber capable terrorists and criminal gangs of the early 2000s, it really didn't make any sense. Sean was still pondering this conundrum when the chief executive beckoned for Mr Hatchet face, as Sean now thought of him, to come forward.

The individual who now had the focus of all their attention introduced himself in heavily accented English as Alek Kulkas. He and his team would be working with the banks crisis management team to try and resolve the current situation and ensure Ceri's safe return. His company, Andriane security specialised in Kidnap, extortion, and cyber threat response. He had apparently flown in early that morning at the request of the bank's board.

The name touched a chord with Sean, but he couldn't quite recall where he had heard it, but he did know Andriane weren't one of the key players providing such services.

'Does anyone have any questions?'

As Sean expected Landec practically fell over himself in his attempt to ingratiate himself with this new obviously important individual. Puffing out his sparrow like chest and flashing his most obsequious smile he asked Alek if there was anything that his team in Sales and Marketing could do to help by way of dealing with any press questions.

'We really need to control the message Mr Kulkas, my team and I can get our PR people working on this now.'

The look that Alek Kulkas flashed at Landec could have curdled milk whilst the barbed verbal response must have sent a shiver down the unfortunate Landec's spine.

'There will be absolutely no contact with any press, and what is said in this room stays in this room.'

In a thunderous voice designed to cow rather than persuade John Covington added.

'If there is even a sniff that anyone has passed on any information to anyone outside those gathered here today, that person's employment will be terminated immediately on the grounds of gross misconduct.'

Alek Kulkas looked around the room before continuing to speak in a very measured fashion.

'We believe this kidnapping is not about the value of the individual, rather it is about the value of what that individual can provide access to. The request for 200 million pounds worth of bitcoin is a sum too ludicrous to make any sense. We believe this request is a smoke screen to hide their true intentions.

We believe that the kidnappers may have attempted, or may currently be attempting to use Ms Gillis's access to systems. As well as her knowledge about the banks security infrastructure to gain access to the banks systems and data.'

Well thought Sean, at least we have someone here who seems to know what he is talking about. However, Sean couldn't help but feel that a more established organisation might have been better placed to successfully resolve the current situation.

Sean's thoughts were once again trampled on by the loud and confident voice of John Covington.

'Our IT team have been very proactive in disabling all of Ms Gillis's access to the bank's systems. In addition, Richard's team have reset all system management passwords that she may have had access to.

Does anyone have any questions?'

The first person to speak was Mary King the Head of Risk and Compliance, who in her usual deferential tone asked.

'So John with our friends from Andraine Security Services are we hoping to negotiate Ceri's release and pay a smaller amount, or are we involving the police in order to secure her release through other means?'

John Covington's jaw clenched, and he practically ground his teeth as he responded to the obviously very stupid question he had just been asked.

'200 million pounds is a amount which would have a detrimental impact on the finances of this institution Mary, and would result in us breaching our minimum capital requirements with the regulators. It would also create issues with the credit rating agencies if this situation were to become known.

What I do know is that we won't be paying two hundred million for Ceri's release. Also, Mary if you had been listening to Alek, you would understand that the request for money is a smoke screen.

This is about gaining access to systems and data. As for the other part of your question I think that is probably a question for Alek to answer.'

Looking directly at Mary King with his cold blue eyes, Alek Kulkas spoke slowly and precisely pausing between each sentence.

'At this point we have no idea of where Ms Gillis currently is.

We have some indication of who the kidnappers may be, but we are totally in the dark as to which jurisdiction they may currently be residing in.

We have advised the board with what we believe is the best course of action and they have agreed not to involve the police at this juncture.

With this group there has always been a suggestion of collusion with the North Korean state. If this is indeed the case, Ms Gillis could already be in the Korean Peninsula.

If that is the situation there is little your local law enforcement can do, and until such times as we know with any certainty that Ms Gillis is in the UK, we will not be involving the police.'

Mary King had a firm belief in rules, regulations, and the banks regulators. She wasn't going to be diverted from the pursuit of all that she believed in, by some hatchet-faced blow in. With her eyes flashing with indignation and steel in her voice, she looked directly at her chief executive challenging him not to answer her next question.

'Surely the board has informed the Prudential Regulation Authority and the Financial Conduct Authority that a senior manager in the bank has been kidnapped and that the banks security may be compromised.'

John Covington glared at the animated Head of Risk and Compliance.

'Ms King the board have chosen at this time to bide our time and review the situation before involving either the police, or our regulators. This is a situation which is still evolving, and we may be able to resolve it satisfactorily without involving others.

It would have a negative impact on the bank for anyone to feel the banks finances are not secure due to either a ransom demand, or a cyber security incident.'

Sean could see Mary King's face and neck take on a more russet hue and heard her voice raise an octave as she responded with obvious indignation to the chief executive.

'John surely our duty of care to a member of staff, and our duty to the financial regulator is such that we should be informing both the police and the regulators of the current situation?'

Struggling to keep the annoyance from his voice, the chief executive obviously not used to such insolent dissent, snapped his response.

'Ms King as an officer of this bank, your first duty is to the organisation and not to the regulators, or police. They will be told what they need to know when they need to know it.

In relation to Ms Gillis, the reputation and security of this organisation is much more important than the fate of any one individual. Now does anyone else have any further questions?'

After the turbulent interaction between John Covington and Mary King, Magda Harte spoke trying to diffuse what she sensed had become a tense situation. Looking directly at Mary King, but obviously addressing the entire room, she spoke in a soft friendly tone.

'Mary, we share your feelings about the current situation, but you have to understand that the bank has enlisted the help of people who are experts in dealing with these matters.

We need to listen to their advice and not overreact, that way we have the best chance of resolving matters satisfactorily.'

Well thought Sean this is a complete Clusterfuck, whilst he had no love for Ceri Gillis, he could see that the board were quite happy to sacrifice her on the altar of corporate expediency. She was no longer an individual needing their help, rather they now had a situation that needed to be resolved satisfactorily.

Sean's sense of justice and fairness and a morality that had been imbued by two loving parents back home in Northern Ireland and time served in the RAF were screaming in anger. As one of his nerdier IT friends would have said, 'His Spidey senses were tingling', something stank, and much as he disliked Landec, he knew it wasn't his breath.

Chapter 3

With no further questions forth coming and everyone suitably cowed by the chief executive's outburst, everyone made their way to the conference room. The crisis team would reside there until such time as the situation had resolved itself.

Everyone that is, except for Sean and Richard Head the IT Director, they were both asked to remain behind.

Well thought Sean perhaps I'm now about to find out why I'm here.

There were now just five people in the meeting room, John Covington, Trevor Reid, Alek Kulkas, Richard Head and Sean.

After a few seconds the chief executive cleared his throat before turning and staring directly at Sean.

'No doubt you are wondering why you have been called here today. '

Sean nodded in affirmation and waited for the head of the bank to enlighten him.

John Covington went into full charm offensive mode as in an oily voice he explained the reason for Sean's presence.

'You are here because Richard believes that you are an individual who is uniquely placed to help us protect the Bank from the threat that is posed by this potential Cyber incident.

He tells me that you have an encyclopaedic knowledge of the security infrastructure that we have in place within the bank. That means you are best placed to help marshal our cyber defences in the absence of Ms Gillis. Do you share Richard's view?'

Sean's response was direct and to the point.

'No sir I am not in agreement with Mr Head.

 I would say that I am best placed to marshal our cyber defences full stop.

Ceri is the Chief Information Security Officer and as such her role is more about oversight, management and presenting a view to the board.

She has nothing more than a general knowledge of how the assets we have in place actually work.'

The ghost of a smile passed across John Covington's face as Sean finished talking, whilst the look on the IT Director's face suggested that he had just had an oversized carrot inserted forcibly between his buttocks.

Buttocks which Sean was sure were so tightly clenched due to the current situation, that if he got up from his seat, his large overly upholstered backside would probably take a bite out of the unfortunate chair.

'Well young man you certainly aren't lacking in confidence', said the deep voice of Trevor Reid the Finance Director.

 'I just hope it is justified or we may have to find ourselves a new IT Security Manager.'

Alek Kulkas who had been staring intently at Sean, stood and a gravelly voice asked if Sean had any observations to make.

Taking a deep breath Sean looked at each of the other four individuals in the room before he spoke.

'I agree with you Mr Kulkas the 200 million pound ransom is complete bullshit.

It makes absolutely no sense for an organisation who have stolen hundreds of millions of dollars from dozens of banks all over the world to resort to Kidnap.

They have Cyber-attack tools that they have used successfully on many occasions without having to resort to kidnap.'

John Covington leant across the table with a look of concern in his eyes.

'What are you saying Sean?

Are you suggesting that Ceri hasn't in fact been kidnapped?'

Sean tried to keep the exasperation from his voice as he replied.

'No, what I'm saying is that this situation doesn't make any logical sense. I would question whether the email you received actually came from Hidden Cobra. There is always the possibility that it came from another source, a lone wolf attacker pretending to be something they aren't.

Has anyone reviewed the email? we could paste the email header information into a trace email analyser tool and see if we can identify the sender, or even the source IP address.'

Alek Kulkas, quickly responded to Sean's question and equally quickly cut-off any possibility that Sean would be involved in any analysis of the email.

'Thank you, Sean, but my team have already carried out that analysis. We have confirmed that the email came from Ceri's corporate email account via her mobile phone.

It is our opinion that Ceri may be under some form of duress. As far as we can tell the mobile is currently turned off and untraceable. However, the last time it was used it had been connected to a mobile cell tower close to Heathrow airport.

So, Sean, if as we suspect Ceri is no longer in the country, and as we have indicated earlier, her access to the corporate network has been disabled can you see any way in which she could be used to gain access to the banks systems or data.'

'The simple answer to that is yes, as Richard knows from the report presented to the board each month by Ceri we have a number of unpatched vulnerabilities in the software we use in the bank.

A number of these vulnerabilities could potentially be used to gain access to a computer from a remote location and use that computer to access systems and data on the network.

Ceri's knowledge of the organisation and individuals within the bank could be used to craft targeted emails carrying malware which could take advantage of any number of these vulnerabilities.
'

A pompous Richard Head, with the shadow of a sneer on his jowly face seeing an insult where none had been intended, stood, puffed out his chest and placed his hands on his stocky waist before interrupting Sean.

'Yes Sean, but as you very well know, we do have tools in place and several different layers of defence to mitigate the risks from these known vulnerabilities.'

Sean paused, tempted to give the arrogant IT director a verbal slap, before continuing to calmly enlighten the select group with his opinion.

'I agree Richard, these things certainly mitigate those risks to a large extent. The other potential attack vector is a direct attack through our firewalls, but the risk of this shouldn't have changed.

If Ceri's still had access to our online password store then I would say that we would have a serious security issue on our hands, but as Richard has confirmed that all her access has been disabled then this shouldn't be an issue. '

As he finished speaking Sean could see the colour drain from Richard's face.

The words that stumbled from the obviously agitated Richard Head came out in a squeak.

'We overlooked her password locker user, it's not on the corporate network and we haven't disabled it.'

Richard's face was transfixed by a look of horror.

Sean's Spidey senses that had been tingling previously literally started screaming as Richard finished speaking.

A blind man on a galloping horse, on a foggy night could have seen that Richard was in the middle of a major panic attack. Alek

Kulkas had none of those impediments, so realised immediately that things had taken a sudden turn for the worse. Turning to Sean Alek Kulkas raised his eyebrows quizzically and asked. 'How big is the problem, Sean?'

Sean's brain whirled as he thought through all the permutations of what Richard has just let slip. Maintaining an unruffled demeanour, which in no way matched the turmoil going on inside his head, Sean responded as calmly as he could.

'Well Mr Kulkas all members of the IT and Information security teams have access to an online password locker. This locker holds all the credentials needed to gain access to core systems, including firewalls and other network equipment.

The password vault as we like to call it holds the IT crown jewels. Ceri has the highest level of privilege within the information security team. So potentially the bank could be in the middle of a major data breach.'

As the significance of what Sean had just said hit home, the carefully curated look of arrogant self confidence that John Covington wore like a shield began to slip. In wide eyed panic, with words practically tripping over each other as they tumbled out of his mouth he turned his attention to Alek Kulkas.

'Alek is something wrong? do we have a problem? Are we in trouble?'

Sean had never seen John Covington project anything but confidence, right now he couldn't help but think he was looking at a very frightened man. As he stared at his anxious chief executive Sean puzzled over John Covington's use of the word "we", if he meant the bank why hadn't he said, "is the bank in trouble?". Sean wondered if perhaps the use of the word "we" indicated a more personal predicament involving John Covington and Alek Kulkas.

Alek seemed completely unphased when he responded to the panicking chief executive, but then he wasn't the one who would be explaining a data breach to the regulators rationalised Sean.

'Yes, John we could have a problem, in fact we could be confronted with a very challenging situation. Right now, Ceri Gillis's credentials could be providing access via the bank's firewalls to all data and systems within the bank.

Is my reading of the situation correct Sean?'

Sean saw no reason to be anything other than direct, a straight question deserved a straight answer.

'Yes Mr Kulkas, that is correct, changing the system passwords will have been a complete waste of time. By using Ceri's access to the password vault the kidnappers will have access to the new passwords.

Potentially they will be able to gain access to all systems and steal the banks data with impunity. Furthermore, with access to those passwords they could potentially change key passwords and lock us out of systems entirely.'

'What can we do?' whispered an ashen faced John Covington.

'Yes Sean, what can we do?' rumbled a slightly less tanned looking Trevor Reid.

Sean as a general rule liked to have all the facts before making a decision, but right now, he knew swift and decisive action was required, if they were going to save the bank from a potentially major data breach.

With everyone else in the room totally out of their depth and looking to him for an answer Sean knew what had to be done. So, speaking in a confident tone that he hoped masked his own concerns he answered their question.

'We can join the rest of the crisis team and discuss all possible actions and potential risks, before agreeing what we do next.

Or we could save ourselves a week of debate and potentially the bank by doing the one thing that could stop all external access in its tracks.

It will have an impact on customer service and the banks access to external services such as email and web services, but this impact will be short lived and should be resolved within 24 hours, the choice is yours Mr Covington. '

'I agree with Sean, we need to act quickly,' squeaked an extremely nervous and somewhat deflated looking Richard Head.

Sean outlined his remarkably simple plan to protect the bank, briefly outlining the issues that would arise as a result of following his plan.

John Covington's demeanour, having fed off the confidence projected by Sean and with safety in sight returned to its usual brash arrogance.

'I don't care about the issues, just do it now! I am the chief executive of this organisation and will take full responsibility. '

Trevor Reid nodded his assent to John Covington's instruction.

Sean couldn't help but think that John Covington would be only too happy to take the credit if things went the way he hoped. He was equally sure that it would be he who would feel the full weight of responsibility if things went wrong. Nonetheless he knew what needed to be done and never one to shirk his responsibility that is exactly what he intended to do.

Chapter 4

After quickly jogging to the IT and Security management office in the Data Centre, Sean did two things, firstly he prayed to the great god of IT Security, that the people who had taken Ceri had not had the foresight to change the passwords on the firewall.

Secondly, he logged onto both the primary and secondary firewall clusters in both data centres and disabled all external interfaces, bringing down all internet connections for the bank.

Finally, he checked on his mobile phone that he could no longer access the Banks online banking site and checked that he was unable to access the internet through his desktop PC. Satisfied with the absence of internet traffic in or out of the bank he sauntered to the conference room to pass on the good news.

All eyes turned as Sean walked into the conference room, including those of Richard Head who was busy on his mobile talking to the IT service desk manager. Sean had warned that pulling the plug as he had so succinctly put it, would result in a very sudden communications blackout. The shit storm that Sean had predicted had no doubt started to make its presence felt, with services used by the bank's staff and customers already being adversely impacted.

Sean's seemingly casual entrance to the room did not go unnoticed by an agitated looking John Covington. His demeanour immediately became more relaxed and confident as he began ushering people towards their seats.

'OK ladies and Gentlemen if we could all take a seat, Sean and Richard will update us as to the current situation.'

Sean took a seat to the right of the chief executive, in the middle of the conference table, whilst Richard sat immediately to the John Covington's left. Sean could feel all eyes focus in their direction.

Sean had been brought up in the wide-open spaces of county Tyrone, a country boy who didn't normally feel comfortable as the centre of attention. Man, and boy he had spent many happy hours walking and cycling in the wet boggy uplands that made up the Sperrin Mountains near the family home.

Many a time he had ventured out on an excursion, in conditions that were only fit for ducks and submarines. As his dad had often reminded him, "what doesn't kill you makes you stronger." Those same tough excursions had helped build the disciplined, confident man who now prepared to inform the bank's upper echelons of the current situation.

Today the excitement of being involved in a high-profile security incident, gave him the adrenaline rush that he had felt during some of his hairier youthful excursions. This coupled with the obvious trust being placed in him, helped overcome any discomfort he felt in the current situation.

Sean cleared his throat; he most definitely didn't want what he was about to say to come out with a squeak.

'Ladies and gentlemen, we believe that with the actions that have just been taken, we have halted a potential cyber breach in its tracks. Now that the incident has been contained there is currently no external avenue by which the bank's systems or data can be compromised.

However, before we can complete the recovery phase there is further work to be done. We first need to ensure that our suspected attackers have not contaminated our infrastructure with malware, which could be used to exfiltrate data once we have restored internet access.

 If we find anything sinister on our network, we need to eradicate it. Only then, can we set about recovering those systems that are currently unavailable.'

Sean then nodded towards Richard indicating that he had the floor.

'Ladies and gentlemen, I am sorry to say that this unfortunate incident and the actions that we have had to take, have resulted in a number of key systems being currently unavailable or severely compromised.'

Richard continued droning on in a monotonous monotone listing system after system that had been adversely affected.

Sean couldn't help but think that Richard was certainly milking his moment of glory. Sean wondered if any of those present knew what any of the systems being listed by Richard actually did.

Sean's impatience grew as Richard continued with his monologue.

'External email services are currently down, however staff can still communicate internally via email.'

Sean supposed the email would at least mean that head office staff didn't need to resort to using paper cups on the end of pieces of string to communicate. Though in his opinion it wouldn't do any harm for staff relations if people had to get up from their desk and actually speak face to face with their colleagues.

Sean's mind sank further into boredom as Richard droned on.

'The bank's online banking service is down and inaccessible to customers, however the banks main website which is hosted externally is still available.'

Well, that's great thought Sean, at least the customers will have access to the telephone numbers and email addresses that aren't currently working.

Eventually after 15, mind numbingly, excruciating minutes, Richard finally sat down. As Richard took the weight off his feet, John Covington got to his and in a commanding voice addressed the room.

'Thank you, Richard, for that scintillating summary of our currently less than ideal situation. We believe that it may take up to 24 hours to resolve the current situation and restore services. Services which our customers and the media are soon going to start noticing are not available.

It is now 10 am and I would expect that sometime in the next two hours we will have to speak to the Regulators and be prepared to field questions from the media.'

Looking directly at Landec John Covington continued with his command performance.

'We need to control this situation and formulate the message that we want to pass to both our regulators and interested parties in the media.

Our message needs to give the impression that there is nothing to see here and that we have had a simple IT systems failure. Under no circumstances should the words cyber incident, ransom or kidnap form any part of the message at this stage.'

Landec nodded his thanks to the chief executive, before puffing up his pigeon chest and surveying those around the table to make sure they were aware of just how important he had just become.

Over the next two hours the assembled crisis team came up with a message that indicated that the current difficulties at the bank had been caused by the failure of a network upgrade, which had resulted in the banks internet connectivity being compromised. The statement also confirmed that customer data and security of systems had not been compromised and the IT team were in the process of rolling back the faulty upgrade.

By twelve noon this message had been relayed to the Regulators by the chief executive and Finance director using their mobile phones. This being the only reliable form of external communication available to them. The same message had also been published on the banks externally hosted Web site by Landec's colouring in department.

Whilst the creative members of the crisis team had been coming up with the usual stock message of IT failure. Sean and Richard had been working with their teams to perform a plethora of tasks.

The IT infrastructure team used their network security scanner to run a scan on the entire bank infrastructure, scanning all attached PCs and servers for any indication of compromise. The antivirus and web filtering management consoles were also reviewed for any potential issues. All of their investigations drew a blank.

Sean and his security team spent hours reviewing the logs on both internal and external firewalls. The logs for the Web application firewalls used by the banks online solution were also reviewed in some detail. Nothing was found to indicate any compromise of the Banks network.

It surprised Sean to find that the logs on the internal firewalls only contained three days' worth of data, but he put this down to there being an ongoing project to implement new rules on these devices.

As part of this ongoing security enhancement project, the bank had implemented an awfully expensive Security Information and Event management solution which gathered information from multiple sources on the banks network. With limited experience on this solution within the bank's IT and security teams this system was being reviewed by a supposed expert who had accompanied Alek Kulkas to the meeting.

He was called Olek, a tall, blond Ukrainian, with a small scar on his right cheek and an excellent grasp of English. Sean noticed that he was probably a big fan of body art as there were the suggestion of tattoos peeking above the neckline of his shirt and just below the cuffs of his shirt sleeves.

Olek's grasp of English unfortunately wasn't matched by his understanding of the security systems that he had been tasked with helping Sean to review. Sean couldn't help noticing the laboured fashion in which Olek navigated a system which to him, appeared to have quite an intuitive interface. It seemed strange to Sean that a supposed expert should make such hard work of traversing the system. On occasion Sean found himself directing Olek on what to do next, on a system which he himself had an extremely limited knowledge of.

When Sean had been offered Olek's help, he had presumed that it would help speed up the investigation process. After all he came from an organisation that apparently specialised in the area of cyber threat response, kidnap, and extortion. Sean had incorrectly presumed, that people from Olek's neck of the woods would be experts in this field, considering how many cyber-attacks originated from that part of the planet.

Sean came to the conclusion, that perhaps the fledging Andraine security company's security expertise lay in the areas of kidnap and extortion. If Olek was anything to go by, their capabilities in the area of cyber threat response left a lot to be desired.

By eight in the evening many hours of pain staking analysis and tests had been run. Everything indicated that there were no issues on the banks network and there had been no attempt to access the network through the bank's external firewalls. Ceri's password locker had been deleted, but again the indications were that the last time this had been accessed, was more than two days previously and during business hours. Sean found the lack of evidence of any breach both perplexing and confusing, given how the day had started.

At eight thirty both Sean and Richard returned to the conference room and indicated that the Banks network and the systems and Data that it contained were secure. This being the case they asked for approval to reinstate the internet connections in both data centres to restore the lost services.

The crisis team readily agreed and once the internet connections had been restored, tests were run to confirm that all IT services were functioning normally. At ten thirty in the evening with all systems functioning as expected an email was sent to the banks supervisors at the Financial Conduct Authority and Prudential Regulation Authority to confirm that the situation had been resolved.

Whilst everyone else was in a buoyant mode over the successful conclusion to the days activity Sean felt uneasy. He couldn't understand why, in the ten hours it had taken to restore secure services to the bank, there had been no further communication from Hidden Cobra in relation to Ceri.

This could have simply been down to external email being unavailable, but tests run since restoration had confirmed that all queued emails had been processed by the banks email server, so the chief executive should have received any emails by now.

Sean had little time to think about this however. With the immediate threat of an IT security issue having been alleviated John Covington thanked Sean for his input during the day and told him that his services were currently not required by the Crisis management team. Sean gratefully accepted the order to take himself home, but keep his mobile turned on in case he needed to be called back to the conference room.

Chapter 5

Sean sat in the cosseting sports seat of his Audi S4 Avant quattro estate thinking about everything that had happened that day. As he ran through the sequence of events in his head, something just didn't sit right.

He realised that he felt sorry for Ceri Gillis, a woman who he had always considered to be a ball busting waste of space. Someone who had been more concerned with proving her importance to the board, than with the accuracy of the information that she used to prove her worth.

But what concerned him more, was the fact that nothing which had transpired today made any sense. Why would Hidden Cobra change their modus operandi and get involved in kidnap. Why on earth had they not used the information that they would obviously have had access to, to completely screw the bank to the wall.

Instead, a gang known for its ruthless pursuit of its goals had given the bank a heads up by sending that email. An email which come to think of it no one else apart from the John Covington and Alek Kulkas had seen. As someone in the business of dealing with a problem logically, nothing about today sat well with Sean.

 Sitting here thinking about it wasn't going to change anything thought Sean as he glanced at his Citizen Skyhawk watch and he had a 40-mile drive ahead of him to get to Sevenoaks and pick-up Otto, his dog. Sean had no doubt Otto would be quite happy sitting on the couch in his neighbour Mary's house being treated like a lord, but Sean still felt that today had been a bit of an imposition on Mary and would take a brief detour on the way home to pick up some flowers and a box of Mary's favourite chocolates by way of thanks.

Otto was the reason that Sean currently drove the Audi estate. Sean's previous car had been a Nissan 370Z coupe. He had loved that car, but when Otto came along it just hadn't been practical to try and squeeze a 100 lb German Shepherd dog into a boot that would barely hold a set of golf clubs.

Sean found the current situation rather ironic. He had bought his substantial three bedroom detached house in Sevenoaks five years ago using inheritance from his late father's estate. For almost three of those five years he had shared his home with Anna Szabo his Slovakian girlfriend. Anna had bought him the Skyhawk watch, she had seen him admiring it in the window of a jewellers on a trip into London one weekend. He had arrived home from work the following week and found the box sitting on his pillow.

He smiled as he thought back to how he and Anna had got together. They had met in the middle of a dance floor at the bank's Christmas party. Sean, well on his way to being the drunkest man at the party, had been making an absolute tit of himself. He had been pogoing around the dance floor with long arms and legs flailing in a manner that suggested all four limbs were dancing to completely different beats.

The totally uncoordinated and massively drunk Sean had collided with Anna. As he spun round to apologise for his clumsiness, he was confronted by two of the most startingly blue eyes he had ever seen. The tall beauty with long brown hair and gorgeous blue eyes graciously accepted Sean's hastily mumbled apology, before turning to join the circle of giggling girls that she had been dancing with.

Sean had left the dance floor and gone straight to the bar and ordered two pints of water. An hour later, a fully hydrated and more in control of his faculties' Sean had bumped into Anna again. This time their coming together had been deliberate and as their eyes met over the evening buffet table, he gave her the full force of what he hoped was an irresistible boyish grin.

The fact that she hadn't immediately taken to her heels gave him the opening to introduce himself as 'Sean from IT', and much to his surprise he found that she already knew his name. The girls she had been dancing with had given her a complete run down on him. Sean cringed when Anna innocently asked him what a skirt chaser was.

Sean quickly realised that she wasn't so innocent when she grinned mischievously at his obvious discomfort and was delighted when she invited him back to her table to eat his food. They spent the last three hours of the party glued to each other, both on and off the dance floor. Sean's dancing didn't get much better when he was sober, but Anna didn't seem to mind.

When the evening ended, they had both exchanged numbers before going their separate ways. The rest of the weekend past for Sean in that haze that comes with a hangover. He lay around his house eating junk food and feeling sorry for himself. When he returned to work the following Monday, he barely had time to get his backside into his seat when his phone rang.

It had been Anna, and she had been straight and to the point inviting him out for dinner at his favourite Italian restaurant the following evening. That first date had been amazing, they had laughed and talked like old friends, totally enjoying each other's company. They had been so engrossed in each other that they hadn't noticed that they were the last people in the restaurant. That was until an apologetic head waiter appeared at their table holding both their coats, as a not too subtle indication that it was time to leave.

Sean had driven Anna home and just before she got out of the car she had turned and kissed him passionately on the lips. The butterflies in Sean's stomach had obviously been taking gymnastics lessons as they all performed triple somersaults. Sean drove home in a happy daze and rang Anna as soon as he reached his house, asking her out for drinks the following evening.

They saw each other every night for the next week before Sean asked Anna if she would like to come to his house for Christmas dinner. He was hosting a few friends and would like it she could be there too.

Anna had accepted and Sean had surpassed himself with the meal that he prepared for everyone. The craic had been fantastic, and Sean's friends had given each other knowing looks as they watched how well Sean and Anna had got on. Eventually everyone had gone home leaving just Sean and Anna alone in the house. They had made love for their first time, that night, on the rug in front of the dying embers of the Christmas day fire.

 After that there was no doubt, they were an item and six months later Anna had moved in with Sean and they had lived in blissful happiness until as Sean put it "He fucked up."

Anna had been good to him and for him, but three months ago he and Anna had parted ways. Sean still couldn't understand how he had let it happen.

He had surprised Anna with an early spring break in Paris. Sean had pushed the boat out and booked them a room in a wonderful five-star hotel in the centre of the city, with a view of the Eiffel Tower. Anna had been delighted by the surprise and they had spent three glorious days exploring Paris and just enjoying each other's company.

Anna had been excited when on the final night of their trip Sean had suggested that they eat out in an expensive restaurant close to the spectacular tower that they saw from their hotel bedroom window each morning.

They had dined Al Fresco, their table heated by a gently hissing gas burner. The setting sun had cast a romantic haze over the cobbled streets, while the sounds of the city were nothing more than a low hum in the back ground.

As he sat across from Anna Sean had felt his heart swell with joy. Anna was beautiful certainly, but there was more to her than that. Highly intelligent she could read him like a book and keep him constantly on his toes. What he loved most about her was her independence, when he was with her he felt free. She was perfection.

The romance had hung heavily in the air that night, Anna had spent the evening rubbing her foot up the side of his leg as they drank prosecco and waited for their food to arrive. They had talked incessantly about their adventures of the previous three days and laughed uproariously when Anna reminded Sean of how he had accidently abandoned her on the Metro. Sean had stepped off the train to facilitate the exit of a rather infirm old lady. Sean had been horrified when the carriage doors had closed in his face leaving him standing on the platform as Anna disappeared into the distance.

Service had been slow, but they didn't care, and had ordered a second bottle of prosecco before their steaks had arrived. Being from Northern Ireland, Sean had a bit of a reputation for having hollow legs and a liver of steel. In Sean's mind he was an Olympic standard drinker, able to drink anything and everything with little ill effect.

Everything except prosecco as it turned out. He could feel his head buzzing and from the way Anna's eyes were glazed seductively he knew she was on her way too. The night was going well, perfect. Sean couldn't help but smile as Anna attacked the mass of meat on her plate.

The sound of a child screaming in protest tore through the romantic ambience as a family with a small child arrived at the restaurant and were ushered to a table close to Sean and Anna.

'This is no place for kids' in Sean's view, and based on the stony glares they were getting from the other diners Sean was sure his opinion was widely shared. But not it would appear by Anna, as he turned to comment on the unwelcome intrusion, he was surprised to see her practically melting as the family were seated.

The little blonde-haired bundle of joy was still screaming and had tears in his eyes.

'Clearly wants a McDonald's,' Sean thought.

Anna had leaned forward in her seat and cooed 'Bonjour' to the upset boy.

He had looked at her with the kind of disdained bewilderment only a child could get away with. The boy's mother at least had the good grace in Sean's opinion to be embarrassed by the disturbance their child was causing and whispered 'We are so sorry, ' with a broad scouse accent.

'He's been fussing about all day; he doesn't mean to be rude. Say hello to the nice lady Adam.'

 As she spoke his name the mother jabbed a finger in his back and almost like a switch went off the boy stood beaming up at Anna. Anna fussed about the boy while Sean continued eating his steak.

'Isn't he the cutest, Sean? ' He looked up to see Anna, the child and his two parents looking at him expectantly. Practically choking on his steak Sean coughed 'Cute wee lad.'

With the family now firmly settled and being attended to by a waiter Anna turned her attention back to Sean.

'Oh Sean he is so perfect! Imagine what a little Sean of our own would look like.'

Sean took a deep swig of his prosecco as he shook his head.

'Fingers crossed there won't be a little Sean for a very, very long time.'

Anna's head tilted enquiringly, and her soft voice took on a harder edge, 'What do you mean for a very, very long time?'

Sean, too far into the second bottle of prosecco didn't catch the warning signs and just let the words spill out without thinking.

'Look, it's not that I don't like kids. It's just I don't like the idea of giving up the freedom we both have. Look at us we're in Paris! If we had a child, do you think we could have gotten here?

For the first five maybe six years of that kids life we'd be unable to go anywhere. We'd spend our time cleaning up poo, pee, vomit and feeding the thing. We would be lucky to get any sleep!'

Anna was getting more agitated as Sean spoke and a look of disappointment and sorrow clouded her beautiful face as Sean continued.

'I'd sooner get a dog than have a baby. At least a dog would be easier to train and be a bit more fun. It would probably cost a lot less too.'

Sean had laughed, pouring himself another glass of prosecco, and topping up Anna's glass.

There were tears in Anna's eyes as she looked up and her voice caught in her throat as she whispered. 'When you invited me to Paris I thought this was it, I thought we were going to... ' she trailed off.

Through the fog of alcohol Sean had sensed that all was not well and reached out across the table for Anna's hand.

Rejecting his attempt at conciliation she placed both hands in her lap and looking Sean straight in the eye and asked, 'Do you ever see yourself wanting a family?'

He could see it now, by God, he had really painted himself into a corner. She was upset and he was starting to panic. Sean rambled on about how he 'didn't want to overpopulate an already overpopulated planet' and realised how dumb he sounded.

Each time he had tried to rescue the situation he had just dug the hole deeper. Anna had cupped her chin in her hands and watched emotionless as Sean tripped up on his words again and again.

She put her hand up to stop him and gave him one final chance to redeem the situation, in a low voice she asked him 'Do you ever see yourself wanting to start a family?'

Sean's lacklustre response of 'I think so,' had elicited a look of despair from Anna. The rest of the meal had been passed in silence with neither of them having the heart to reopen the discussion.

The journey home the next day had been painful, Sean had tried to make light of the situation, while Anna just felt his attempts to lighten the mood trivialised a serious question that needed to be answered.

Sean loved Anna intensely but had a stubborn streak a mile wide. Eventually after three days in a fit of ill-judged pique he gave Anna an answer. He told her that he enjoyed the lack of responsibility of not having kids to worry about and didn't see why they should tie themselves down just yet.

Anna had been upset at what she saw as his lack of commitment to their relationship and had immediately applied for a transfer to work in the bank's Bratislava branch. She said it would be close to home and close to people who loved her and would give him time to sort out the priorities in his life. Sean had compounded his initial mistake, by making the more massive mistake of calling her bluff and found that she hadn't been bluffing.

Chapter 6

After Anna had left Sean had realised that living alone was not something that he enjoyed, but neither did he enjoy admitting that perhaps he had been on the wrong side of the disagreement that had resulted in Anna leaving.

Noel one of Sean's friends had decided that Sean just needed in his words, 'to get back on the horse'. So he had organised a night out for himself and Sean with two of his close female friends. Noel had a firmly held belief, that if you couldn't be with the one you loved, then love the one you're with.

Noel was sure all Sean needed was a bit of close female companionship. However, after a couple of drinks Sean had realised that the evening Noel had planned just wasn't for him, his heart very much still belonged to Anna. So making his excuses he left and went home to an empty house.

Sean was lonely, but another woman was out of the question. In his head no one could replace Anna, unfortunately he was also bone headed and couldn't yet bring himself to ring Anna and apologise. So when the opportunity arose to acquire a well-trained German Shepherd to keep him company Sean had jumped at the chance.

Another of Sean's mate's Andy, a dog handler with the metropolitan police, had been training Otto to be a service dog. Unfortunately for Otto, whilst he had all the attributes required, strong, extremely alert, disciplined, and obedient, he had a fear of the dark.

Whilst out on a shout with Andy one night he had point blank refused to chase a pair of thieving scrotes across a dark field after they had abandoned the car they had stolen and embedded in a hedge. Otto's fear of the dark had proven to be extremely limiting for his career as a police dog.

Sean had taken up the chance of adopting Otto without a second thought about what it would mean for his life. Having to get rid of his beloved Nissan had been an early indication that owning a big well-trained dog was not necessarily going to be as easy of he had imagined.

Now here he was driving that big family estate that he had never wanted, or seen the need for, with all the responsibility of looking after a 100lb boisterous child, who needed walked, fed, and brought to the toilet.

Sean had spent a small fortune, having a new pen and dog run built in his large back garden, in preparation for the big day when Otto would arrive. Money that he soon realised had been wasted.

On his first night, after Sean had put Otto to bed, within five minutes a heart wrenching howling had emanated from Otto's pen. Sean had tried everything, bribery with food, taking him for a walk through the deserted lanes around his house and so long as Sean was with him Otto had been quiet. However as soon as Sean put Otto back in his pen and walked back to the house the noise began again.

Eventually for the good of his relationships with his neighbours and the need to get some sleep, Sean had given in and brought Otto into the house to sleep. Exhausted by the ordeal Sean had felt completely powerless to stop Otto as he followed him up the stairs to sleep at the foot of his bed and there he had slept ever since.

It was close to midnight by the time Sean and Otto got home that night. Sean had picked up Otto from Mary's house and thanked her profusely for being so understanding, presenting her with the flowers and chocolates that he had picked up in a motorway service station on the M23 as a token of his gratitude.

Sean awoke, conscious of a low rumbling coming from the foot of his bed, Otto snoring was a completely new experience for him. Then he realised it wasn't snoring, it was a low guttural growl. Reaching his left arm across to the bedside table he touched his mobile phone the display lit up to show 2:30am.

A tired Sean whispered to his hairy and obviously upset roommate.

'Otto, what's the matter boy?'

Hearing Sean's voice Otto momentarily quietened down, then Sean heard what sounded like a creak on the stair and the rumbling coming from Otto took on a deeper resonance. There is someone in the house! the realisation hit Sean like a sledgehammer. Obviously, the kidnappers had failed to use Ceri to get what they wanted and had identified him as the next best option.

Sean's heart was pounding so hard in his chest that he was sure the intruder or intruders were bound to think he must be playing bongos in his bedroom. With adrenaline now coursing through his veins, Sean threw back the covers in preparation for the pending confrontation with his unwanted visitors.

Before he could even set a foot to the floor, his bedroom door opened wide to reveal a short, shadowy figure standing in the doorway. The undersized assassin, highlighted by the light coming through the landing window behind him, appeared to be dressed all in black, including a ski mask.

Before Sean could say a word three things happened. The figure took a single step into the room, the low rumbling that had been coming from Otto became a full-throated growl and the mound of fur and teeth that had been lying by the foot of Sean's bed launched itself across the two metres or so that separated the bed from the door.

Sean heard a loud grunt as the speeding Otto connected with the mystery figure followed by a loud and somewhat high-pitched scream as Ottos impressive dental work connected with the family jewel area of Sean's erstwhile assailant. The scream soon turned into a full-blooded roar of agony, as Otto shook his head from side to side in an attempt to disengage the offending items from the body to which they were attached.

Sean leapt naked out of bed to go to the assistance of Otto and put some light on the subject by switching on the bedroom light. He had half expected his room to be overrun by a horde of reinforcements, coming to the aid of the unfortunate individual, currently losing out in a wrestling match over the ownership of his wedding tackle.

Instead, much to his surprise he heard a familiar voice say, 'Good morning Sean could you possibly ask your dog to give my friend Martin his toys back, we have a lot that we need to talk about.'

As he stood there naked, bathed in the unflattering light of a 100Watt bulb, he could see the figure of a fully clothed Ceri Gillis standing on the landing illuminated by the same light that clearly showed his current state of undress.

Quickly recovering his composure and equally quickly covering his exposure by donning the dressing gown hanging on the back of his bedroom door. Sean gave Otto the command to release his captive.

Now unattached to Otto the unfortunate Martin curled himself into the foetal position, cupped his badly abused nether regions in both hands and lay on the floor sucking in huge gulps of air, as Sean headed into his ensuite bathroom with an armful of clothes.

Sean wasn't a great believer in the old saying 'Clothes maketh the man', but he certainly believed that a lack of clothing could maketh a man very uncomfortable.

After two minutes Sean emerged back into the bedroom fully clothed and buoyed by the fact that his house hadn't actually been invaded by a gang of inscrutable Cyber criminals. He called Otto to his side and silently stood and contemplated the two intruders who had disturbed his sleep.

Ceri broke the silence first, 'Perhaps we could head down to the Kitchen and talk over a coffee, and perhaps you would be kind enough to provide Martin with a bag of frozen peas to try and help the bruising.'

Sean nodded and then looked at Martin, 'look on the bright side buddy, if their sore their probably still attached and what doesn't kill you makes you stronger as my old da would have said.'

With that Sean and Otto stepped over Martin, walked past Ceri and headed downstairs to the kitchen.

For the life of him Sean couldn't figure why Ceri and her vertically challenged friend were in his house in the wee small hours of the morning. It wasn't as if he and Ceri were friends.

Truth be told Sean had no liking for the woman, she epitomised everything that he currently hated about the bank's management culture. He had a cold hatred for the dehumanising corporate culture that she stood for.

When she had first joined the bank less than a year ago, she had made it her mission to get someone fired for a data security breach within the first two weeks of her tenure. The poor unfortunate who had been sacrificed on the altar of better data security, had committed the cardinal sin of accidentally including an external recipient on an email meant for internal viewers only.

The fact that the information had been purely product analysis information meant for the board and had not been in any way sensitive, hadn't been accepted as a mitigation.

Sean had been aware of the situation and had tried to reason with Ceri on the individual's behalf to no effect. He had then spoken to Landec the sacrificial lamb's boss and tried to get him to see reason. Finally, he had written an email to John Covington the chief executive, an email that had gone completely unacknowledged.

All his protestations came to nothing, no one in management gave a rats ass about someone who had worked for the bank for the last ten years. Ceri Gillis had an example to set and important board information was perfect as far as she was concerned. The marketing assistant was gone in days and the fear of god was put into all staff. Ceri had made her point, data security was important and by definition as guardian of all thing's security, so was she.

So why was the princess of darkness here in his house? what was going on? Yesterday in work had been a weird day to say the least, right now Sean felt like things had just taken a surreal turn for the worst.

Chapter 7

In the kitchen Sean filled the kettle, rummaged in the freezer for a bag of frozen peas, which he sat on the kitchen counter. He then sat himself down in the easy chair with Otto lying at his feet, leaving a small couch for his visitors.

'OK Ceri so what exactly do we have to talk about? I have to say the only thing that surprised me more than finding you on my landing in the dead of night, is the fact that you have managed to escape from your North Korean kidnappers.'

Sean could see from the puzzled look that appeared on Ceri's face that she didn't have a clue what he was talking about. Remembering his mother's advice, "you should listen twice as much as you speak", he thought it would be best to keep quiet and let Ceri do all the talking for now.

As the kettle had finished boiling Sean stood up and set about making the coffee. He handed Ceri her coffee, before providing Martin with both a coffee and the pack of frozen peas wrapped up in a tea towel, before retaking his seat.

With everyone sitting comfortably, Ceri began to relate the events of the previous two days which had resulted in her turning up at Sean's house.

As part of the new IT Security enhancement program that the bank was implementing Ceri had been working with the external consultants who had been implementing new zero trust rules on the internal firewalls and configuring the new security information and event management system.

Sean mused that Ceri's version of working with probably meant sitting and watching, as opposed to doing any actual work.

Ceri continued by explaining that as part of the project the internal firewalls had been put into learning mode. This allowed the normal flow of traffic to be identified and taken into account when creating new rules to block abnormal traffic. Whilst reviewing the firewall logs with a consultant called Jim, they had noticed some odd-looking traffic patterns.

'What exactly do you mean by looked odd' interrupted Sean, 'surely this was only normal internal bank network traffic and if it wasn't it should have generated an alert on the external firewalls.'

'Yes, it was all normal internal traffic and none of it would have raised an alert on the firewalls or the Security Information and Event management system, but to the human eye it looked strange' replied Ceri.

'Jim noticed that a lot of database traffic had been coming from three specific servers outside of the normal hours of business. The servers were in Prague, Krakow, and Bratislava.

I assumed this was simply due to the one-hour time difference between London and Eastern Europe. However, Jim explained that this traffic wasn't early morning network traffic, rather it was traffic coming in after eight pm GMT or nine pm local time.'

A tired Sean found nothing interesting in anything that Ceri had just, so he struggled to sound anything other than bad tempered and bored when he spoke.

'OK Ceri, so we have people working late in our Eastern European branches displaying an admirable work ethic. That's no reason for you to be sitting in my kitchen at three in the morning depriving me and Otto of our beauty sleep.'

There was a hint of desperation in Ceri's voice as she responded to Sean's total lack of interest.

'Sean please hear me out. I thought off all the things that you are thinking now. If it was as simple as that I wouldn't be sitting here now, on what I have to say is a very uncomfortable sofa'

Sean gave a non-committal grunt and waved his hand to indicate that Ceri should continue.

'I had Jim monitor the traffic and this allowed us to identify a number of accounts that had either been created or transacted upon during the unusual time widow.

Using the details that we had gathered I then logged onto the bank's core account management system to view the accounts and transactions. The accounts looked pretty ordinary; however the account creation and transaction time stamps were all recorded as being between 11am and 1pm. That didn't make any sense, I had sat there while the monitoring took place, between eight pm and ten pm in the evening.'

Sean was quietly impressed that Ceri had been working late, it wasn't something that he would have given her credit for. Resisting the urge to interrupt, Sean allowed Ceri to continue her story.

'I gathered screen shots from each of the sample accounts, copied these to a secure area on the network. I also copied everything onto a thumb drive so I could analyse the information at home.

I then made the mistake of telephoning John Covington requesting a meeting to discuss what I had found.'

Sean could contain his cynicism no longer. 'Obviously, you thought this was going to be another feather in your cap, another chance to show how wonderful you were.'

Ceri glared at Sean before continuing.

'At the meeting with John I explained what Jim and I had found on the firewalls and showed copies of the screen shots that I had taken. I then explained the anomaly with the date time stamps.

 He thanked me for the information and said that he would have a word with the Operations Director about why the three branches might be opening accounts outside of normal business hours.

He suggested that due to the popularity of the accounts on offer there may well be service issues which were requiring staff to work late.

I wasn't completely happy with John's view. So, after leaving his office I asked Jim to carry out further monitoring that evening to verify that the unusual traffic patterns were still occurring.'

Sean couldn't stop himself from once again sniping at Ceri, not that he tried very hard, his dislike of the woman gave his words a sharp edge.

'Well Ceri having worked with you; I don't need much imagination to know that it would be very upsetting for princess Ceri to be ignored. I'm with John Covington, the only problem I can see right now is the fact that I am going to have bags under my eyes in the morning from lack of sleep.'

Martin who had been sitting quietly nursing his battered wedding tackle had had enough of Sean's comments. Quivering with outrage Martin jumped to his feet, pointing aggressively at Sean with his right hand.

'I'm not sure what your problem with Ceri is, and to be honest I don't really care. I have known this woman for more than ten years and if she says something smells bad then believe me it stinks to high heaven.

She isn't the highly strung princess that you seem to view her as. Me and her have been through shit together that would turn your hair grey. She isn't spinning you some yarn; she is as honest as the day is long. So, do yourself a favour, stop being a dick and listen to what she has to say.'

Otto wasn't amused by the display of aggression towards his master. His hackles were raised, and his lips drawn back to expose his impressive array of teeth as a low rumble emanated from his throat.

Sean placed his hand on Otto's back and leaned in to whispered calming words, into ears that were laid flat against the big canines skull. His actions were mirrored by Ceri, who placed a calming hand on Martin's arm and gently tugged him back to his seat.

Ceri's voice took on a conciliatory tone.

'Sean, I know you don't like me, but could you please put your personal feelings to one side and listen to the rest of what I have to say. It's important that you understand what has happened and don't let your views on me cloud your judgement.'

After a brief pause to allow her request to register, Ceri continued with her story. She explained that she had gone back to her office to review the sample accounts and to her surprise found that withdrawals had been made, which brought the account balances down to virtually zero.

Looking at the withdrawals she could see that all funds had actually been sent by internal transfer to two different accounts both of which were holding around one million euros and both of which seemed to have received internal transfers from multiple other accounts.

She had taken more screen shots of those accounts and again copied these to a secure area on the network and to her thumb drive. She had then emailed John Covington to request a further meeting, before heading home for the night.

The next morning when she came into work, she went to speak to Jim. She couldn't find him at his desk so had assumed that because he had been working late he would be in later.

Once back at her desk she had received a phone call from John Covington asking her to come to his office. There she had been introduced to Alek Kulkas and been told that his team would be taking over the investigation into the anomalies she had found. Ceri had then been asked to pass over all the information that she had gathered to Alek's team.

Finally the chief executive had told Ceri that Alek would be reporting directly to him on this matter and It might be a good idea for her to take a few days leave whilst the investigation progressed.

By the time Ceri had walked back to her desk she found that her access to the banks systems had been disabled. By the time she had got to her car she realised that her mobile no longer worked. Indeed, it appeared that it had been remote wiped so that nothing relating to the bank, emails or applications were accessible on the device, so she had turned it off.

'That I have to admit is strange,' said a now more interested Sean.

'Alek Kulkas was introduced to me this morning as someone who had been brought in to investigate your kidnap, yet here you are sitting in front of me. Contrary to what you have just told me, there was no indication given that he had been investigating anything else.'

Once again Sean got a puzzled look from both Ceri and Martin. An obviously angry Ceri, straining to keep her voice level leaned forward and spoke calmly to a now puzzled Sean.

'I met Alek Kulkas two days ago, he was brought in to investigate a potential IT security incident. An incident which the banks Chief Information Security Officer has been excluded from.

Since meeting with him, I have lost all access to the banks systems and been excluded from doing my job. Not only that, but other things have happened which have made me think that I am in danger.'

Sean had to admit that if there was any truth in what Ceri was saying, then something strange was definitely going on, but he remained to be convinced. There were still a whole lot of questions that still needed to be answered.

What were the other things that she was referring to that made her fear for her safety?

Why were they here and how on earth had they been able to get into his house?

Sean vocalised his second question, indicating that with the locks he had installed their presence indicated skills that he wouldn't expect of a completely honest person.

Sean's question had elicited a grin of obvious pride from Martin, who was only to happy to respond.

'It wasn't Ceri who picked the lock on your back door Sean, it was me, but yes I have to admit they are good, it took me a good ten minutes to get us inside.'

Sean turned and looked at Martin, 'So what you're saying Martin is that Ceri is completely honest, she just keeps bad company.'

Ceri interrupted the exchange between the two men, with an unmistakeable tension in her voice.

'Sean I'm frightened, yes I was worried about my job, but other things have happened that have made me more worried about my safety.

I've known Martin a long time and we have had a professional relationship and friendship that goes back many years. After what happened in work I needed advice from someone I could trust, so I went to Martin.'

'Sorry Ceri, but the person you trust most in this world is a burglar, that doesn't say much for the rest of your friends.'

Martin brindled at Sean's insult to his professional abilities.

'Sean I'm not a burglar, lock picking is just one of the many things I do well. Perhaps if you would get your head out of your ass and put aside your obvious dislike for Ceri you might understand what Ceri is trying to tell you.

I've known Ceri a long time and I know she can be a pain in the arse, but I've never known her to be over dramatic. You haven't heard the rest of her story, because if you had you wouldn't be such an arsehole right now.'

Sitting back in his chair Sean looked at the diminutive figure of Martin with some admiration. Despite the discomfort of the injury, to which he was still assiduously applying the frozen peas and unperturbed by Sean's physical presence. Martin had shown a loyalty to his friend which Sean couldn't help but admire.

Perhaps he did need to wind his neck in and listen with a more open mind to what Ceri said, she was obviously frightened and that did seem unlike her.

'OK Martin, as you have asked so nicely, I will listen, but before Ceri continues with her story, perhaps you could both explain just how you fit into Ceri's life and why I should trust your opinion.'

Chapter 8

Ceri adjusted herself in the obviously uncomfortable sofa. Sean smiled, Anna had chosen it for its aesthetics rather than its practicality and Sean's two unexpected house guests were now suffering for Anna's fashion sense.

'Sean, Martin and I have known each other for more than ten years. We both started out as ethical hackers for the National Cyber Security Centre in London.

After several years we both realised that our skills were very saleable in the private sector and we pooled our skills to setup a small Security consultancy business.

We advised clients in both the private and public sectors within the UK and Europe, on how to protect digital assets, physical property, and how to ensure personal safety.

My role had been to meet with clients, discuss concerns and maximise the services we could sell and thus the income from any particular contract.

Martin wasn't particularly good in front of customers, as you have seen he can be quite blunt. Diplomacy is not one of the skills that he possesses, so he focussed on testing the cyber and physical security of our clients to destruction. '

Sean sensed an almost childlike excitement in Martin's voice as he took up the story.

'Yes, my role was to prove that clients were not as secure as their security teams had led them to believe. I would deface websites in small ways to prove it could be done. I would breech firewalls and leave files on servers to show that systems could be accessed by unauthorised individuals.

The thing I loved doing the most, was gaining access to premises to test the physical security controls that were used to protect a building and its contents.

It never ceased to amaze me; how otherwise intelligent people would quite happily accept a total stranger tail gating them through a door, which they had just opened with a security pass. Peoples innate sense of good manners and a fear of offending is something which time and time again has a negative impact on security.'

Ceri explained that once Martin had completed his work, she would then provide a risk assessment report detailing weak areas in computer security, personnel risks, and building access.

Sean couldn't help but feel quietly impressed by Ceri's life before she had joined the bank, and he wasn't afraid to admit, just a little bit jealous. It sounded like an interesting job and going by what he saw the bank spend on consultancy it could have been quite lucrative.

Ceri explained that the work had indeed been interesting and financially rewarding for them both. Right up until the point that Martin got a little bit carried away with one particular job.

They had been awarded a contract which involved assessing the security of police stations in London. The Home Secretary had ordered that a security assessment be carried out by all police services in England and Ceri and Martin had been successful in winning a small part of the resulting business.

However, quite early into the job they came up against a Chief Inspector who had been totally against the assessment, seeing it as a pointless exercise, "this is a police stations, who is going to break into a police station".

The result of his reticence was that his senior team did their best to block the work being done by Martin and Ceri.

Martin had taken this as a personal challenge and without telling Ceri exactly what he planned to do, had taken things just a little bit further that was advisable for a professional security consultancy business.

Ceri had obviously touched something of a raw nerve as Martin felt the need to interrupt her story.

'Hell Ceri, they were in total denial and I thought a short sharp shock would give them a kick up the pants.'

Ceri smiled indulgently, a smile which certainly softened some of those hard edges that Sean had attributed to her.

'Yes in order to provide the necessary kick up the pants Martin had accessed the police services web site and configured the content management system to replace the pictures of all senior officers on the site with those of farmyard animals at 11am the following morning. The Chief inspector's picture was to be replaced with a picture of a rather large fat pig.'

Sean could see the smiles on both Ceri and Martin's facing broaden as Ceri continued in a more exuberant tone.

'Never one to rest on his laurels, Martin then accessed the logon server for the police service and setup a timed batch job to change the logon message to say, "Hello Lard ass, shouldn't you be out chasing criminals instead of playing on a computer!", from 11am that same morning.

Finally, his piece de resistance had been to break into police headquarters, walk into the Chief Inspectors office and borrow his police issue laptop.

When Ceri and Martin had turned up at 10am for their planned meeting with the Chief Inspector to review the observed security issues, things had started fairly amiably.

However, the atmosphere had soon turned frosty when Martin produced the Chief Inspectors laptop out of his brief case and explained how he had acquired it.

Sticking to the script, Ceri had then pointed out that Martin had been able to easily gain access to both the police services website and its internal systems. The Chief Inspector had expressed his doubts at Martin's achievement. Ceri had informed him that as was normal practice Martin had left evidence of his successful incursion.

When the Chief Inspector took a call during the meeting his complexion had taken on a very ruddy glow. At this point Ceri had started to get the feeling that perhaps things weren't as normal as she had imagined.

As the Chief Inspector's telephone conversation continued, she could see his complexion becoming a much deeper shade of red and she couldn't help but notice a large vein start to throb at the side of his forehead.

During the entire telephone conversation Martin simply sat beside Ceri saying nothing, maintaining a stupid grin on his face.

When the telephone conversation ended, they both found the office had suddenly become very claustrophobic as four police constables entered, with the purpose of escorting them from the station.

To say that the Chief constable had been apoplectic with rage was an understatement. By the time he had finished calling into question their professional abilities and the marital status of both sets of parents, Ceri was sure that steam had been whistling out of his ears.

Sean could see a glimmer of what Martin's grin must have been like that day, as Ceri told the story, but there was possibly a little sadness too, when Ceri explained that job had been the last for their firm.

News of Martin's exuberant but unprofessional work soon got around and no self-respecting organisation was going to hire them. So they had to do the unthinkable and find jobs working for someone else.

Ceri using her abilities as a saleswoman who knew the theory of security intimately had been able to talk herself into the high-profile job of Chief Information Security Officer for Credit Finance Bank. Ever mindful of the lessons learnt by the fiasco which had destroyed their company she became a stickler for the rules.

Martin on the other hand had struggled to find a regular job and decided to stick to what he knew and continued to provide hacking and security assessment services, ethical and sometimes not so ethical to those willing to pay him.

Sean was impressed, realising that perhaps there was more to Ceri Gillis, than he had given her credit for.

Chapter 9

Sean's demeanour had changed considerably when in a more positive tone of voice he asked Ceri to continue.

'OK Ceri you now have my full attention, please continue with your story about the bank.'

Ceri drained the remainder of her coffee, before starting to speak, this time to a more attentive Sean.

Ceri explained that she had worked in a security role long enough to know that the situation that she had found herself in wasn't normal. So after briefly returning home she decided to visit Martin in East Hampstead and ask his opinion.

They had discussed the situation long into the night over a bottle or two of wine, without coming to any concrete conclusions. Due to the late hour and Ceri having consumed more than her fair share of the wine, she stayed the night in Martin's guest bedroom.

When she returned to her house the following morning, she found two police cars parked outside in the street and scene of crime officers wandering in and out through her front door. Not knowing what she might be walking into, she drove past her home and straight back to East Hampstead.

Ceri explained that she had a state-of-the-art security system in place at her home paid for by the bank. Normally she could access the system through her mobile phone. However, without a working mobile she needed Martin's specialised skills to allow her to review the footage from the system.

Using Ceri's credentials Martin had been able to log onto the web backup copy of the security system footage. Looking at the video from the external cameras they saw two tall individuals wearing ski masks and nondescript black clothing enter through the rear door of Ceri's home.

'That seems to be quite a common occurrence at the moment,' said Sean. 'It might have been easier and a lot less painful if you had knocked on my front door and asked to come in for a chat.'

Martin laughed readily acknowledging that he had come of worst in his unexpected battle with Otto.

'Once you hear what Ceri is going to tell you, you'll understand why we didn't come to your front door.'

Ceri nodded her thanks to Martin before continuing in an obviously angry voice.

'The video from the internal Cameras in the living room and Kitchen showed the two men looking very thoroughly for something, and not taking a lot of care of my property, as they ripped drawers from units and threw open doors.

After five minutes of tearing the house apart they were disturbed by Mrs Jones from next door. We observed her through the footage from the doorbell cam ringing the bell.

She had obviously heard all the noise and had come to investigate.

The video feed then showed the two men leaving through the back door, carrying my laptop bag, which they had found during their search.

As they left the house, they removed their ski masks giving the security camera a great view of the back of their heads.'

Ceri and Martin both felt that the two intruders were familiar with the security system that the bank had installed in Ceri's home. They obviously were aware of the placement of the cameras that the bank had installed.

However, the intruders hadn't been aware, that after a spate of car thefts, and attempted burglaries Ceri had installed additional covert cameras to the rear of her house at the end of her garden.

Sean listened intently as Ceri continued the story.

'On the footage from one of these cameras we saw the faces of the two men. There was a blond-haired individual who I didn't recognise. He had a broad face, prominent cheekbones, a small nose and a small scar on his right cheek. Quite a handsome individual in a scary sort of way.

When I saw the face of the other guy, my stomach did somersaults. It was the same man that I had been introduced to in John Covington's office as Alek Kulkas.'

Sean was dumbfounded by what Ceri had just told him.

'Hold on Ceri so you are saying that the security company who have been employed by the bank to investigate your apparent disappearance have broken into your house. If that's true, then you certainly have a problem.'

Ceri was practically in tears, as she snarled indignantly at the man she had come to for help.

'What do you mean if ? Sean, we can show you the footage if you don't believe me. I'm telling you the bank has had someone break into my house and I'm afraid they are going to come back.'

Martin put his arm protectively around Ceri's shoulder and whispered gently in her ear in an attempt to sooth her, while at the same time glowering at Sean.

Sean wasn't a man who liked to see a woman upset and whatever else he might have thought of her, Ceri did fall into that female category. Taking a deep breath, a more contrite Sean tried to placate the obviously upset Ceri.

'Listen Ceri, I'm sorry for upsetting you, but I do actually believe you, the other guy you described may well be Olek, one of Alek Kulkas's team. He worked with me today and it makes sense that his skill set is more in the line of breaking and entering, because his knowledge of IT security systems is woeful.'

Martin's scowl softened and Ceri sniffed and wiped the back of her hand across her eyes as Sean finished speaking.

An obviously relieved Ceri speaking softly thanked Sean before an animated Martin started to speak.

'Sean, I think you have to agree with us that someone at the bank intends to cover up what Ceri has found. Obviously, they broke into Ceri's home hoping to find either copies of the information she had gathered, or worse case to find Ceri.'

A pensive Sean sat for a few moments chewing his bottom lip and contemplating what Martin had just said. Looking Martin square in the eye, Sean spoke slowly, considering each word.

'I assume your theory about the bank is the reason Ceri decided to do a disappearing act and send an email pretending to be kidnapped by Hidden Cobra?'

Martin looked quizzically at Sean before leaning forward in his seat and speaking to Sean as if addressing an exasperating teenager.

'What is this bloody email you keep harping on about? Yes, we were concerned that the cover up by the bank might include causing Ceri physical harm. I thought that it might be a good idea to lay a false trail suggesting that she had left the country. That way she could keep a low profile and keep out of harm's way.

We drove in convoy from East Hampstead to Heathrow airport and parked Ceri's car in the long stay carpark at terminal two. We then turned her bank mobile on for twenty minutes before turning it off and returning to East Hampstead in my car.'

In a final attempt to clarify the situation, a puzzled Sean couldn't help but ask the question one more time.

'So you didn't send any email pretending to be kidnapped?'

It was now Ceri's turn to express her exasperation.

'God almighty Sean, have you not been listening, my phone had been wiped and I had no facility to do anything apart from turn it on and off.'

Sean held up his hands apologetically as the situation suddenly became clear to him. Obviously, Ceri's mobile number had been transferred to a new Sim by someone within the Bank, no one else would have had the authority to do it, or the ability to remote wipe Ceri's phone. The email had been a complete fabrication, invented to explain Ceri's absence. But how could they maintain that fiction when Ceri reappeared, they couldn't, and then another thought hit him.

Looking directly at Ceri, Sean spoke quietly and firmly.

'Ceri, I agree with Martin, you need to keep a very low profile. I don't think Alek Kulkas and Olek were at your house for the good of your health. People at the bank have fabricated an email saying you were kidnapped to explain your absence, and I think we need to make sure that doesn't become something more permanent.'

There was a silence as Ceri and Martin absorbed what Sean had just said.

As the silence deepened Sean's mind started working overtime. Everything pointed towards Ceri having stumbled across something illegal that was of major concern to senior people within the bank.

Everything that had happened to Ceri suggested that something illicit was going on. Why else would the bank have their so-called security consultant break into Ceri's home, why else would they pretend she had been kidnapped and clone her phone in order to support this assertion.

But something still puzzled Sean, turning to Ceri with a perplexed look on his face he asked, 'So why have you broken into my house in the middle of the night and why have you come to me for help?'

Ceri's answer was very forthright and showed an understanding of Sean's character that Sean didn't think she would have possessed.

'That's simple, Richard Head may well be involved, who else would have instructed his team to disable my network access and mobile phone, and Richard does an even better job than me of kissing the boss's ass.

You on the other hand seem to have no love of authority, you're intelligent, honest and you have an intimate knowledge of the Banks Security systems, that is something we will need to identify what is going on, so it can be exposed.

Just as importantly you are known to dislike me, and no one would think that I would come to you for help, and I hoped we would be able to use your network connection to the bank to gather more information.'

Sean abruptly got out of his seat, followed by an anxious Otto, before he turned and addressed Ceri with just a hint of anger in his voice.

'You don't know me and yes you're right, I don't like you, so why on earth should I help someone who as far as I can see has no concern for anyone but herself, why should I get involved and put myself in jeopardy to help you?'

Ceri looked up at the imposing figure of Sean and paused before speaking softly.

'Because I think you are honest and are fair in your dealings with people, I know you spoke to John Covington and did you best to get the Marketing Assistant reinstated after I had her fired. If you and Martin are right, this situation isn't about someone's job, this situation is potentially life and death and I need your help.'

Ceri hadn't been wrong, Sean did have a strong sense of fair play, equally he had absolutely no tolerance for dishonesty. From Sean's perspective, whilst John Covington seemed to have mislaid his moral compass; he still had a firm grip on the difference between right and wrong.

Sean had no love for Ceri, and he didn't know Martin well enough to have an opinion about the guy. What he did know was that the pair of them were up shit creek without a paddle and his bosses in the bank seemed to be up to their eyes in something very shady.

As things stood, Sean knew he needed to help them in whatever way he could. After listening to Ceri's story, he certainly had some sympathy for her. Besides, he had been brought up to believe, "Never do a bad turn if you can do a good one." His mind made up, Sean decided he would dig deeper into what they had told him and if things were as bad as they seemed he would do his best to help fix it.

Ceri and Martin had both been sitting staring expectantly at Sean as he considered his options.

Sean's mouth creased, showing the hint of a smile as he spoke.

'OK, I am going to help, but as for using my network connection to gather more information, that's the stupidest thing I have ever heard.

Do you not think at this stage that they will be monitoring all connections for unusual activity?

Using my connection is going to tell them exactly where you are and exactly who might be helping you.'

As he spoke, he could see the tension drain from Ceri's face and for a moment Sean felt a twinge of pity for the woman who he had always seen as a right royal pain in the ass.

Obviously deep in thought Sean continued speaking giving voice to his inner thoughts.

'We don't have enough information yet to determine what is going on, we need to gather more information from the bank's core systems. Hopefully through analysis of that information we can identify some sort of pattern which will help to show what is going on.'

Ceri, obviously happy at now having Sean in their camp gabbled excitedly.

'That's exactly what Martin and I had hoped we could do using your home network connection. We weren't aware of the excitement at the bank today. Obviously it would be difficult to proceed with our plan given the state of alert that is now in place with the banks security systems.'

Sean laughed in response to Ceri's animated outburst.

'I would replace the word difficult with suicidal. Trying to extract the volume of data required, using an external connection would in all certainty generate an alert on the banks intrusion detection and prevention system. We may as well stick a neon sign on my roof saying "Ceri's here".

Likewise trying to extract the data using another server, or PC on the banks network would generate similar alerts on the internal firewalls which have been configured to identify the extraction of large volumes of data and shutdown connections that were identified as potentially malicious.'

Sean leaned forward in his chair bending down to stroke Otto's coarse fur as he contemplated their options. After a few moments of consideration, he spoke with an infectious confidence in his voice.

'There's more than one way to skin a cat

All we have to do is ensure that the extraction of data is not highlighted by any of the bank's security systems. To do that we just need to ensure that the data is generated on and extracted directly from the database server.'

Sean explained that he could logon to the database server from his office PC. He would then run SQL commands on the database server which would generate files containing the account and transactional information, required for them to carry out their analysis.

This data would be generated on and output directly to the database server, so this process should trigger no alarms.

To extract these files from the database server he needed to gain physical access to the database server in the Banks data centre. He would then be able to copy the datafiles from the database server onto a thumb drive, before deleting the files from the server to remove evidence of what had been done.

As Sean finished speaking, Ceri looked pensive, speaking hesitantly she expressed her concerns with his plan.

'Sean the bank has software in place that will raise an alert if a thumb drive is inserted into any of the banks machines.'

Sean smiled, 'It does indeed Ceri, but that system is only installed on client PCs. Servers in the data centre are not monitored by this software.

The access to the data centres themselves is monitored and restricted to a small number of key IT and security staff.

As you know, no one will question the reason for a member of the IT team visiting either of the data centres. We will retrieve the data during what looks to all intents and purpose like a normal maintenance visit.'

Having agreed on a basic plan Sean showed his guests to the door, telling them he would be taking Otto for a walk in Bradbourne lake park around eight pm the following evening and would meet them at the large stone at the park entrance. Then he headed off to bed with Otto in the hope of gaining another three hours sleep before leaving for work in the morning.

Chapter 10

The next morning after leaving Otto with Mary, Sean had headed into the office to find that things had changed significantly.

During the night, the crisis team in the data centre conference room had been stood down and the bank rumour mill had kicked into overdrive. Apparently, Alek Kulkas's team had discovered that Ceri Gillis had stolen sensitive bank information. She had then sought to extort money from the bank by pretending to have been kidnapped by Hidden Cobra.

Alek's team, who from what Sean could gather consisted of Alek and Olek, had discovered a copy of the data that Ceri had stolen on an encrypted thumb drive in her office. The customers involved had apparently been informed of the breech by the bank and their money had all been moved to new accounts to protect their funds.

Ceri's position with the bank had obviously been terminated immediately on the grounds of gross misconduct.

Within fifteen minutes of arriving in the building, Sean had been summoned to John Covington's office where he found Richard Head, Alek Kulkas and Trevor Reid already sitting around the meeting table.

John Covington welcomed Sean and offered him a coffee before briefing him on what Alek's team had apparently discovered the previous night after his departure.

In words dripping with honey John Covington was unstinting in the flattery that he bestowed on a completely underwhelmed Sean.

'It looks like your suspicions were correct Sean and Ms Gillis has not in fact been kidnapped. The bank cannot thank you enough for the quick and decisive action that you took yesterday.

You saved us from what could have been a very difficult situation. A situation that would have been all the more embarrassing given that the rogue member of staff who broke our trust, turned out to be a member of our senior team.

You will be happy to know that as far as the bank is concerned the incident is now over. Ms Gillis from what we can tell is now out of the country and your actions have ensured that the banks systems and data are secure.

With the thumb drive containing the stolen data that Alek and his team were able to secure yesterday evening, now in the bank's possession, things can get back to normal don't you think?'

Sean was sure he had never in his entire life had so much smoke blown up his ass. Presumably, he was being given the feel-good treatment to encourage happy thoughts and discourage him from asking any awkward questions. That might work in his world, thought Sean, but not in mine.

A cynical Sean couldn't help but throw a cat amongst the pigeons. So in a completely innocent voice he asked a question which he already knew the answer to.

'So Mr Covington what do you think happened at Ceri's house. It doesn't make any sense for her to have attracted the attention of the police.'

John Covington paused and glanced across at Alek Kulkas, who gave an almost imperceptible nod. Before the chief executive continued in a conspiratorial tone.

'Alek believes that the disturbance at her house had been a ruse to divert attention and suspicion away from Ceri in the event of a successful data breach being discovered.'

Alek cleared his throat and leant back in his chair with an arrogant smile on his face, as he prepared to give Sean the benefit of his sage wisdom.

'Yes, Sean in my experience people often attempt to hide their illicit activities behind a smoke screen or create a distraction which obscures their real intentions.'

Summoning all the righteous indignation at his disposal Sean left his audience in no doubt about how dishonest activities should be dealt with.

'I hope that the bank regulators and the police have been informed of what transpired yesterday. I would hope that anyone who has been given a position of trust and authority will be seen to be punished to the fullest extent of the law when they have broken that trust.'

All those around the table nodded in agreement with Sean's view, but John Covington explained in a very reasonable voice that as the incident had been resolved highlighting what had happened could only serve the aims of the erstwhile member of staff and embarrass the bank. This being the case the board had decided to protect the bank's reputation and take the issue no further.

Trevor Reid explained that all members of the crisis team had signed a non-disclosure agreement before going home the previous evening and it would be greatly appreciated if Sean would do the same.

Without any further preamble John Covington pushed a small sheaf of papers across the table towards Sean.

Looking Sean in the eye Trevor Reid smiled before speaking in his most patronising corporate voice.

'The bank and particularly the board has greatly appreciated your efforts and the loyalty that you have shown to the bank. We would hope that you would continue to be a loyal member of the team and sign the non-disclosure agreement that John has just provided. But … we will obviously understand if that is not the path you wish to continue to follow.'

Sean had long been a firm believer that everything before the "but" was bullshit and the obvious implication was, sign this or pack your bags. It appeared to Sean that when it came to John Covington and Trevor Reid, loyalty was very much a one-way street.

If anything, the current situation solidified in Sean's mind that he had just been fed a load of guff by this collection of cockwombles. If he had any doubts about the conspiracy theory laid out by Ceri the previous evening they had just evaporated like dew on a sunny morning. It was now obvious to Sean that more than one director at the bank was involved in these shady goings on.

After giving the paperwork a cursory once over Sean signed the last page as requested before saying, 'I really appreciate the trust that you all placed in me yesterday, but … there is no need for thanks, I was only doing my job.'

With the paperwork signed, John Covington reached across the desk to retrieve it.

'Thank you Sean, after all the excitement yesterday I'm sure you have a lot of work that you would like to catch up on.'

Doing his best to keep the disgust that he felt from showing on his face, Sean put on his best 'Fuck You' smile before taking his leave and heading back to the relative safety of his own office. Once seated back at his desk, Sean reviewed the skeleton plan he had formulated the previous evening and started to put some meat on the bones.

One of the life lessons that Sean had learnt during his time in the RAF was 'those who fail to prepare, prepare to fail, or as his old commanding officer used to put it 'proper preparation prevents piss poor performance'

Using the information that he had gleaned from the conversation the previous night Sean first wrote a piece of SQL code that he would use to extract all transactions in the last two months from the three Eastern European branches.

He then wrote a further piece of code to extract the account and customer details associated with the suspect transactions.

Having written his code and tested it on a test database, Sean logged onto the bank's primary database server and executed the two procedures, saving the output into two innocuously named files in a temporary folder on the server.

Sean then zipped up and encrypted the two files into a single file that looked to all intents and purposes to be a server patch.

Sean knew that what he had done had stepped way over the border of what could be considered legal. He was about to steal data from the bank, the very thing that he had spent his career trying to prevent. He didn't care about what John Covington, or Trevor Reid might think, but it troubled him that he had betrayed the trust of the guys that he worked with daily.

Best case if he got caught, he would be sacked and escorted quietly from the building with his reputation in tatters, he would be a pariah. Worst case, well he didn't want to think about the worst case, he just knew that something was going on that needed to be stopped and he wasn't in the mood to stop now.

Having extracted and packaged up the data, the next phase was the tricky part of his plan. He needed to get physical access to the data centre and connect a thumb drive into the server so he could download the files, hopefully without raising any suspicion. That could prove to be difficult, given everything that had happened in the last 24 hours.

Under normal circumstances it would have been quite normal for Sean given his security role to visit the data centre. However, given what he was in the process of doing, Sean felt that a certain degree of caution on his part might be advisable.

Downloading the latest service pack for the banks database servers onto a thumb drive Sean asked one of his junior colleagues James, to visit the primary data centre and connect the thumb drive to the database server.

Sean felt a twinge of guilt as he spoke to the junior member of his team.

'James this drive contains the latest security patches for the two database servers. They should have been installed yesterday, but other things got in the way. Unfortunately, the current project to update the internal firewalls is making it difficult to remotely load the patch software.

If you could head to the primary data centre first and attach the drive, I'll be able to copy the patches directly onto the server. Once I've finished with the copy process you can then take the thumb drive to the secondary data centre where we can repeat the process.

Once both copies have finished just return to the office and give me back the thumb drive.'

James smiled, 'that's not a problem Sean, only to happy to help, glad to get away from this madhouse for a few hours.'

Sean hated himself for lying to his enthusiastic young team member but managed to return James's smile as he patted him paternally on the back.

'Thanks for your help with this James, I really appreciate it. I'm a bit snowed under today and really can't afford the time to drive between the data centres.'

When James arrived at the primary data centre, he rang Sean to confirm that the thumb drive had been connected. Sean quickly copied the patches into the temporary directory on the server before copying his encrypted file onto the thumb drive.

As planned, James retrieved the thumb drive before visiting the secondary data centre and returning to head office, to give the drive with its additional payload of encrypted data back to Sean.

Once he had the thumb drive back in his possession Sean copied the encrypted file onto his laptop. Extracted the transaction, customer and account data into a test database and then began his analysis.

Sean's initial analysis suggested that the information relating to all three branches did indeed show that things were not as they should be. All three branches showed a high level of what Sean considered suspicious transactions.

Sean could see that the few accounts that Ceri had looked at were but the tip of the iceberg. He identified thousands of what he considered to be suspicious accounts and tens of thousands of suspicious transactions. Just how big this iceberg was, could take some time and effort to identify, time and effort best not expended in the office.

What he couldn't understand is how these accounts were being created and how the funds were being posted to the accounts without arousing any suspicions.

The bank had reporting procedures that staff would use if they had identified any suspicious transactions. Not only that, but the bank had installed an automated suspicious transaction management system that had been necessary to keep their regulator happy. Surely that system should have highlighted the suspicious transactions, even if the staff hadn't.

That evening after work Sean left the office, carrying the laptop which contained the database that he was going to analyse in more detail in the comfort of his own home.

He also took with him, a set of plans for the top floor of the bank headquarters building. He had already formulated a plan in his head as to how they might gather further evidence and he had a suspicion that the plans might prove useful.

Chapter 11

Once home, Sean picked up Otto, fed both himself and his canine companion and set about analysing the mass of data that he had extracted from the bank's database.

Deciding to ignore any accounts or transactions that had been processed via the Bank's online customer portal Sean began to analyse the branch-based account openings and transaction processing only.

The first thing he noticed was that ninety percent of the account openings and roughly the same percentage of the transactions were time stamped between 1pm and 3pm. There were literally hundreds of transactions and account openings occurring in a very constrained time window each day in all three branches.

Now Sean had been at the bank long enough to know how long it took a cashier to open a new account especially with all the money laundering checks that had to be carried out.

A lot of the recent major corruption and money laundering scandals such as the Russian and Azerbaijani Laundromats and Operation Car Wash in Brazil all had one thing in common. They relied on European banks to pay bribes, transfer illicit funds, and hide the proceeds of corruption.

Sean knew from reading some of the justifications that had been put forward by the bank's compliance team in relation to implementing new money laundering systems that the amounts of money involved had been immense.

The Russian Laundromat alone involved more than 13 billion dollars of illicit funds. Funds that had been transferred via Latvia to banks located in Cyprus, Denmark, Estonia, Germany, Netherlands, Sweden, and the UK.

One of the outcomes of these scandals had been the levying of billions of dollars in fines by U.S. authorities on European banks, for deficiencies in monitoring money laundering.

The nett result of this was that Credit Finance Bank, in common with all its peers had implemented more stringent systems and procedures for account opening in order to prevent money laundering and fraud.

From the point of view of a customer this meant that it could take up to ten minutes to open a new account with the bank. The fact that hundreds of accounts were being opened every hour during the identified two-hour window wasn't feasible without dozens of cashiers.

Like all banks Credit Finance bank had encouraged more of its customers to go online, by reducing its level of service in its branches. This meant none of the bank's branches had more than six cashiers, with fewer in the fledgling Eastern European branches.

Anna had left Sean to go work as assistant branch manager in the Bratislava branch, managing a total team of ten staff dealing with mortgages, loans and savings and current accounts.

What Sean noticed next made staff numbers totally irrelevant. The data showed that all suspicious accounts and transactions were tagged with just three operator codes.

The three remarkably busy operators were K Robocie in Krakow, B Avtomaticen in Bratislava and P Robota in Prague. This suggested to Sean, that all these transactions and accounts were being generated by some sort of batch process.

Certainly the bank had processes for generating transactions from files received from other banks, or through the Bank Automated Clearing system. There was no such system to Sean's knowledge for the generation of accounts, so these were not standard batch processes. Especially since all batch processes were run by IT staff in Head Office.

The data also appeared to contain a lot of duplicated customer data. Normally when an account was opened in a branch the first thing a cashier would do would be to check if the customer was already known to the bank and if so, attach the new account to the existing customer.

From what Sean could see the same customers with the same names, dates of birth and addresses had been duplicated more than twenty and in some cases thirty times. This was totally against bank procedure and Sean couldn't for the life of him understand how this was happening.

From experience he knew Anna was a stickler for procedure and her branch would appear to be every bit as bad as the other two in relation to the creation of duplicate customers.

When he looked at the amounts involved, Sean found that all cash receipt transactions were for amounts between three thousand and four thousand Euro. These smaller amounts from hundreds of low value accounts were then being transferred into a much smaller number of larger value accounts.

These larger accounts were then being used to transfer funds out of Credit Finance bank to accounts in other financial institutions. From what Sean could see millions of euro were being processed each day across the three branches. This was then being siphoned into a dozen or so accounts, which were then being used to transfer around 60 million euro to other banks at the end of each month.

Sean realised that if this rate was maintained over the space of a year these suspicious transactions would total over 700 million Euro. An eye watering sum so huge that he had to recheck his calculations twice.

Obviously whatever Ceri had stumbled upon, involved an extremely large volume of cash and at least some of the directors within the bank. But where did Alek Kulkas the mysterious security consultant fit in?

At seven forty-five, with a thumb drive holding a copy of the data, Sean put Otto into the boot of his estate and headed to the Park to meet with Ceri and Martin. They were going to have a lot to talk about. If Sean's suspicions were right the bank was involved in a major money laundering operation.

Chapter 12

It was the height of summer, so the park was busy when Sean pulled into the car park. He popped the boot before getting out of the car. When he reached the open tailgate, he found Otto sitting patiently, waiting permission to exit the vehicle.

Sean quickly clipped Otto's lead onto his collar. Whilst Otto was a very well trained and well-behaved dog, Sean had found that a lot of people found a large unrestrained German Shepherd a bit intimidating. So, to keep the peace and not get involved in unnecessary altercations with other park users, Sean kept Otto on the lead during his park walks.

Walking towards the entrance Sean couldn't see any sign of Ceri, but he did see Martin standing eating an ice cream near the large stone at the entrance. The stone according to local legend was a druid stone, what exactly this meant was lost on Sean.

As Sean walked towards him, he could see Martin glance uncomfortably at Otto and shift from one foot to the other as he remembered his last encounter with Sean's roommate.

As Sean walked up to Martin he smiled as if just noticing an old friend and greeted him with some convivial banter.

'Hello Martin, long time no see, fancy joining us for a walk, I'm sure Otto won't mind. And don't worry he's just been fed. So, he won't try and take a bite out of your … ice cream.'

Martin grimaced, but he responded in a light hearted manner to Sean's teasing, just like an old friend would.

'Very funny Sean, I'm still walking with a limp, but yes if you keep the beast on a leash, I'll come for a walk with you.'

As they walked away from the entrance and the swirl of people who gathered taking selfie pictures around the Druid stone Sean enquired as to Ceri's where abouts.

Martin waved his hand vaguely across the expanse of water that they were walking beside and whispered out of the side of his mouth.

'She's waiting on us at the other side of the lake, there were too many people at the entrance for her to feel comfortable.'

After ten minutes of walking along the track that hugged the edge of the lake, they came across Ceri in black Jeans and a dark hoody sitting on a bench throwing bread to the ducks.

Sean sat at one end of the bench with Otto by his side, Ceri sat in the middle and Martin sat at the other end of the seat. It was as if the men and dog had automatically created a protective cordon around the ex-Chief Information Security Officer.

Sean quickly went over the things that he had discovered whilst analysing the data and waited on a response.

The first one to speak was Martin. He spoke in an excited and rather high-pitched voice that made Otto's ears twitch. 'Robotics, they are using Robotics to open accounts and process transactions. The cheeky sods aren't even attempting to hide it, Robocie is polish for robot.'

Looking thoughtfully down at his phone he then added in a more subdued tone, 'avtomaticen is something to do with automation in Slovenian and Robota is Czech for Robot.'

Sean knew that Credit Finance bank had as part of its digital transformation process looked at using robotic process automation as a quick and easy way to streamline some of its processes.

They had even looked at it as a possible way to provide an online app to supplement the banks online website. Using robotics, they had experimented with feeding data to internal processes, to open new accounts and accept payments.

However, as the previous IT director had pointed out much to the annoyance of the board; it was no more than a short-term fix and not a long-term intelligent automation strategy for a bank intent on doing more online.

From a security perspective, Sean had pointed out that using internally developed robotic processes would create potential update issues and security exposures. Especially when they were providing direct access to internal processes and systems from the web.

Sean had agreed whole heartedly with the previous IT director when she had pointed out that money would be better invested in purchase of application programming interfaces. These would allow both the banks website and any newly developed apps to communicated efficiently and securely with the bank's core systems.

The project had been dropped after nine months. Not because of the advice from Sean and the former IT director. Rather, it had been because as predicted, trials had shown that the interface between the webapp, robotics and core system was slow and flaky and a simple upgrade on the banks core system had caused it to fail completely.

Even so what Martin had just said made sense. During early testing of the robotic process automation Sean was aware that things had gone very well. Batches of test data had been fed in from spreadsheets to generate new accounts on the test system in a matter of seconds.

It was only when they had tried to integrate the backend robotic processes with the web application that the cracks had appeared.

Sean couldn't hide his excitement, his voice reverting to his Northern Irish roots with the words coming out in an exuberant rush.

'Ceri, I think Martin has hit the nail on the head. They are using an automated process to open multiple accounts and generate receipts into all those accounts.

Under normal circumstances they would be banging the drum about how they have improved customer service.

But this isn't about improving customer service, at least not to our genuine customers. All the transactions I've looked at were posted as cash. That suggests that someone is using our three new bank branches in the east to launder vast sums of money.

Ceri raised her hand laughing, 'Slow down Sean, take a breath.'

Sean did as Ceri suggested, took a deep breath, before continuing to speak at a speed that Ceri and Martin could follow.

'More importantly, this is being done with the approval and full knowledge of directors within the bank. Think about it, your home has been targeted by the security team hired by the bank. Your reputation has just been trashed within the bank by John Covington and Trevor Reid. They are doing their best to cover up the financial shenanigans that you stumbled across.'

What I don't understand though, is how the system the bank implemented last year to identify suspicious transactions hasn't highlighted any of this activity.'

Ceri sat back on the bench and breathed out deeply before responding.

'That's simple Sean, that system has been configured to highlight cash transactions over 5000 pounds or 5000 euros. The transaction amounts they are using have been carefully chosen not to trip any alerts.

We need to report this to the police and to the regulators right away.'

Sean frowned and shook his head in disagreement.

'Catch yourself on Ceri, what are we going to tell them? … that we have a strong suspicion that its highly likely some senior members of the bank management team are involved in an international money laundering scheme. But we can't be sure who, we can only guess at how, and we don't really know why.'

Martin who had been sitting quietly listening to the exchange put his hand on Ceri's knee and spoke softly.

'Sean's right Ceri. We need to be sure of what is going on, who in the bank is involved in this, how they are benefitting and who they are laundering the cash for before we involve the authorities.'

Sean hadn't known Martin long, but he could see he was a sound wee man with a lot of common sense.

After nodding his thanks to Martin, Sean continued to lay out the facts as he saw them.

'Normal procedure would be to report this to the bank's Money Laundering Reporting Officer and let the MLRO make a suspicious activity report to the police.

We don't know if the MLRO is involved in this, and we will have shown our hand if she is. No we do not involve the authorities until we are sure of who and what we are dealing with.

From what we know at the moment, we could be dealing with a case of bank capture, where the money launderers are running the bank.'

Sean wasn't an expert, but through the regular online courses run by the compliance team, that he had forced himself to sit through. He knew that money laundering consisted of a three-phase process, with the placement into the financial system being the first phase.

Detection risk is greatest during the placement phase due to large-deposit reporting requirements that had been put in place at financial institutions at the behest of the regulators.

However, in this case those depositing the cash were using hundreds of accounts with deposits well below the banks reporting limit to circumvent the bank's automated reporting system.

Worse still it would appear that the bank had been facilitating the layering process. Internal transfers were being carried out which moved the money to other accounts within the bank, before transferring the funds onwards to other financial institutions.

Turning his head so that he could see both Ceri and Martin, Sean spoke slowly with assurance.

'To be clear we need to find out where this money is coming from, who in the bank is helping with its placement, how the placement is actually being done and finally how the bank is layering the cash to make it look legitimate.

The data I have extracted is going to need a lot more analysis, someone is going to need to identify what banks the money is being transferred on to. That I think is a job for you Ceri. I still have a day job and I need to keep it if we are going to want a man on the inside.'

Sean took the thumb drive that he had been carrying out of its pocket and passed it to Ceri. Then turning to Martin, he said, 'we are going to need to make use of your special collection of skills to help answer one of our other questions. We are going to need to bug the chief executive and the finance director's offices. We need to listen to their conversations and phone calls and see if we can find out who else is involved.'

Sean explained that he wanted video and audio devices planted in both rooms which could be used to view and listen in on any meetings or conversations which might take place in the two locations.

To facilitate Martin's planning for this Sean produced the architects plan for both rooms, highlighting all electrical and network points in the rooms. These were the plans that he had taken with him when leaving work that evening.

Having outlined what needed to be done Sean stood up to go and was about to suggest a further meeting in a few days, when Martin handed him a mobile phone.

'We need a better channel of communication that doesn't consist of wandering about in a park. This phone is password protected and encrypted in case you lose it, or it gets stolen.'

After giving Sean the passcode, Martin showed him the encrypted messaging app which could be used for messaging, and video or audio calling. Martin explained that all alerts were silenced on the telephone so that Sean's possession of it would not be inadvertently advertised to anyone.

'If you are happy with the phone Sean, could I suggest that we follow a secure protocol when trying to communicate with each other.

If you need to speak send a message requesting a call. We will message you back if its safe to talk, then you can ring us.'

'That's grand Martin, I certainly wouldn't want you guys ringing me whilst I'm in ear shot of John Covington, or Trevor Reid. That could prove to be very awkward.'

Sean shook Martin warmly by the hand and nodded his goodbyes to Ceri. He then tugged gently on Otto's lead and he and the dog headed off around the lake to complete their walk.

Chapter 13

The next day in work Sean sat at his desk unable to focus on his work feeling angry that people in positions of great responsibility who's behaviour should be beyond reproach were involved in shady and dishonest business.

His mind then turned to Alek Kulkas, who was he? why had he been called in by the bank? and why were he and his team still here if the issue had been resolved as the chief executive had indicated? Sean decided that he would pay Mr Kulkas a visit. Alek had taken possession of Ceri's office.

Sean found the office door closed when he arrived but knocked politely before opening the door and entering. He found both Alek and Olek sitting in front of Ceri's PC and laptop with their jackets off. Olek had on a short-sleeved shirt which exposed an impressive set of tattoos on both fore arms. His right had a beautifully crafted picture of a snarling wolf, whilst on his left Sean could make out a picture of what could have been a Russian church resplendent with several onion shaped domes.

Both men had looked up as Sean had entered, with Alek raising an enquiring eyebrow. Sean cleared his throat, and put on his best boy scout voice, 'Mr Kulkas I was wondering if I could be of any further assistance to you and your team? The fact that you guys are still here would suggest that there is still a potential problem and with my knowledge of the banks systems I could be of some assistance.'

Alek looked at Sean, giving a smile that never quite reached his eyes.

'Thank you for the offer Sean, but with the help of Richard we have gained access to Ms Gillis's devices and Olek and I are just reviewing them to see if we can identify any potential clues to her where abouts. Her company car has been found in one of the car parks at Heathrow and is currently being retrieved.

We have not been able to find any trace of Ms Gillis on any flights out of Heathrow or any other London airport on the day she went missing, so we assume she has either slipped out under another name, or is still in London.

As you yourself have already said, Ms Gillis needs to be punished, so Mr Covington has instructed us to find any information which might identify the alias she used, or indeed where she might be now.

Once she has been found I can assure you that she will be punished properly for her disloyalty to the bank. I will be sure to make Mr Covington aware of your commitment to the bank. Now if you'll excuse us we really have quite a bit of work to do.'

As Alek gave a final cold smile Sean took one last look at Olek's arms before turning and walking out of the office, hoping that the panic he felt didn't show on his face. Once they had that car back, they could check its sat nav system to see where she had been and what if Ceri had information on her devices that pointed to Martin and her current location.

He needed to contact Ceri and Martin right away, they were going to need to relocate in a hurry.

Once back in his office, Sean took the encrypted mobile from his inside jacket pocket entered the pin code and typed in a message, explaining that he needed to speak to Martin and Ceri right away.

Whilst he waited on the response, he paced around the office thinking about the conversation he had just had with Alek. What Alek Kulkas had said troubled Sean, but he couldn't quite put his finger on why. Then it dawned on him, Alek had said, "We haven't found any trace of her on outbound flights", he hadn't mentioned the authorities.

Sean knew with certainty that the bank's hierarchy were involved with a very serious criminal gang. A gang that had sufficient connections to get information on all travellers out of all four London airports. As he thought about the brief conversation, Sean's concern for Ceri rose, Alek had indicated that Ceri would be punished for her disloyalty, he hadn't said that they were going to pass the information onto the police. Sean had seen enough Hollywood gangster movies to know that punishment would be a lot more painful that a slap on the wrist.

Finally, after five anxious minutes the acknowledgement message came through from Martin, Sean made the call and Ceri answered immediately. Sean wasted no time in explaining the situation with the car; however, Ceri sounded totally unconcerned. She had parked the car twenty minutes' walk from Martin's house on both occasions. The chances of them finding Martin's home amongst the thousands that would be within reasonable walking distance of her parking location were slim to non-existent.

Next Sean explained about what he had found in Ceri's office and asked if there could be any possibility that she had details on any of her devices that would point to Martin, or his home. Sean didn't try to sugar coat his concerns.

'Ceri, If these guys identify your location I don't think they'll be calling the metropolitan police to slap the handcuffs on you. I think the bank is involved with some very bad people.'

The line went quiet as Ceri thought for a few moments, Sean sensed a hesitancy in Ceri's voice when she finally responded.

'Sean, I don't think there is anything that could lead to our location, I never put any of my personal contacts onto my address list in work.'

Sean noticed the hesitancy in Ceri's voice and as firmly as he could he restated his concern.

'Ceri, you need to be absolutely certain, because if you're wrong Alek and Olek could soon be knocking none too gently on Martin's door and they won't be there to deliver flowers.'

He could sense her thinking at the other end of the line. When she spoke again Sean could hear the tension in her voice.

'There may be some old documents relating to the company that Martin and I used to have on the laptop. Whilst they didn't have Martin's address, they will have his name and professional details.'

Sean interrupted Ceri before she could say anything else.

He spoke with an urgency that he hoped Ceri understood.

'You both need to get your arses out of Martin's house now. These guys might not be up to much when it comes to IT security, but they seem to have access to considerable resources.'

Resources which could be used to trace Martin's home and your location. Get out now, leave nothing relating to the bank behind and find somewhere that is safe before contacting me again.

Ooh and bring your passports we might need to visit foreign parts to sort this out. The physical evidence that we are going to need access to is in Eastern Europe in John Covington's new branches.'

Once sure that Ceri had got the message and was going to do just as he suggested, Sean hung up the phone and put it back into his inside jacket pocket. Then very calmly he sat down to do his day job, after all the bank was still paying his salary.

Chapter 14

Sean had attended a number of meetings that day but had found himself distracted by the current situation. He had nothing concrete to go on, but he knew to his core that Alek and Olek were not good people. Who were they working for? and apart from John Covington and Trevor Reid, who else in the bank had a part to play in what was going on?

He had overheard another member of staff mention that Alek and Olek were dropped off each morning and picked up each evening by a black S Class Mercedes limo. Not the usual mode of transport for an IT security consultant, no matter how well paid they were, they didn't normally turn up to work in a chauffeur driven limo.

So that evening Sean sat in his car close to the carpark exit and waited on the limo to arrive. Shortly after six the car arrived, and Sean scribbled down its registration.

He then telephoned his mate Andy and after a brief conversation about Otto, Andy's old police dog Sean asked Andy if he could do him a favour.

'Andy, we have had a bit of excitement at work and I've been on edge a bit. It's probably my imagination working overtime, but I've noticed a suspicious vehicle parked outside my house on a couple of occasions this week.'

Andy had known Sean for many years and knew he wasn't the type to frighten easily. So, his voice echoed the concern he felt when he asked Sean for clarification.

'What do you mean by suspicious Sean? If you are concerned for your safety, you should ring 999 and report it.'

Sensing that he had perhaps over played the frightened card, Sean lightened his voice and spoke in a more jocular tone to his long-time friend.

'Well, that's why I'm speaking to you buddy. I don't want to look a fool by reporting a car that's there for completely innocent reasons. For all I know it's a pair of door-to-door salesman selling satellite TV to the neighbours.

Any chance you could maybe do me a favour and do a quick check on the car registration to see if its stolen or linked to a criminal gang.

It's a black Audi saloon car with blacked out rear windows and it had at least two people sitting in it.'

'OK Sean give me the registration, like you say I'm sure it's completely innocent, but if it helps you sleep better then I'm happy to help.'

Sean looked at the scribbled note sitting in his lap and gave the registration for the S class Mercedes he could see parked in front of him, with its engine now turned off.

Sean waited as Andy typed in the registration all the while watching the blacked-out limousine. After thirty seconds or so Andy spoke, he sounded just a little confused.

'You sure it's a black Audi mate? according to the system that registration belongs to an S class Mercedes registered to a company called Odessa securities with an address in Kensington Palace gardens.'

Sean did his best to keep his voice steady and not give away the excitement that he felt at now having an address linked to the enigmatic Alek Kulkas.

'100% positive Andy, I drive an Audi myself and I would recognise that badge anywhere.'

'In that case Sean if you see that car again contact the local police, because it has false plates, and you were right to be suspicious. I'll flag your address on the system so that you can be sure of a quick response.'

'Thanks buddy, if I see that car again, I'll be straight on the phone to report it.'

After hanging up his phone Sean got out of the car and walked the two minutes to Canary Wharf underground station.

When he reached the station, he telephoned his neighbour Mary, to apologise, explaining that he would be late picking up Otto tonight. He then got himself a ticket to Notting hill Gate. Sean knew that driving through central London at this time of the evening would be a bit of a nightmare and the nine miles or so from docklands to Kensington palace gardens could take an hour. On the other hand taking the tube and travelling the jubilee and central lines should only take about thirty minutes.

After a totally uneventful tube journey Sean got off the jubilee line train at bond street and changed to the central line and a train which then took him all the way to Notting hill. The whole journey took him forty rather than the expected thirty minutes. Sean was unconcerned by the delay, he knew from experience that

Alek and Olek would still be sitting in traffic, as their driver fought the good fight with central London traffic.

After leaving the tube station Sean walked west for five minutes, passing a modern looking concrete building that purported to be the Czech embassy. Before reaching a pub at the top of Kensington Palace Gardens.

Looking at his watch Sean could see that just over forty-five minutes had passed since he had started his journey, so he expected the black limo to arrive shortly. Taking a seat outside the pub he ordered himself a pint of cider and decided to sit and enjoy the sunshine whilst he waited on Alek and Olek.

Halfway through his pint and twenty minutes into his wait, Sean spotted the car as it turned into the street opposite him. Standing up Sean walked casually across the road following the car as it drove slowly down the tree lined street past a large imposing building with a shining brass plaque that trumpeted the location of the Russian embassy.

About two hundred metres ahead of him the car pulled in and stopped. Sean turned and pretended to read the noticeboard attached to the wall of the Russian embassy whilst watching the car out of the corner of his eye.

The driver a large individual, who looked muscular rather than fat and the two back seat passengers all got out of the vehicle and walked up the steps of a substantial four story white Georgian building.

Sean waited until all three men had disappeared, before walking down the street and past the building. As he came adjacent to its façade, he took out his phone and whilst pretending to make a call took a few pictures of the brass plaque on one of the pillars at the bottom of the steps leading up to the front door. Sean put his telephone to his ear to complete the illusion of making a telephone call as he continued to walk down the street until eventually, he came to Kensington high street.

Taking the tube again, this time utilising the circle and jubilee lines Sean made it back to his car and headed for home. He knew from a quick online search that the London offices of Andriane security were nowhere near Kensington Palace Gardens so who owned the building that Alek and Olek had disappeared into.

Sean hoped that when he analysed the few pictures, he had taken that he would be a little closer to identifying who exactly Alek and Olek were and what their interest in the current situation at the bank could possibly be. He knew one thing with certainty, John Covington's explanation as to their presence didn't hold water.

Chapter 15

Once home Sean sorted out dinner for Otto and himself, before settling down in front of his PC. Firstly, he transferred the pictures from his telephone onto his computer. By increasing the magnification on the pictures on his twenty inch monitor he succeeded in making out the name on the brass plaque, luckily one of his pictures had the plaque pretty much in the centre of the image.

The name on the plaque was "Odessa Capital overseas Investments". Putting the company name into his search engine Sean found a limited liability capital management company registered in Florida, with a principle and mailing address in Odessa in the Ukraine.

The company apparently specialised in real estate investments. By reviewing the online company listing Sean identified the Chief operating officer as an individual named Alexander Kulkas. Sean wondered if Alek and Alexander were one and the same person.

Sean broadened his search looking for any reference to Alexander Kulkas and bingo he found a PR photo showing Alexander Kulkas President of Andriane security Inc. Hatchet face was smiling for the camera, the skin stretched taught over his high cheek bones, as he celebrated the opening of the Florida office.

The story alongside the picture made much of the organisation's multinational Cyber Security capabilities, with offices in London and Florida. Alexander and Alek Kulkas were definitely the same man. Even more amazing was the fact that the petite chief executive of the organisation standing smiling beside Alek Kulkas was none other than Magda Harte. Now Sean understood why the name Andriane security had been so familiar, when Alek Kulkas had first been introduced.

It also explained why Alek and his team, a team which in his opinion were severely lacking in cyber expertise, were now in the bank. Obviously, the easiest way to ensure secrecy was to bring in a company managed by the Chairwoman of the bank's board.

Sean wasn't sure of the ethics of that situation but had to admit there was probably nothing illegal in the arrangement. But if you wanted to be cynical it just went to prove the old adage, "it's not what you know, but who you know."

Hoping to find some information on Olek Sean took a look at the website for Andriane security Inc. If Olek was a senior member of their kidnap extortion and threat response team he should find information about him on the site. Sean found information relating to over 20 senior consultants at the organisation, as well as the usual director profiles, but not one of them was Olek.

Either they have sent one of the office juniors, or Olek works for a different part of the Kulkas group, thought Sean as he returned his focus to the other Kulkas enterprises.

Continuing his search, he also found a limited venture and development capital company registered with companies' house in London with an address in Kensington Palace Gardens. According to the registration details the company had two directors. Dimitri Kulkas and Iryna Kulkas.

The snapshot of the accounts that Sean could see suggested a highly profitable organisation. It would appear that the Kulkas family had quite the business empire spreading from Ukraine through the UK and onto the USA and possibly beyond.

Having identified two individuals associated with the address that he had been to that day. Sean started another search using both names, hoping to find something on social media that would at least help him to see what they looked like.

He immediately found an unsecured social media profile for Iryna Kulkas. Some people never learn thought Sean, in their rush to share their wonderful lives with friends they give the whole world access to some of their more intimate moments.

Trawling through the many pictures available through her profile on the social media platform he could see she was an extremely attractive blond woman. With if the pictures were anything to go by a large number of extraordinarily rich friends. There were the usual pictures of Iryna posing in front of outrageously expensive sports cars and standing around on yachts. Her Social media posts definitely gave the impression that she enjoyed an incredibly lavish lifestyle.

One of the nautical pictures grabbed Sean's attention. Much to his amazement Iryna was standing in a swimsuit on the back of a yacht beside a smiling and bare-chested John Covington. His curiosity well and truly aroused he kept moving through Iryna's digital life until he came across a photo of her in a wedding dress. There were two tall men standing to her left, one was Alek and the other slightly older man had got to be Alek's brother, their obvious resemblance made it impossible for him to be anything else.

On Iryna's right hand side stood John Covington, dressed in an immaculate three-piece suit with a flower in his button hole smiling for the camera like he had just won the lottery. The caption with the photo said "So glad my husband and I could share our special day with my brothers Dimitri and Alek".

Then it hit Sean like a sledgehammer, Iryna Kulkas was now Iryna Covington, the wife of his boss. Iryna must have been at least 20 years younger than her new husband John Covington. Sean was sure that women of a certain age would see him as a handsome man, but he couldn't understand how a young woman in her twenties could have the same attraction.

Then perhaps the choice hadn't been hers. Perhaps one of the two older brothers who were standing like two predacious sentinels in the background had made the choice. The smiles painted on their faces for the photo looked every bit as cold as their inky black eyes. They were the closest thing to walking air breathing sharks that Sean had ever seen. The well fitted expensive grey suits they were both wearing, just added to the squaloid image in Sean's head.

It looked like the Kulkas family empire had extended its tendrils to include Credit Finance bank. Sean sat and scratched his head trying to make sense of what he had just found. The bank that he worked for had personal and professional connections with an apparently successful and highly profitable Ukrainian business empire.

The spiders web of connections in itself wasn't illegal, nor were there any ethical issues with the connections that he was aware of. But he knew that John Covington and Trevor Reid were doing their best to cover up financial irregularities at the bank. Sean's gut told him that the duo were doing their best to protect themselves rather than the bank.

Setting what he had learnt about the Kulkas family and its connections to one side, Sean once again set about searching the internet for information that could help shed some light on the goings on at the bank. He next focussed his attention on Olek, Alek Kulkas's side kick and apparent partner in crime.

Sean had no idea what Olek's second name was and even if he did, could he even be sure it was his real name. What he did have was a very clear picture in his head of the two tattoos on Oleks arms. So focusing once again on his PC, he did an online search for "snarling wolf tattoo". He found nothing of particular interest.

When he then did a further search for "Russian Church tattoo" the second page that appeared related to Russian criminal tattoos. The church, or kremlin tattoo apparently indicated that the wearer had spent some unwanted holiday time in a government institution.

On this page he also found a reference to an "Oskal tattoo", these were tattoos showing snarling tigers, leopards, or wolves, it indicated a hatred of the authorities. It certainly looked like Olek had not been a particularly law abiding citizen and may well have criminal connections.

Sean had found a lot of dots, but didn't quite have enough to join them, just yet. They needed to follow through with the plan to bug and put cameras in John Covington and Trevor Reid's offices.

Chapter 16

Before heading off to bed with Otto, Sean took a quick look at the messaging app on the telephone that Martin had provided him with. There was a brief and to the point message, 'Safe, call when you can'. Taking this as an invitation he made the call to the other encrypted mobile.

A cheerful Martin answered after only a few seconds, 'Hi Sean you were right we had visitors to my house, before you ask, we weren't there when they called.'

'So how do you know you had visitors?'.

'I left a few hidden cameras and hidden microphones strategically placed around the house, linked up to the security App on my phone. We had three armed individuals come straight through my front door all wearing masks literally 30 minutes ago. As far as I could tell they sounded Russian, or at least some of the words they used whilst ransacking the house were Russian.'

Sean asked Martin to put the phone on speaker whilst he recounted everything that had happened that day, as well as everything that he had been able to find during his trawl of the internet.

Once Sean had finished speaking Ceri explained that she and Martin had carried out more detailed analysis on the data that he had provided. The data suggested that an electronic smurfing operation was being run at Credit Finance Bank.

Sean's only knowledge of Smurfs were that they were little blue people popular in children's cartoons. Ceri assured him that this was nothing to do with children's cartoons.

'Smurfing is a money laundering term, where a lot of individuals make small deposits under the money laundering reporting cash threshold. This makes it harder to detect that money laundering is happening because it looks like a bunch of different individuals are depositing the money.

In the case of Credit Finance Bank, these small deposits are we believe not being made by people, but are being carried out electronically by a process within the bank. The money from thousands of smaller accounts is then being transferred internally within the bank into a dozen or so much larger accounts.

These accounts all appeared to belong to what appears to be legitimate, property management, property development, investment, or transport and logistics companies. The money in these larger accounts is then transferred out at the end of each month, using the banking system to other accounts in the UK, Europe, USA and Cayman Islands.

We believe the next transfer is due to take place in ten days time.'

Sean could hear the excitement and trepidation in Martin's voice as he interrupted Ceri's narrative.

'They transferred just over 50 bloody million euros last month Sean. They aren't laundering money for some back street brothel; this operation is big and involves a lot of people who are making a lot of money. We need to be incredibly careful, I'm sure we are all only too aware that people have died for a lot less.'

Sean could sense rather than see the reproving stare that Ceri must have given Martin as he mumbled an apology and left Ceri to continue her spiel.

'Martin's right Sean, if a little dramatic. We have noticed something very interesting, multiple bank transfers are being carried out on each account at the end of each month. 70% of the value goes in one large transfer with the other 30% being split between a bank in the USA which gets 25% and two accounts in the Cayman Islands which get 2.5% each.

What we haven't been able to do yet is identify the actual owners of any of the bank accounts to which the money is being sent, that will take a little bit more time.

If we take everything we have found so far including the Odessa connection. Sprinkle in the break ins at both mine and Martin's homes, I think we have the recipe for a major money laundering operation involving the Ukrainian Mafia and the bank. in fact It looks like we have our very own "Financial Mafia" working in the bank.'

Sean wasn't at all surprised by what Ceri suggested, but still felt the need to clarify his understanding of what had just been said.

'What you're saying Ceri is that the bank we work for is being used to facilitate money laundering for a Ukrainian organised crime group.'

It was a request for clarification that Sean was soon about to regret as Ceri went into full presentation mode. Sean needed to be educated and Ceri felt she was most certainly the person best placed to do it.

'That's exactly what I'm saying Sean. One of the downsides of the collapse of the former Soviet Union was the rise of criminal gangs in the former Soviet republics. Ukraine was no different.

When the Russians pulled out, they left behind large stockpiles of arms and ammunition. The Ukrainian Mafia grew from illicit international trafficking in these arms.

By all accounts Between 1992 and 1998, some 32 billion dollars in military material disappeared from military depots in Ukraine and ended up in West Africa, Central Asia and even Afghanistan.

Having dipped their toe into the murky pool of illicit trafficking in arms, it was only a short step for the Ukrainian crime syndicates to get involved in the international trade in illegal drugs.

Using the criminal connections, they had already built up, they soon became a major player in the narcotics trade between Central Asia, Afghanistan, and Central Europe.

When a number of Eastern European countries then joined the European Union, the same Ukrainian criminal organisations expanded their reach to become involved in people smuggling and prostitution. They take advantage of the open borders within the European Union to profit illegally from the human misery.'

Ceri paused for breath, but Sean could hear the disgust in her voice when she spoke again.

'Ukraine is a source, transit, and destination country for men, women, and children trafficked transnationally for the purposes of commercial, sexual exploitation and forced labour.

It Is also a major player in drug trafficking from the middle east and Afghanistan and our three branches are in countries which border Ukraine.'

Sean couldn't help but be impressed by Ceri's grasp of the subject and the depth of her knowledge, amazement that he found it impossible to hide.

'How the hell do you know all of this Ceri ?'

Sean was equally amazed when Ceri explained that she and Martin hadn't just been involved in corporate security assessments. They had also been involved in a little bit of freelance Cyber surveillance work for the security services.

According to Ceri the security services had their hands full with simply focussing on home grown terrorists. So they outsourced some of the less urgent intelligence gathering to people like Martin and her. Ukraine and Ukrainian Cyber criminals had apparently been on the security services watch list for some time.

As the story unfolded, it turned out Ceri also had a personal interest. Her brother Adam had been working for an international anti-slavery charity in eastern Europe when he upset the wrong people.

He had been instrumental in rescuing over 30 young girls who were being smuggled across the Ukrainian border into Poland. They were headed for the sex trade in western Europe.

Two weeks later Adam had been attacked as he left his office to go to a planned meeting with local police. He had been shot in the spine and was going to spend the rest of his life in a wheelchair.

At this point in her story Sean sensed Ceri getting a little emotional and by the sound of things slightly tearful. He could hear Martin making soothing sounds in the background. A slightly choked Ceri nonetheless continued her story.

'It could have been worse, the doctors didn't expect him to live, but its been difficult for him to adjust to life in a wheel chair. But at least he is still alive and is still doing his best from behind a desk to continue the fight against human trafficking.

So yes, I have first-hand experience of the misery that these people cause. They are a classic example of mans inhumanity to man, guns, drugs, people. It doesn't matter to them the misery they cause, so long as they get their filthy money.

All of these activities produce massive amounts of cash and it would appear that the bank for which we both work is being used to launder this cash. Worse it would appear that the bank's senior management are directly involved in the illegal activity.'

Sean was quiet and obviously contemplative when he eventually responded after a few moments of silence.

'Yes, Ceri but how do we prove it, and what do we do about it. We need to get more proof. We need to follow through with the plan to bug the offices of John Covington and Trevor Reid

We also need to get our boots on the ground in Eastern Europe and see what is actually happening in the effected bank branches.'

A cautious, but determined Ceri responded with steel in her voice.

'I totally agree Sean, but we need to be very careful. These people have a distorted sense of honour that is about protecting the organisation and their fellow members, whatever the cost to others. My brother Adam is living proof that they will have no qualms in dealing with someone who threatens their business interests.'

Martin's cheerful voice broke the sombre mood.

'Don't worry Ceri, me and Sean will be like Cyber Ninjas, they will never know we have been there.

Which branch should we visit first on our holidays Sean? And should I pack my swimmers?'

'We will go to Bratislava first Martin, I have a personal contact in that branch, who just like us will want to stop what is going on and should be able to help us gain access to the building.

Besides there's something I need to apologise for and it's the sort of apology that is best-done face to face.'

Sean couldn't let Martin's flippant comment about swimmers' slide, so laughing he told him,

'Bring your swimmers and a pot of Vaseline just in case wee man. We might have to grease you up and squeeze you through the branch letterbox to get in, if all else fails.'

Once the laughter had subsided, Sean quickly laid out the next steps in his plan.

He planned to be working late that Thursday on a network upgrade which would have an impact on several different floors of the banks head office building.

If Martin could acquire all the covert surveillance equipment they needed by then. Sean could get him access to the director's floor under cover of the ongoing upgrades.

Sean's voice took on a challenging edge obviously directed at Martin as he finalised his plan.

'If I can get you onto the directors' floor, I'm sure a man who broke into a Chief inspectors office in the middle of a police station should be well capable of getting into the two target offices.'

Martin, a man confident in his abilities quickly accepted the gauntlet that had just been thrown down.

'That's a challenge I could hardly refuse.

I'll be with you on Thursday night with everything I need. By the time I'm finished we'll be able to hear a mouse fart and see the cockroaches playing in the wastepaper bin.

There won't be anything they say or do in either of the two offices that we won't be able to see and record in glorious high-definition video and full surround sound.'

Chapter 17

That Thursday evening Sean made sure the network switches that powered and connected to the Banks security camera system were undergoing their upgrade at 8pm the time Martin had indicated he would be at the bank.

Sean had told Martin to come to a side roller shutter, used by the Banks management for weekend access to the under-building car park. Security at that location consisted of nothing more than monitored security cameras, which thanks to Sean, were currently providing as much coverage as a G string made of dental floss.

When Sean raised the motorised shutter, Martin walked calmly into the car park and shook his hand.

'So how do I get to the two offices from here Sean?'

Sean handed Martin a security pass.

'This card will open all necessary doors, apart from the two directors' offices. They are protected by traditional 5 lever locks; which I am sure you should have no problems picking.'

Sean then pointed towards a door labelled service stairwell.

'You need to go through that door and take the stairs to the 15th floor. Avoid using the lifts as they are still being monitored through a separate system.

The two offices that you are interested in are at the end of the corridor that you will find when you leave the stairwell. The doors are labelled so you should have no problem identifying the target offices.'

It was apparent that Martin had a distaste for all things athletic and he was quick to vocalise the horror he felt at the thought of the physical ordeal that lay ahead of him.

'Jesus Sean, 15th floor! if I'd known that I'd have spent the last two days training on a stair master. Keep your phone handy, you might have to come and get me if I have my first heart attack.'

Sean smiled fondly at his diminutive partner in crime and slapped him none too gently on the back.

'It'll be no problem to you Martin, you're a cyber ninja after all.'

Martin laughed and Sean watched his short companion jog purposefully towards the service stairwell. Sean gave him a head start of 2 minutes before following him through the door.

Whilst Martin made his way to the 15th floor Sean exited the staircase on the 2nd floor ostensively to check on how his IT colleagues were getting on with the upgrade and replacement of the network switches in the second-floor comms room.

Martin stopped twice on his way to the 15th floor, even so within ten minutes of leaving Sean, he stood panting, his forehead bathed in sweat, in the corridor in front of the two target offices.

Martin quickly picked the lock for John Covington's office before entering the well-appointed and rather opulent space. Once inside he wasted no time on starting the installation of the surveillance equipment. The plans that Sean had provided him with, had proven to be very useful and he already knew exactly what he planned to install and where.

Martin quickly upgraded two of the existing network points in the office and replaced them with new units. These units not only allowed the existing network connectivity to continue unabated, but also provided the facility to allow high-definition video and audio to be captured and streamed automatically to an internet hosted recording system using a 4G mobile connection.

Power for the newly installed equipment would be taken from the power over ethernet network connection provided by the bank's own network equipment. The system would continue to function so long as the network points were connected to the bank's corporate network.

The final pinhole camera, this one without audio was installed in the celling just above John Covington's desk. To the casual observer it looked just like a Philips head screw. Unfortunately, due to its location Martin had to install a battery power source above the celling which would power the camera for 60 days. Martin was sure that this would provide more than enough time to achieve what they needed to do.

Martin had suggested that they also bug the phones in both offices, but Sean had told him this would have been a pointless exercise. Sean pointed out that when anyone rang the bank they were greeted with a message saying , "Your call may be recorded for training and monitoring purposes".

Due to the recording of calls, it had been accepted practice for bank staff to use their mobile phones for difficult phone calls. This meant that any calls that might come back to bite them on the ass weren't recorded.

That being the case, it would be highly unlikely that John Covington and Trevor Reid would be using a desk phone connected to the banks call recording system to make anything other than purely legitimate calls.

Having installed all his devices in John Covington's office Martin verified that he could access them via the app on his mobile phone before relocking the office and replicating the operation on Trevor Reid the finance director's office.

Whilst Martin worked on the 15th floor, Sean spent the next two hours apprehensively waiting on the call which would tell him that Martin was ready to leave. It was essential that Martin finish the installation of the equipment and be ready to leave before the IT guys had completed their upgrade.

The plan necessitated Sean and Martin mingling with the rest of the team as they left the building. Bringing the security camera network down twice in one night might just be a little bit too suspicious, so Sean planned to hide Martin in plain sight amongst a gaggle of IT staff to get him safely out of the building. The security guys wouldn't pay any attention to another IT nerd leaving the building, after all they were there to keep undesirables out.

Finally, at ten thirty Sean's encrypted phone started to vibrate in his pocket, Martin had finished and as agreed was standing in the stairwell outside the door to the second floor, Sean's floor.

After retrieving Martin Sean checked with the network team leader as to the state of play with their nights official work. He informed Sean that everything had gone to plan, and the team would be completing their final checks by 11pm with the intention of leaving shortly after that.

At 10:45pm Sean and Martin came down the service stairwell to the ground floor and took two seats in the atrium close to the lifts and sat in apparently deep conversation so as to discourage any curious security staff from coming up for a chat.

At 11:05pm the lifts opened and disgorged the ten IT staff who had been helping with the upgrade. Sean waved generally in their direction getting a brief acknowledgement from several of the team as they focussed on getting themselves out of the building after a long day at the office.

Waiting until they were a few metres in front of them and heading for the exit , Sean and Martin nonchalantly got up from their seats. They followed the main body of staff through the security turnstiles, Martin using the card that Sean had provided him with earlier. Once through the turnstiles there was nothing to stop them as they walked straight out through the front door.

As they exited the building they parted, Martin walked across the front of the building heading towards the tube station, whilst Sean headed for the car park. Sean walked quickly and caught up with the IT team leader, taking the opportunity to get a quick debrief on how things had gone.

 Just because his primary concern this evening had been getting the surveillance equipment installed didn't mean that he didn't care about the guys who were working for him and it would have seemed out of place if he hadn't asked.

After finishing the conversation with his colleague, Sean bade him good night before getting into his car. Leaving the carpark, he headed for the tube station, where he stopped briefly to pick up

Martin who was by now halfway through a king-size pasty that he had picked up in one of the kiosks in the station entrance.

'I get hungry when I get excited,' mumbled Martin around a mouthful of pasty, as he spilled himself and a generous sprinkling of pastry crumbs into the passenger seat.

Ignoring the casual vandalism that Martin was inflicting upon his pristine car interior Sean pointed his car in the direction of Euston station and spent the next hour listening to Martin as he explained what he had done in the two offices.

During the briefing, Martin took Sean's encrypted phone from him and loaded the surveillance app that would allow him to access the audio-visual streams from the devices that had just been installed. He then gave Sean a very brief run down on how to operate the app in order to view either real time, or recorded video and audio footage.

At 30 minutes after midnight Sean dropped Martin outside Euston station. Martin had around 6 hours to wait on his train, but they both thought it best that Martin not be seen at Sean's house.

Sean stopped at the sparsely populated taxi rank outside the station to let Martin out. As the car stopped Martin turned and handed Sean a small canvas bag.

'I brought some extra equipment with me tonight; it might not be a bad idea if you beefed up your own security just in case'.

Sean took the bag without comment depositing it in the back seat as Martin got out of the car. As Martin disappeared through the station entrance Sean pulled out of the taxi rank and headed for home. Sean finally got his head down around 2am, leaving Otto to enjoy an undisturbed night at Mary's.

Chapter 18

The next morning Sean went into work a couple of hours late, after all he had been working late the previous night. On his arrival he found Alek sitting in his office waiting on him.

'Good morning Sean, we would like to take you up on your offer of help. Olek and I have not had much success in tracking Ms Gillis down. We have identified someone who may have been an old friend or colleague during our investigation, but unfortunately, we have not been able to speak to the individual.

However, we have concerns that the skill set that this person possesses may be of use to Ms Gillis if she were to try and gain access to the banks systems.'

Sean's response was dismissive.

'The bank's systems are tied up tighter than a ducks arse, and that's water tight.'

Alek smiled condescendingly at Sean's interruption before continuing.

'We appreciate that, and we appreciate that you have a pride in the security infrastructure that you have helped build here. But I have spoken with Mr Covington, and he has requested that I ask you to carry out a further detailed review alongside another member of my security team. We want to focus on all means of external access into the bank's core infrastructure.'

Alek paused distorting his face into a facsimile of a smile, which from Sean's rather cynical perspective looked more like the pained grimace of a man with grumbling haemorrhoids.

'Given your confidence, I am sure the review will allow us to close this unfortunate situation down and provide the bank with certainty which will allow it to dispense with our services for now.'

Sean couldn't believe his luck, with these guys off site he would be able to implement some minor changes on the firewalls which would give him unfettered access to the banks systems without alerting the security monitoring systems.

Sean couldn't have been more surprised when an hour later, instead of another hulking Eastern European, a short bespectacled individual in a long raincoat knocked on his door. The archetypal IT nerd introduced himself in a broad Dublin brogue as Phil Donaghy.

As it turned out Phil didn't work directly for Alek, rather he worked for a well-known Cyber security business based in Manchester, who's name Sean immediately recognised. His organisation had been contacted the previous day and asked to complete a thorough review of the Banks Firewalls.

Phil pompously explained that he had been tasked with carrying out two key operations. Audit the firewall rule change process and then audit the firewall rule base itself. Phil estimated that this process would take the best part of two days.

For the rest of that day Sean sat with Phil as he explained the bank's overall change control process and how it was applied to firewall changes. Phil seemed particularly interested in how the requester of a change was recorded and who verified their authorisation to request the change.

Phil extracted a sample of the change request forms which had exclusively been requested by Ceri Gillis, and had Sean show him on the firewalls how these changes had been implemented.

By the end of the day Sean had become conscious of a definite pattern in Phil's work. It was obvious that Phil had been given specific instructions to review any work that had been requested by Ceri Gillis in the last 12 months. The thankfully short time he had spent with the irritating Phil had done nothing to change Sean's view on IT auditors as being individuals who would always rather be right than reasonable. Watching Phil pack up, Sean knew with an unshakeable certainty that he would rather slide down a barbed wire banister into a bath of disinfectant than ever do Phil's job.

After showing Phil out of his office for the day Sean checked the messaging app on his encrypted phone and saw a message from Martin asking that he give them a call as soon as he could. He responded that he would call once he reached home.

On reaching home Sean immediately went to Mary's to retrieve Otto, much to the big dog's obvious delight. The excited canine managed to decorate both Mary's hall carpet and Sean's brown brogues with a welcoming jet of pee.

After helping a laughing Mary to clean up the mess Sean headed home and set about getting food together for both himself and Otto, before ringing Ceri and Martin.

The ever cheerful Martin answered the call immediately, and an impatient Sean got straight down to business without any social preamble.

'Hi Martin, so what have you found?'

Martin's concise and business-like response took Sean just a little by surprise.

'Well Sean, we've been able to trace a number of the accounts that money is being sent to. From what we can see they all appear to be legitimate business, or personal accounts. Ceri thinks that isn't really that unusual, I'll let her explain.'

Sean could hear Ceri take a deep breath as she prepared to give Sean the detail of what they had discovered.

'What Martin has just told you is fairly typical of the final, integration stage of the money laundering process. The dirty money that has been washed through the financial system ends up in seemingly legitimate accounts.

One way of integrating large amounts of cash is through the procurement of property, either by buying it, or building it and then selling it on.

A lot of the companies we have identified are property and investment companies, much like those owned by the Kulkas family. We have also identified a number of logistics organisations.'

Ceri paused for breath and Sean detected a little hesitancy in her voice, as she started to speak again.

'I wasn't sure where this information was leading us, so I spoke to my brother Adam, and asked for his opinion.

In his experience with human trafficking, seemingly legitimate construction companies with connections to organised crime frequently use trafficked men as cheap labour and trafficked women to provide sexual services to their male labour force.

As for the logistics companies these are probably the people who are doing the drug and people trafficking into Europe. Whilst smuggling the weapons in the other direction. The same weapons that create the mayhem that the trafficked people want to escape from.'

This was all very interesting background information but didn't actually change much from Sean's point of view and he made no attempt to hide his impatience.

'OK Ceri, so what you and Martin are saying is that everything you can see in the data is confirming what we already know. An as yet unconfirmed number of the senior management team in Credit Finance bank are allowing the bank to be used in a major money laundering operation.'

Ceri had obviously been holding back, because she seemed very pleased with herself when she next spoke.

'Not just that Sean, we may also have an answer as to who in the bank is directly involved. Martin has been able to identify the owner of the account in the US which is receiving 25% of all transfers. This account is owned by Odessa Capital overseas investments LLC in Florida. That organisation is linked directly to Alek Kulkas.

But more importantly Martin has been able to identify the owners of two accounts in the Cayman Islands. The owners are John Covington and Trevor Reid.'

The phone went quiet as Ceri let Sean absorb what had just said, before continuing in a more animated tone of voice.

'It would appear from the money trail that the Kulkas family are using the bank to facilitate a major money laundering operation and are receiving a 25% cut for their services.

We have also now found a financial connection between Alek Kulkas and the chief executive and the finance director at the bank. I think we can see with a high degree of certainty that John Covington and Trevor Reid are directly benefitting from the proceeds of money laundering.

That explains why they were so nervous about what I found; it was just the tip of a very dirty iceberg.

We have evidence that those greedy bastards at the top of the bank, not satisfied with their fat salaries and big bonuses have been benefitting from human misery and lining their pockets with dirty money.'

A more cautious Sean tried to curb Ceri's enthusiasm.

'Ceri, I understand what you are saying, but We don't have evidence. You and Martin have done great work, but all we have at the moment is a connection.

We still need to see the cash coming into the bank, We need to go to the branches and see for ourselves how the money is coming in. When we have that we are in a position to do something about the whole rotten situation.'

Ceri raised her voice obviously impatient with what she say as Sean's lack of enthusiasm.

'Sean, Martin and I are both on board with what you have suggested, but what do we do next, what is your plan?'

Sean needed Ceri to understand that this wasn't something they could rush, so taking a considered tone he explained the next steps.

'We need to take one step at a time, and at the moment I have a situation in work which I need to deal with. Alek Kulkas has called in another security consultant to review our security infrastructure. He seems to have concerns that you and Martin might be planning to get up to no good.

This guy Phil seems to have been given specific instructions to check to see if you had authorised anything which would facilitate someone getting unfettered remote access to the bank's network.

Of course, you haven't, and he isn't going to find anything, but once Phil has left the building, I will be making a few minor adjustments of my own.'

Sean spelt out how he intended to provide a backdoor into the banks firewall, which would give them direct and unfettered access to all systems currently operating within the bank.

He would then book himself a couple of weeks leave. That should give him and Martin enough time to get their boots on the ground at the branches that were being used for the money laundering.

Sean was confident that If he did his job right, by tomorrow evening they would have the ability to access all the banks systems. Including the security systems in the three branches that were being used for the money laundering. Using the back door into the banks systems provided by Sean, Martin would be able to disable the security systems and allow easy access to each of the branches. Once inside they would plant further surveillance equipment which would allow them to gather direct evidence of the criminal activities being facilitated by the bank.

Ceri had listened patiently as Sean laid out his plan, but it was obvious that she wasn't completely happy with what she had just heard.

'I appreciate that you want to be careful Sean, but once we gather that evidence what are we going to do? You are in the happy situation that Alek Kulkas and our friends at the bank see you as an asset.

Your house hasn't been invaded by unwanted visitors who want to do you harm. Just gathering the evidence and passing it to the authorities isn't going to make the problems that Martin and I have go away.

As far as these guys are concerned Martin and I are public enemy number one. An investigation into the bank, which doesn't involve their immediate incarceration is going to leave us in a difficult situation.

They will quite rightly assume that Martin and I had a hand in their legal woes and will do their best to ensure that we aren't around to further complicate their legal situation.

We also have the more immediate issue of how we even get out of the country. From what you have said there is every possibility that they are monitoring the London and possibly other UK airports to see if Martin and I appear.'

Sean thought carefully before he spoke again, he knew Ceri was agitated and could understand why. She was right he could walk away now without any real concerns for his safety.

Ceri and Martin on the other hand were being actively sought by people who were trying to protect a multimillion-euro operation that profited from human misery. If they were found, both Ceri and Martin would be in grave danger.

'I agree with you entirely Ceri, but I don't have all the answers just yet. What I do have is a way to get you both safely out of the country. Once I get home tomorrow night I will ring, and we can sort out travel arrangements.'

Sean's voice then took on a more encouraging tone as he addressed Ceri's other concern.

'What we need is a way of misdirecting the attention of Alek Kulkas, John Covington and Trevor Reid when the authorities come calling. They have already opened the door to the possibility of an intervention by a cyber gang. Why don't we use that possibility to muddy the waters?

If you both put your heads together, I'm sure you'll be able to come up with something that will redirect their attention long enough for us to get them behind bars. With the experience you both have in targeting Eastern European cyber criminals I'm sure you can come up with something plausible.'

Sean could hear Ceri grunt non-committaly on the other end of the phone. Martin on the other hand was audibly exuberant at the thought of letting his mischievous side go wild to create mayhem for Alek his co-conspirators.

Sean couldn't help but think, that if life had handed Martin lemons, he would have made lemonade, then gone out and found someone who had been handed vodka and had a party. Martin's cheerful demeanour was certainly growing on him he thought, as smiling he ended the call.

Chapter 19

The next day a very impatient Sean sat with a very annoying Phil going through the tedious process of reviewing the network diagram for the bank and cross referencing this to the rules that were configured on the firewall.

Eventually a very pedantic Phil closed his Laptop, satisfied that all points on his checklist had been met to his satisfaction. Looking at Sean he asked if he could possibly be brought to Mr Covington's office, so he could provide a preliminary verbal report of his findings.

Sean took Phil to the lift and after hitting the button for the 15th floor he queried Phil as to whether anything needed immediate remediation, or had he found things to be satisfactory. Phil bent forward and looking over his glasses at Sean, told him that he had been instructed to report directly to the chief executive and no one else, however he had found nothing that Sean should be concerned about.

Reaching the 15th floor Sean took Phil to John Covington's office and knocked before opening the door, to see both Alek and Trevor Reid sitting in front on the boss's desk.

'Come in Philip' said a beaming John Covington, 'We have been awaiting your report with some trepidation. Sean would be so kind as to close the door on your way out.'

Getting back to his office Sean decided that it might be useful to listen in on the conversations that were currently taking place in the chief executive's office.

Closing his door and attaching the earphones to the encrypted telephone Sean opened the app in real time mode so he could listen to the conversation currently taking place in the chief executive's office.

At the end of an hour when Phil had completed his report, Sean sat back and smiled thinking that's an hour of their lives they are never getting back.

It had been a painful hour for Sean and must have been excruciating for the three amigos as they listened to Phil drone on about proper protocol, fully integrated security systems and effective change control. Especially when all they wanted to know could have been summed up in his final sentence.

'Your network is effectively managed and secured and is secure if not more secure from hostile access than any I have seen.'

Once Phil had left the building Sean logged onto the firewall stack, temporarily disabled logging and made the configuration changes required to give him complete and unrestricted remote access to the bank's IT network.

Re-enabling logging Sean logged out of his computer and left the office, content that should it be required he had the ability to access all systems and data on the banks network from wherever he might be during his pending two weeks off.

Arriving home that night he picked up Otto as usual, but took the opportunity to explain to Mary that he would be going to Bratislava to visit Anna and wondered if she would be able to look after the big dog during his absence.

A beaming Mary told Sean she would be only too happy to keep Otto, she also expressed delight that Sean had at last seen sense. With her agony aunt hat firmly attached, Mary left Sean in no doubt that resolving his difficulties with Anna would be the sensible thing to do. She had missed Anna and she had no doubt that Sean had missed her even more. So, giving Sean a supportive hug, she assured him that Otto would be perfectly safe with her whilst he sorted out his life.

Once home Sean fed Otto and himself before ringing Martin and Ceri to discuss travel plans. However, before he could start, Ceri spoke.

'We think we have found a way to close this down safely for all of us.'

Ceri explained that she and Martin had been watching the video feed from John Covington's office that evening.

'So you saw Phil giving them the good news that they had nothing to worry about?'

'We did indeed Sean, and I am sure you felt immensely proud when he gave his final summary,' Laughed Ceri.

Sean's mother had often told him that sarcasm was the lowest form of wit. On this occasion he was happy to let it slide, as Ceri was obviously feeling in much better form than yesterday evening.

'After Phil left, Martin and I continued to watch the video feed and we saw something very interesting. We watched John Covington take a laptop out of his top desk drawer and log into his Cayman Islands bank account.'

'What's so interesting about that Ceri, we already know he has a Cayman Islands account?'

'Yes, but now we also know the bank that he is using, his user id, his password and four of the digits for his passcode.

Obviously this isn't quite enough to be sure of getting access to the bank account, but we are sure, given time we can gather the remaining digits of his passcode and get access to his bank account.

We suspect but can't be sure yet that Trevor Reid will have a similar arrangement for keeping his Cayman account details safe and we will be reviewing the video footage from his office to confirm this.

Assuming we have both their login details and a security authentication device from the bank that they are using we can reallocate the illegal wealth that they have gathered to a more deserving cause.'

'Ceri, I hope you're not suggesting that we steal their money and reallocate to the bank of Ceri and Martin. That will just make them all the more determined to find you and make you disappear.'

'Ooh get off your sanctimonious high horse Sean, we are going to give it to the authorities as part of the body of evidence we are going to provide.

But you're right we will be muddying the waters somewhat, so they can't attribute it to us.'

Martin then explained that using the access that Sean would provide they were going to do two things. Firstly they would destroy the pipeline that has been supplying Covington and company with their ill-gotten gains. Then they were going to redirect all of the funds that would normally be going to the criminal organisations into a financial black hole.

Martin was certain that if shutting down the pipeline didn't do it, then the actual loss of money should put the three amigos on the shite list with their business partners. That should give them a lot more to think about than him and Ceri.

As Martin cheerfully put it.

'If they are busy covering their backsides and trying to avoid being given a pair of concrete slippers, they will be too distracted to pin anything on any of us.'

The plan sounded simple if you said it quickly, but Sean had concerns which he made very clear to Ceri and Martin at the other end of the phone line.

'That's all very well and good, but how do we get access to a security authentication device and how do we get access to their money without them knowing?'

Ceri had no such concerns, as she eagerly outlined an embryonic plan.

'The Security device is the easy part, all we have to do is open an account with the bank, but to do that we need to get to the Cayman Islands. As for accessing their cash I'll leave that to Martin, what we are going to need to do isn't entirely legal.'

Martin admitted that over the last year or so he hadn't always been able to get access to the type of work that he carried out when he and Ceri had worked together. Indeed, on occasion he had resorted to doing work of dubious legality for some unsavoury individuals.

Martin sounded buoyant when he finished his story.

'To be honest if you were standing at the legal end of the scale you would have needed the Hubble space telescope to find me. This is an opportunity to get some pay back and rebalance things in favour of the good guys.'

Sean couldn't help but laugh.

'Well Martin, its wonderful that you've had this sudden epiphany and I'm all in favour making the world a better place. But how do we do this without ending up with our balls in a Ukrainian vice whilst they tear out our toenails?'

'Yes Sean we will need to be careful', interrupted Ceri , 'But like you said, we need to take this one step at a time and the next step is getting us out of the country. That is going to be tricky with all the airports being watched from what you have told us.'

'Not that difficult if we don't use the airports.'

Sean then updated Ceri and Martin on his proposed plan. Very simply they were going to take the ferry to Ireland. Sean explained that strictly speaking British and Irish citizens didn't need a passport when traveling between the two countries.

So, Ceri and Martin just needed to use their contacts to get themselves photo ID in a different name, something like a photo card driving licence. Then book themselves onto the Holyhead to Dublin ferry as foot passengers.

Sean would book himself onto the same Ferry with his car and would pick up the two foot passengers at the other end of the ferry journey in Dublin. His going to Ireland under his own name wouldn't register as unusual as his mother still lived in County Tyrone.

Once in Ireland they could use a well-known travel website to rent themselves a country cottage for a few days whilst they finalised their plans.

Chapter 20

That Saturday as Sean sat in a queue in lane four of the parking area, waiting to drive his car onto the Ferry, he saw Martin and then Ceri walk up the covered walkway onto the ship separated by around 20 other foot passengers. Good to see that they were taking precautions and doing their best not to be seen together thought Sean.

At last after another 15 minutes, the queue in lane four started to move and Sean drove up the loading ramp onto an already half full car deck. After carefully parking under rapid fire instructions and hand signals from the deckhand, Sean made his way via the internal stairway up to the passenger deck on the ferry.

The ship was noisy and thankfully busy, best place to hide is in a crowd thought Sean. From the conversations that were going on around him in an excited Dublin brogue, Sean realised that many of his fellow passengers had just come from Chester racecourse.

Most seemed to be in great form, doing their best to celebrate a successful day at the races for either themselves, or their travelling companions. It was apparent that the celebrations had started well before they had boarded the ship as quite a few of the celebrants were already a bit unsteady on their feet and the ship hadn't even left its moorings.

From the crowd of well-dressed men and women that had gathered around the bar at the front of the ship it was plain that the erstwhile race goers fully intended to continue the assault on their livers until the ferry docked in Dublin.

It going to be carnage in the toilets today thought Sean, I just hope the crossing isn't rough. It's going to be bad enough wading through ankle deep urine in the gents, without having to negotiate piles of sick.

Finding a seat in the middle of the passenger deck away from the bar, Sean sat down and took out a book and prepared to chill out during the short sea crossing. Just opposite, one lucky individual, probably tired and emotional after his visit to Chester had commandeered a bench. The bench which normally seated four had morphed into a bed, which the inebriated man lay sprawled across snoring with gusto, his head resting on a 24 pack of Guinness that he had bought in the onboard shop.

Sean smiled, that reminded him of his time in the RAF. With a weekend pass in their pockets, he and his mates had been able to travel to different RAF bases in Europe on scheduled supply flights free. Once there, they had been able to enjoy the nightlife in the local towns before flying back in an alcohol induced coma strapped into a jump seat.

That had been great craic thought Sean, up until the point he and two of his mates had missed the return flight from RAF Akrotiri and ended up being confined to base for a month after getting stranded in Cyprus for three days.

Twenty minutes after he set down Sean felt the Ferry judder as it pulled away from the dock and started the crossing to Dublin. During the three hour crossing Sean did his best to drink as little as possible whilst he read his book, and booked a small cottage on the outskirts of Dublin. Unfortunately, two hours into the crossing he had to eventually give in to a call of nature and go to the gents.

As he stepped over the threshold into the men's toilets Sean was thankful that he'd had the foresight to wear a stout pair of waterproof gortex boots. As he splashed his way towards the urinals, he fought valiantly to ignore the stink that arose from the disgusting mess that rippled around his feet. It's like a pigs paddling pool, God help anyone wearing flipflops he thought as he released the contents of his bladder and beat a hasty retreat back to his seat.

Fifteen minutes prior to the ferry docking in Dublin an announcement asked all car passengers to make their way to their vehicles. Sean joined the stream of rather unsteady humanity as it headed towards the car decks. He really hoped the designated drivers had stuck to the plan, otherwise the disembarkation might get a little hairy.

Much to Sean's surprise the Ferry disgorged it's cargo of vehicles without any drama. Once on terra firma Sean left the Ferry terminal and found a quiet stretch of road just outside the entrance to the terminal to await the arrival of Ceri and Martin.

Ten minutes later Sean saw the two figures approach in his rear-view mirror. Hitting the remote release for his boot he encouraged them to deposit their backpacks in the boot of the car before getting in. Ceri got into the back seat and Martin joined him in the front of the Audi.

Punching the address details of the cottage into cars sat nav, Sean pulled the car away from the kerb and headed for Dublin Harbour tunnel, before heading north and following directions to the quaint Irish cottage that they would be renting for the next two weeks.

It took them just over an hour to reach their destination in Ashbourne Co Meath, having stopped on the way to buy some provisions. At the property They were met by a very friendly middle aged and very matronly Irish woman. The very thoughtful lady insisted on explaining how both the broadband and satellite television worked before handing Sean the keys and bidding them good night.

They all quickly threw their rucksacks into their chosen bedrooms before returning to the kitchen. Once there, Martin threw some frozen ready meals and garlic bread into the oven before joining Ceri and Sean at the table.

As they sat around the table awaiting on their food to cook, they started to make plans for the two weeks ahead. Whilst Sean and Martin were going to fly from Dublin to Vienna, before taking a train to Bratislava, Ceri planned to fly out of Dublin to the Cayman Islands.

On arrival in the Cayman Islands, she would open a new account in the same bank currently receiving funds for John Covington and Trevor Reid. Once she had completed the account opening process, Ceri would pass the details of the account to Martin and Sean so that the account could be funded electronically by transfers from Credit Finance bank.

'So how exactly are we going to fund this account from Credit Finance bank?' asked Sean.

'That's very simple' said a smiling Ceri. 'You are going to use the remote access you have given yourself to login to the banks systems. Then you are going to change the nominated bank account for the dozen or so interbank transfer accounts we have identified, so that all funds are sent to my newly opened Cayman Islands account.'

Sean stared at Ceri, aghast, surely, she couldn't be serious.

'Now hold on Ceri, this is the Ukrainian Mafia we are dealing with, when they find out their money has gone to Ceri Gillis, you'll be top of their shit list'.

Ceri smiled, completely unphased by Sean's outburst and confidently continued with her explanation.

'I'm touched by your concern Sean, but my name won't have any connection with this money. Whilst getting our fake photo ID for the trip to Dublin I took the opportunity to furnish myself with a fake passport.

Whilst the passport probably wouldn't pass muster going through immigration, I'm sure it would pass casual inspection when I use it as ID to open the new account in the Caymans. The person who is going to be on the shit list will be Iryna Kulkas and by extension the rest of the Kulkas clan, not to mention her husband John Covington.

Once the account has been funded, I should then receive my security device from the bank. Using that and the login details for our two favourite directors we will transfer the contents of John and Trevor's accounts to mine, or should I say Iryna's account.'

'I can imagine the conversation over cornflakes the morning John realises Iryna has stolen all his money,' laughed Martin.

Sean nodded, quietly impressed by the apparent simplicity of Ceri's plan, but a cautious inner voice reminded him that that other elements of the plan might not just be as straight forward. He and Martin still needed to get into the three branches to place cameras so they could gather evidence to go with the money they were going to send to the authorities.

They needed to find how the money was being fed into the bank and by whom. They also needed to place hidden cameras and listening devices in all branches to get as much evidence as possible. Martin thought the icing on the cake would be recording footage of John, Trevor and Alek having to explain themselves to their criminal colleagues in glorious technicolour with full surround sound.

Their discussions were suddenly interrupted by the high pitched throbbing of the smoke alarm, as a column of dark smoke had started to escape from the oven.

'Time for dinner' coughed Martin as he opened the oven door to be assaulted by a face full of eyebrow singeing smoke and hot air.

As they sat drinking the last of the red wine, surrounded by the remains of what had turned out to cremated garlic bread and a lasagne that could well have been made in a tire factory. Sean's mind couldn't stop spinning, how on earth were they going to get into three secure bank branches without setting off any alarms?

With what they were planning Sean simply couldn't walk through the door, flash his ID and say 'Hello I'm Sean from Head Office.' They had to do this under cover of darkness without being seen. Not only did they need to disable the alarm system, but they also needed a door card which would provide access to all rooms. Sean realised that he had a lot of thinking to do, as he reminded himself "Proper preparation prevents piss poor performance."

They needed to perform a proper reconnaissance of their chosen battlefield, namely the three bank branches. They could do some of this using the banks own security systems which he could access through the trap door that he had created in the bank firewalls.

Equally importantly they needed information from someone on the ground. And much as he hated the thought of putting her in any danger Sean knew that he needed Anna's help.

Sean had difficulty sleeping that night as he worried about Anna's safety if he got her involved. He had no doubts about Ann's honesty he had always found her to be forthright and brutally honest, sometimes too honest he thought. He couldn't help but smile, as he thought of some of the very blunt things she had said to him, during their three years together.

Anna left you under no illusion if she thought something needed to be said, she said it. His smile broadened, as he remembered the day he made the mistake of suggesting his jeans had shrunk in the wash. Anna had looked at him and said, 'No your jeans haven't shrunk you have gotten fat, you need to do more exercise before your ass takes on the shape of that chair you sit in every day.'

Taking Anna's encouragement onboard, Sean had joined a Gym already attended by Anna and she had taken on the role of trainer. He couldn't help but admire her dedication and stamina in the Gym and had been amazed with her level of fitness, less of a surprise was the fact that she looked pretty amazing in her well fitted gym gear.

After using the various cardio and weights machines Anna would get them both an exercise mat and they would do what Anna called core exercises together. It was whilst doing these exercises that Sean had realised just how far he had let himself go since his days in the RAF.

Sean remembered that early on whilst doing Russian twists, he had complained that his legs hurt. Anna had set the kettlebell that she had been using on the floor and turned to Sean and said, "You cry like a little girl, getting fit is hard, but feeling weak is hard, you must choose your hard." Sean had chosen to get fit. 'Yeah' thought Sean 'add inspirational to that list of things I love about her.' As he rolled over on his side and tried to get some sleep.

Chapter 21

The next morning being Sunday Sean knew Anna would be at home so decided to take the bull by the horns and ring her.

'Hi Anna it's me, Sean, long time no speak,' he said tentatively when she answered his call. Sean's heart was in his throat as he waited for a response, there was a deafening silence, as Sean presumed, she was deciding whether to put the phone down or not, but eventually she spoke.

'Hello Sean' she responded with that languorous Slavic accent that he had always loved. Just hearing her voice now made his heart beat faster. How could I have let her go, what an dickhead I've been, he thought.

'So why are you choosing to ring me now, when you haven't cared to be in touch for the last three months?' She asked in her usual blunt eastern European matter of fact way. Her question brought Sean back to earth with a bump.

Sean knew that he missed Anna and had made a mistake letting her go and not making the commitment that she so obviously wanted. He also knew that it would be a big mistake to say that before asking for her help.

'I need your help Anna, we have uncovered something at the bank involving your branch that needs to be fixed.'

Anna's clipped tone suggested that Sean had a lot of work to do, if he wanted her help.

'So why are you calling me, surely your friends in head office are better placed to fix a problem, if it exists?'

Sean knew that he had just one chance to get her on board and saw no other option that to tell her the whole story. As Anna listened silently, Sean spent the next ten minutes giving her a run down on everything that he, Ceri and Martin had discovered.

Anna was curious rather that hostile when she asked her next question.

'So why are you helping Ceri Gillis?' asked Anna, 'I thought you had an extreme dislike for the woman.'

'Because it's the right thing to do' said Sean 'all it takes for evil to prevail is for good people to do nothing. I simply can't stand by knowing what I know and do nothing.'

'Yes, you always were a stubborn man, with an over developed sense of right and wrong' said Anna.

Sean couldn't help but think he detected a tiny hint of affection in her voice as she spoke, perhaps it was wishful thinking, but as his father would have said, "nothing ventured nothing gained."

'Anna I will be in Bratislava tomorrow evening, can I take you out for dinner so we can talk about how you might be able to help us?'

'No' came the abrupt response and Sean's heart sank, 'No we will not go out for dinner, you will come to my apartment, and we will talk in private about what can be done and whether I want to help you.'

Anna gave Sean the address for her department before reminding him that as she was providing the food he would be responsible for bringing the wine.

Before hanging up Sean said 'Anna; I am really sorry that I forced you to go to Bratislava, I have really missed you.'

Anna paused before replying, 'yes Sean you were a complete asshole, but I miss my girly gym buddy too. See you tomorrow night'. With that she hung up, leaving Sean to stare at the now inactive mobile in his hand.

After getting a shower and putting on some fresh clothes Sean headed into the kitchen to find Ceri and Martin already busy in the kitchen.

Martin had ensconced himself in front of his laptop, whilst Ceri busied herself cooking breakfast. As Sean entered the room Ceri momentarily turned her attention from the sausages sizzling in the frying pan, 'Martin has used your credit card to book two flights tomorrow morning to Vienna and two train tickets to Bratislava, hope you don't mind?'

Sean realised that he had left his wallet sitting on the kitchen table the previous evening and it now lay open in front of Martin. 'Of course not Ceri, you guys have already put my life and job in jeopardy, why not go the whole hog and screw my finances as well', Sean answered sarcastically.

'Don't worry Sean once this is all over we'll pay you back for everything, including my flight to the Cayman Islands which leaves at 5pm this evening,' said Ceri with a cheeky grin as she started plating up the breakfast.

Martin had been watching Sean and saw his jaw clench in anger. Ceri had wound Sean up, and Martin realised he needed to take some heat out of the situation. Looking directly at Sean and clearing his throat to attract his attention, Martin gently explained why the perceived liberties had been taken with Sean's credit card.

'It would be for the best if mine and Ceri's bank accounts remained inactive for the time being. As you are the only one not currently on the Kulkas most wanted list, it was only logical that we use your bank cards.'

Martin then tapped his rucksack and added 'I have a few thousand Euros in my bag so once we get to Europe, I'll treat you to a couple of beers.'

'And I have enough cash in my bag to get a few nights in a swish hotel in George Town with no questions asked', added Ceri.

Sean's face softened, he took a deep breath and nodded his agreement.

'Yes Martin, I know you're right, but next time do me a favour and ask before going through my wallet.'

'Understood Sean, by the way who is the girl who's picture I found in your wallet? Lovely girl I have to say'.

Sean's demeanour changed immediately; his face was lit up by a smile as he happily answered Martin's question.

'That's Anna my ex, I'm meeting with her tomorrow night in Bratislava to see if she can help us. We're meeting at her apartment, and before you ask buddy the invitation only extends to me, you'll have to sort yourself out for something to eat tomorrow night.'

Martin could see that Sean thought a lot of Anna, so he just couldn't resist yanking his chain.

'Well Sean I can understand why a big ugly lump like you, wouldn't want me around, they do say good things come in small packages. The lovely lady probably wouldn't be able to contain herself once she laid eyes on me and my small package.'

Sean couldn't help laughing at the smaller man's self-deprecating good humour.

'I think she might have a smaller uglier cousin who might be right up your street Martin. I'll be sure to get her number for you.'

Ceri had been listening to the exchange between the two men and could sense the developing friendship. She just hoped their jovial mood wasn't going to distract them from the job in hand.

'listen boys the next transfer is due to take place in five days. We need to focus, this isn't a holiday.

In the time we have left I need to tie up things in the Cayman Islands. You two need to have planted your equipment in three branches in three different countries. And Sean you need to have updated the bank details on our list of accounts before the transfer takes place.

So can I suggest that we all review what needs to be done in the time we have remaining today.'

The ever hungry and impish Martin knew exactly what was required.

'Well Ceri, the first thing we need to do is to eat that breakfast that you have so lovingly prepared. Sean and I have male metabolisms that won't survive on fresh air and happy thoughts. So if you don't mind throw those plates down here and lets get on with our day.'

After breakfast had been cleared away, Sean and Martin sat down at Sean's laptop and connected onto the banks systems via the unmonitored link that Sean had created. Sean quickly gained access to the database server and spent an hour writing a piece of SQL code which would change the nominated bank account details for all the accounts that they had identified.

To sow further seeds of confusion, he made sure that the changes would have an audit record which showed the change had been made by John Covington.

Leaving the SQL to one side, he next set up a link which allowed him to get access to the bank's security camera system. Once he had achieved a working connection Martin used this to access the security cameras in the three branches which they intended to gain access to.

The cameras from what they could see gave all round coverage of the exterior of the branches and good coverage of the banking hall and back office area in each of the branches.

Next, they tried to gain access to the alarm systems. Sean had considerable doubt as to whether this was going to be possible, and had reconciled himself to having to disable the alarms the old fashioned way, using a code entered into the alarm keypad.

There had been a data breach at a major US retailer in 2013 which resulted in the credit and debit card details of over 100 million customers being stolen. The attackers had hacked their way into the retailers corporate network by compromising a third-party supplier, who's refrigeration control systems had direct access to the corporate network.

After news of this breach became common knowledge It had been Sean's strong recommendation to the board and advice to the Richard Head's IT team that any such potential compromises be addressed. It became recognised best practice at the bank to keep service networks accessed by external providers off the main network

Much to Sean's amazement Martin found that the alarm systems for all branches and head office could still be accessed on the bank's corporate network. Sean's amazement turned to professional disgust when Martin gained access to the systems by using a default user and password which had not been reset. How someone could leave a password of "Changeme" unchanged was beyond his imagination.

His relief at having a means of controlling the alarm systems was tempered somewhat by his disappointment that people he knew could have been so sloppy in relation to the security in the bank.

Martin sat back in his chair with an air of satisfaction.

'OK Sean I'm onto the alarm systems for all three branches and they seem to have been configured for three zones. Banking hall, back office, and back corridor. When I look at how each of the zones are configured I can see alarm keypads, motion sensors and door sensors all of which I can disable through this system.'

Martin paused and continued with just a hint of anxiety in his voice.

'I am slightly concerned that the alarm and camera zones don't match. We have no apparent cameras covering the back corridor.'

Where Martin saw a challenge, Sean saw an opportunity.

'That can only mean one thing Martin, the back corridor is where we need to be and where we need to plant our own cameras. Obviously the powers that be in the bank, don't want any video evidence of what is happening there.

I dare say one of the alarm door sensors is for a backdoor which is not covered by any of the exterior cameras and that could be our way in. Whilst we can't see what is happening there, the upside is that once we are inside there will be no video evidence that we have ever been there.'

As Sean finished speaking Ceri stood up and placed her hand gently on his shoulder, 'it's time for you to drop me at the airport Sean.'

Leaving Martin to continue his trawl through the alarm and camera systems Sean got his keys and escorted Ceri to the car. On the way to the airport the atmosphere in the car was slightly strained. Both of them knew that what they were about to do could be putting everyone in great personal danger.

As Ceri went to get out of the car at the airport Sean put his left hand gently on her shoulder and as she turned in her seat he held out his right hand. Ceri stared ad his hand for a moment before the gesture registered and she took his hand for a good luck handshake.

Only a few days ago Sean couldn't have ever imagined feeling any concern for Ceri, but right now he felt protective towards the woman sitting beside him.

'You be careful Ceri, I have the pocket ninja to look after me where I'm going, you need to look after yourself. Besides I don't know if I could survive two weeks on Martin's cooking.'

Ceri laughed.

'I know, Martin is one of the few people I know who can burn boiling water, I think the smoke alarm is probably his biggest fan in the kitchen.'

Ceri paused and looked Sean in the eye.

'You be careful too Sean, and look after Martin for me, he has a habit of getting himself in trouble. He's my dearest friend and I'd never forgive myself if anything happened to him on my account.'

Sean nodded in acknowledgement as Ceri swung round in her seat and got out of the car. At the end of the day, thought Sean, we are all ordinary individuals who have found ourselves in an extraordinary situation and are pretty much making this up as we go along.

Sean's old commanding officer in the RAF had often said "No plan survives first contact with the enemy, so we should always have a plan B a plan C and a plan D". Sean just hoped that their plan A worked, and they didn't end up with a plan Z which resulted in Otto becoming an orphan.

Chapter 22

After dropping Ceri at the airport Sean drove straight back to the cottage. Martin had shut down the laptop, having seen all he needed to see and had just put on the kettle to make a pot of tea.

'I'm going to need your ex's address Sean' said Martin as he poured them both a cup of tea. 'Why? she hasn't agreed to help us so no point sending her flowers just yet'.

'Because I need to order equipment and we don't have time to get it delivered here, before we need to travel to Bratislava. We need to send it by courier to a secure location and her apartment is the only one I can think of right now.

Sometimes it's better to seek forgiveness than ask for permission. Give me her address and you can tell her you're sorry tomorrow evening.

I'm sure if she kicks you out, she'll probably throw the box of equipment out the door after you. Personally, I don't care if she hands it to you, or throws it at you, just so long as we have it.'

Sean reluctantly passed him the pad where he had written Anna's address. Martin then picked up his phone and called his usual equipment supplier. After listing all the equipment he required, he provided Anna's address for delivery and finished the call by requesting that the cost be added to his account.

They finished the evening in fine style having beans and toast and sharing the last four cans of beer before heading off to bed. They had an early start in the morning with their flight scheduled for 7am.

Getting up at 4:30am the next morning they both quickly showered, before loading the car for departure. Breakfast could wait until they had passed through security at the airport. Sean hid the keys for the cottage under a large stone in the flower bed beside the front door, before getting into the car to drive the 12 miles to the airport.

Parking the car in the long stay carpark, they jumped onto the waiting shuttle bus, which dropped them outside terminal one.

After using an automated check in kiosk at the entrance to the terminal, they negotiated Security without any drama. They then found themselves a table in a bar, where Martin ordered two full Irish breakfasts and two pints of Guinness.

'Its my treat', said Martin as Sean looked at him quizzically. 'We need to look like two guys on holiday and the Guinness just adds to the illusion, besides its too early in the morning for coffee, it'll just keep us awake on the flight.'

Breakfast and Guinness both finished, the well fed and watered pair made their way nonchalantly through passport control. They then found themselves two comfortable seats close to the gate, whilst they waited on their flight being called.

As they sat awaiting their flight, Sean couldn't help but wonder how things were with Ceri. She should have arrived on Grand Cayman by now.

Whilst Sean and Martin were sitting in Dublin airport, Ceri was sitting in a taxi taking her from Owen Roberts international airport. She was heading for a hotel in Georgetown that she had booked when she arrived in the airport. The clock on the taxi dash said it was just after midnight, but her body clock told her a different story. After a 12-hour flight with little sleep she was looking forward to getting checked in and getting her head down, before she went to the bank in the morning.

On reaching the hotel a bleary-eyed Ceri had a brief altercation with the desk clerk who insisted on her using a credit card to pay for the room. Ceri had demanded that the night manager be summoned.

She explained that her visit to the Island related to a very delicate financial transaction which she didn't want her husband to know about. She had then opened her shoulder bag to reveal a substantial bundle of 100-Dollar notes.

The very understanding night manager smiled, 'I understand completely madame, I will be only too happy to personally deal with your check-in and resolve any boring procedural issues, that only serve to complicate matters.'

Ceri counted out enough 100-Dollar notes to cover four nights at the hotel. She then looked at the night manager, thanked him for his understanding and proffered her hand, obviously in expectation of a handshake. The beaming night manager grasped her out stretched hand and delicately extracted the 400 dollars which had been nestling in her palm and transferred it nonchalantly to his back pocket.

After thanking Ceri for choosing to stay with the hotel and wishing her a successful trip, the somewhat richer night manager disappeared back into his office, leaving the tight lipped and scowling desk clerk to give Ceri her key and directions to her room.

Once in her room Ceri quickly showered, before jumping into bed with the intention of getting a full seven hours sleep, before preparing herself to go to the bank.

Sean and Martin had meanwhile boarded their plane and had settled down with the intentions of sleeping through most of their three-hour flight to Vienna. With a remarkably busy four days ahead of them, they may as well sleep while they could.

Chapter 23

At 11am local time Sean and Martin's plane touched down in Vienna. After breezing through passport control and customs, they made straight for the train station at the airport and got themselves two tickets to Bratislava.

Whilst Sean searched for the correct platform for the train, Martin followed his stomach and nose and bought two Bosna. A local interpretation of a hotdog, which consisted of grilled white bread, stuffed with two large sausages, onions, and a spicy sauce. The heart burn inducing snack had been completed by Martin's thoughtful addition of a lemon beer for himself and Sean.

Sean reckoned Martin must be getting excited again, because there was no way he should be hungry after the breakfast they'd had in Dublin airport less than four hours ago. Nonetheless Sean took the proffered food and did his best to at least make some sort of dent in the Bosna. The lemon beer on the other hand went down very easily.

After standing on the platform for fifteen minutes, during which time Martin demolished his own bosna and half of Sean's the train arrived. Sean had travelled extensively in Europe, and it never ceased to amaze him just how clean, punctual, comfortable and congestion free the trains were, today's train didn't disappoint.

Stepping onto the antiseptically clean carriage indicated on their tickets, they found their seats close to the doors in the middle of the carriage and settled down for the one hour and twenty-minute journey to Bratislava. At just after one pm, right on time, they stepped off the train onto the platform in Bratislava's Hlavna

Station just north of the city centre, about twenty minutes' walk from their first target branch.

As they walked through the city centre on their way to find the branch, they bought a pair black baseball caps festooned with a white red and blue 'I love Slovakia'.

The caps served two purposes. First with their back packs and caps they looked like two unremarkable tourists. Secondly the peaks of the caps would do a good job of obscuring their faces as they did a walk by at the bank.

They found the branch in a pretty street, lined on one side by quaint looking three-story apartment blocks. Some of the blocks had ornate archways which gave access to an inner courtyard. Everything had been painted an inoffensive and very uniform cream colour.

The side of the street which contained the bank on the other hand seemed to be entirely commercial, with an eclectic mixture of different colours and materials. Some buildings such as the bank made extensive use of glass, whilst others were very utilitarian using grey metal sheets, or plain unpainted concrete.

The bank was a nondescript two-story building, with the ground floor frontage made up almost entirely of metal and glass. On their first walk past, they noted two security cameras mounted at each end of the building pointing along the front of the branch. At the end of the branch in a gap between the bank and a neighbouring building site, stood a large metal gate.

Just as Sean and Martin walked past they heard a metallic screech as the gate began to slide open. Martin immediately came to a halt, causing Sean to almost trip over him.

Martin took off his rucksack and started to sort through his possessions, before pulling out what looked to all intents and purposes like a street map. To any casual onlooker they were just two tourists who had lost their way.

As they stood perusing the map a security van pulled out of the yard, which evidently belonged to the bank. With the van safely in the street, the gate started to slide closed again.

The thirty seconds this took to complete gave them time to see an armoured metal door set into the side wall of the bank with what looked like a digital keypad beside it. They were also able to spot what looked like two security cameras pointing towards the door from either end of the side wall. A high-end executive saloon car sat parked in a spacious parking space to the rear of the yard.

Slipping the map back into a side pocket on his rucksack, Martin hoisted his bag back onto his shoulders before turning and walking purposefully back the way they had come. 'I just want to verify there are no other cameras,' he whispered to Sean out of the side of his mouth.

'Those cameras on the side entrance aren't registered on the banks security system for this branch, just want to make sure there are no other unexpected complications.'

Where Martin saw the glass as being half empty, Sean's view optimistically saw it as half full.

'Every cloud has a silver lining Martin, not only have we spotted cameras that we weren't aware of, but we also know how the bank is moving the cash out of the branch.

That companies cash handling operation is picking up all cash from the branch, probably on a daily basis. No doubt the laundered cash is being treated the same as legitimate cash coming in through normal accounts and is probably on its way to the clearing bank's cash handling facility. Once it hits Credit Finances bank's clearing account it can be to be sent through the banking system to anywhere in the world.'

'Yes Sean, but we are none the wiser as to how the cash is getting into the bank, and how exactly the process of creating the accounts is being facilitated. Yes, we know they are using robotics, but how are they getting access to all the personal details that they are using to create the smurfing accounts?

But I agree every cloud does have a silver lining, not only do we know there is a secondary security system. But we have also found our way into the bank. We will use that building site that neighbours the bank to gain access to the yard, but only after we have resolved the camera situation. Then I can take my time with that digital keypad and get us access through the door.'

They had booked themselves into a budget tourist hotel for the night with Sean's credit card and so having carried out their reconnaissance on the bank that's where they headed next.

Chapter 24

Whilst Sean and Martin were making their way to their hotel, Ceri was preparing herself for her appointment at the Great Cayman Investment Bank. She had made an appointment by telephone as soon as the bank had opened and had an appointment to see the bank manager at eleven that morning.

Standing in front of the floor length mirror in her room Ceri studied the woman that she had just become. In a pair of moderately expensive neutral coloured heels, a blond wig, a powder blue dress and a large pair of sun glasses she certainly looked like a woman of means.

Behind the sunglasses Ceri wore a pair of blue contact lenses, they would disguise her own eye colour when she removed the sunglasses in the bank and would not look out of place with the blond wig she was currently wearing.

Satisfied with the woman looking back at her Ceri lifted her Chanel handbag off the bed, put the Iryna passport into the internal pocket and left the safety of her room to make her way to the bank.

Avoiding reception, she made her way through the hotel bar and out through the side entrance before turning to walk across the front of the hotel and head towards the bank.

At the bank she introduced herself at the reception desk using a high-class English accent and informed the well dressed and heavily made-up young lady behind the desk that she had an appointment with the manager.

She had been asked politely to have a seat in the very plush waiting area whilst the manager was informed of her arrival. Within a few minutes, an immaculately dressed man in a three piece suit stood in front of her, welcoming her to the bank.

Enough time had elapsed to ensure that Ceri understood she had been granted an audience with a terribly busy and important man, but not so much that she would feel insulted. Following the manager who had introduced himself as Julian Besoin, Ceri found herself in a very well appointed air-conditioned office.

She relaxed into the usual small talk about her trip to Grand Cayman, and was only too happy to discuss the glorious weather and beautiful senary on the Island paradise, over the proffered coffee.

Having finished with the expected pleasantries Julian sat back in his well stuffed leather chair and looked at Ceri over the rim of his glasses. 'I believe you wish to open a private account with our bank ?'

'Yes Julian, my husband is in the process of re-structuring his wealth, and his financial adviser has indicated that he should place some of his available liquid assets in my name.'

'Your husband obviously thinks a lot of you Mrs Kulkas, and is willing to place a great deal of trust in you.'

'Yes that is very true Julian, but he is also a financially astute man who is well aware of the tax benefits that accrue from taking sound financial advice.

My husband's financial adviser has informed us that the most efficient way to do this is to open an account in the Cayman

Islands and possibly set up a small shell company which can be used to manage the assets that we place here. So here I am.'

Julian, obviously having been through this scenario on many other occasions had a glazed look that indicated a growing boredom with the situation. However, when Ceri mentioned the amount of money that her husband was re-structuring Julian suddenly became very attentive.

'I am expecting a small initial transfer of around 40 million euro from my husband's bank in the next few days.'

At the mention of such a substantial sum, and the suggestion that there may be more to follow, Julian's ears pricked up. When Ceri mentioned that she would require the ability to carry out funds transfer and required one of the banks exclusive black debit cards she could see the dollar signs appear in Julian's beady eyes.

'I am working within very tight timescales which I hope you can facilitate. My husband's financial adviser has indicated that I would need the account to be available within the next three days.

He has also indicated that there is a certain degree of urgency in carrying out the re-structuring of my husband's funds.'

Julian gave Ceri his most beaming smile, showing a mouthful of teeth that a great white would have been proud of.

'You can be assured that we will do our best to meet your requirements. All we need is a passport as proof of ID and a small number of forms completed and we can have your account opened this very day.

You will of course understand that the funds transfer facility that you require places a certain administrative overhead on the bank. But this two can be provided once the account has been funded.

You will be pleased to know that we charge a very reasonable half of one percent for any international transfers, with an even more reasonable 0.1% for any transfers to local financial institutions.'

'Thank you, Julian, I can understand why my husband's adviser sent me to your bank. I will be sure to tell him when I return home how helpful you have been. I presume the news on my new black debit card is equally as positive.'

'Of course, Mrs Kulkas, our very exclusive card comes with a miniscule annual fee of 1000 dollars, and we charge a minimal fee of 0.1% on any transactions over fifty thousand dollars. You can be assured that your card will be available to you, once the account has been funded.'

Two hours later a very relieved Ceri left the bank having opened an offshore account in the name of Iryna Kulkas. Julian had also very kindly provided Ceri with the contact details of a lawyer. A "personal friend" of his, Jason Connors, who could manage the setting up of a shell company, for yet another small fee. Ceri had no doubt that the emphasis would be on the word fee, with small being very much a matter of opinion.

In his efforts to be seen as offering a complete service Julian had even organised an appointment with Jason Connors for the following morning at 10am. Ceri had no doubt that part of the small fee would find a welcome home in Julian's back pocket.

Before shaking hands and showing Ceri out, Julian had reiterated that as soon as the expected funds arrived in the account, she would be able to pick up both her debit card and the security device, which would allow her to carry out funds transfer.

This was the same device which unknown to Julian, Ceri planned to use to clean out the accounts held by John Covington and Trevor Reid. She smiled as she thought once John found out that Iryna had taken his money, it would made for a very frosty morning over the coffee and croissants.

As soon as Ceri stepped out of the bank, she took a photo of the account's details for the new account that she had just opened and emailed it to Martin. She then made her way to the next bank on her list.

She had no intention of keeping all her eggs in one basket and had made several appointments that day. She fully intended to have a portfolio of Cayman bank accounts to place under the control of the shell company, she intended to set up the next day with Jason Connors.

Where Credit Finance bank had been used to consolidate funds from a lot of small accounts to hide the source of the funds. She now needed to be able to disperse the funds that they would be appropriating to hide its final destination. It was going to be a long, but hopefully very productive day.

Chapter 25

Once they had checked into their twin room, Sean and Martin had made their way directly upstairs. Once in the room Sean had dug out his laptop and connected onto the banks systems, before passing the laptop to Martin. He needed to find the system that controlled the two cameras that monitored the back door that they were going to have to use to get into the bank.

Whilst Martin worked, Sean extracted his best Shirt and a clean pair of jeans from his rucksack. After running the iron over his chosen attire for the evening he got himself a shave and a shower. After a long days travel he smelt a little sporty and he didn't want Anna to think that his hygiene standards had slipped just because she wasn't around.

A six pm Martin continued to trawl through a small number of systems that he had found after doing a rescan of the network. Most of the systems Sean had been able to identify which left just three that Martin was having to investigate individually.

'If we can't find the secondary security system and temporarily shut down those cameras, we are going to be in diffs' said Martin.

'We'll be able to get in and out without tripping any of the main alarms, but if anyone is reviewing footage of those cameras, they will see they have had visitors.

Not to put to fine a point on it, we will be fucked if they turn up to investigate whilst we are still installing the kit. Even if we can get in and out before they show up, their bound to investigate why two unknown individuals were in the bank and find the equipment we are going to plant.

I also have no doubt with my overactive imagination that by the time we get to the next branch we would have welcoming party. Who will be only too happy to attach our balls to the nearest electrical socket in order to find out who we are and what we were doing?'

Sean agreed entirely with Martin, but he had other things on his mind, and he didn't have any immediate answers.

'Martin I totally agree, it would be suicide to go into the bank with those cameras active. This is the stuff that you do for a living and I have every confidence that you will find a way. Right now, I need to go see Anna, if you find anything, or run out of ideas ring me, I will be in Anna's apartment, and it should be safe to talk.'

With that Sean lifted the bottle of prosecco that he had bought in duty free out of the mini bar fridge and left the room heading for the street where he grabbed a taxi to take him to Anna's apartment.

Anna had answered the door in a very light and floating knee length summer dress that showed off her well-toned and very tanned legs beautifully. Sean's heart had been in his throat as once gain his inner man castigated him for being a complete asshole, for letting her go.

'Hello Sean' she said with that voice that had always sounded sweet and melodious to his ears.

'I see you remembered that I like prosecco.' The smile that touched her lips made his heart pound.

'By the way a parcel has arrived which I assume is for you, my neighbour called with it when I arrived home from work today.'

Dumplings, sheep's cheese, cabbage, and pork featured highly in the traditional Slovakian cuisine. Thankfully, Anna knew him well enough to know that none of these were high on Sean's list of must eat foods. Instead, she had made one of Sean's favourite meals an ideal accompaniment to the Prosecco. Taggliatelli Carbonara, delicious ribbons of pasta coated with bacon eggs and cream and a side of garlic bread.

Their chat initially had been tentative and polite, but after two glasses of prosecco the mood had relaxed, and Sean admitted that having missed Anna he had acquired Otto. Anna for her part told Sean that she missed their home in England, she missed her garden and the green fields and parks that they had shared so much time in.

As the evening wore on, the two of them settled into an easy conversational rhythm, talking about memorable moments from their life together, before catching up on what had happened in the previous three months.

With the food finished, the mood relaxed and them both sitting with a half glass of prosecco, Sean decided it was now or never. The words tumbled out of his mouth in a cascade.

'Anna, I want you to know that I'm sorry, I was wrong, I should never have pushed you away. I miss you and want you back in our home. I want us to be a couple again, I want us to have kids, please forgive me Anna, please say you'll come home.'

Anna looked at Sean and smiled.

'I think perhaps once again, you have had too much prosecco Sean.

Yes you were wrong, but perhaps you were not the only one.

You made me angry when you said you didn't want a family, so I thought I would punish you by saying I would come home to mine. When you didn't try and stop me, I thought you didn't love me, so I did leave.

I have hated being here without you, there is no other man for me, you are the one I love. But I couldn't ring you and tell you that, I couldn't bear the thought that you might tell me you didn't love me, that would have broken my heart.'

An overjoyed Sean struggled to contain his excitement, as an enormous boyish grin lit up his face.

'Anna, I do love you and have never stopped loving you, when this is over I am going to come back for you. I am going to ask your father for your hand in marriage, we will be married, and we will have kids, six if you want'.

Anna gave a deep throaty laugh and reached up to seductively push a wayward strand of blond hair back behind her left ear.

'Sean in Slovakia the groom asks for the father's approval on the wedding day, so you might be slightly premature talking to my father.

Besides you would really need to be asking your prospective bride if she has any interest in marrying you before you start planning a wedding.'

A look of consternation crossed Sean's face, before a laughing Anna put him out of his misery.

'Don't worry Sean when you ask I will consider your proposal positively.'

Sean's hand reached across the small table to be met by Anna's and a smile lit up both their faces.

They both stood up and Sean enfolded Anna in his strong arms before leaning into her upturned face for a lingering kiss. Just as they both came up for air the encrypted phone in Sean's pocket started to vibrate, 'great timing Martin', thought Sean. 'Sorry Anna, this will be my friend Martin, I told him to ring if he needed help.'

Sean reluctantly answered the call as Anna stood with her arm round his waist.

'Hi, Martin, this had better be important, or me and you are going to have words.'

By the sound which exploded from the phone, even Anna was able to tell that Martin thought it was important.

'Of course its fucking important Sean, do you think I'd be interrupting your conjugal visit if it wasn't. Now put me on speaker so Anna can hear what I'm about to say.'

Once on speaker, an excited and slightly exasperated Martin explained that he had found the secondary security system. However he had been trying for the last hour to figure out the password, but whoever had installed this system had been careful to change all default passwords. Martin therefore wanted to know if Anna knew about this system and did she have access to it?

Sean glanced round at Anna who had been leaning her head on his shoulder whilst having both arms wrapped round his waist.

'Can you help us with this babe?'

Anna pursed her lips in deep thought.

'My asshole branch manager Pavel Chenko will probably have access to it on his office PC. He's a micro-managing control freak, who doesn't let anyone else have access to the system that monitors the bulk cash office, and he has his own office in the same corridor so he can be close to it.'

'In that case I would presume that you aren't going to have the passcode for the digital keypad on the armoured door at the side of the building', asked Sean expectantly.

'Yes I do, we all do. From time to time if there is no corporate cash to be picked up a member of the banking team will have to deal with the cash transit people. The code is 13579.'

Martin did you hear that? you will need to get yourself logged onto the branch managers PC to get access to that system. Is it safe for you to do that ?'

'Yes the alarm has been set so there is no one in the building. I can see twelve PCs on the branch network, but I think I know which one it is. Your machine naming conventions in the bank leave a lot to be desired from a security point of view.'

Martin quickly opened a remote connection to the branch managers machine.

'Right Sean, I have administrator access, so now I need to change Mr Chenko's password so that I can log in as him on this Machine. I have no doubt he will be calling the service desk in the morning.

He will be trying to log in with his old password and will only succeed in locking out his account.'

Sean agreed with Martin, that it would be better for the lock out to be registered on the network logs in the morning, rather than that night. Password failures outside business hours were a red flag as far as the banks IT security team were concerned and were viewed as suspicious activity. It would be best that they didn't raise any alerts at this stage.

Sean and Anna could hear the clicking of keys as they listened to Martin working on the other end of the phone. Then after about 30 seconds they heard a triumphant 'bingo'.

'Our friend has very kindly allowed the web application he is using to manage the secondary camera system to remember his password. I'm into the system and can see the feeds from all cameras.

You really need to do a security awareness course at the bank Sean and teach your staff how peoples lazy habits make life for undesirable's like me so much easier. It's a hackers dream for an application to use saved passwords, it allows us to log straight into the application without having to waste his time trying to crack the password.'

'It's bad manners to gloat Martin, and right now I think we should accept any breaks we are handed with good grace. So forget the lectures and tell us what you can see.'

Martin confirmed that the were four cameras, two door sensors and two motion sensors on the system. The system also had its own currently armed, silent alarm which had been configured to send SMS alerts to a mobile number. Martin made it very clear that If they had just walked in through the back door after disabling the main alarm system, they would have found ourselves in deep shit.

As he continued to review the system, he clarified that as well as the two external cameras that they know about there was a camera in the hallway and another inside a room. From what he could see the room contained a single PC and a trolley containing what looked like cash bags.

Anna leaned closer to the mobile in Sean's hand so Martin could hear what she was about to say.

'That's the bulk cash office and they will be for the cash pickup tomorrow.

'We have a number of large corporates who Pavel deals with directly. They deliver cash to the bank for lodgement to their accounts. Pavel and his assistant deal with all of that, including the paperwork relating to the banking of the cash.

Any cash lodged through the banking hall is dealt with by me and a separate banking lodgement is done for that. Pavel then transfers that cash and paperwork to the cash handling room.'

Anna explained that they would normally have a cash pickup each day around three when the security company would pick up all, both the corporate cash and the cash received through the banking hall.

She didn't understand though, how there could still be cash in the cash office, as it should all have been picked up at 3pm by the security company.

Martin however had no such confusion in his mind.

'That is the cash that has been laundered through the banks systems tonight after everyone has gone home. That corporate cash as you call it is reason we are here.

Thanks for your help Anna.

Sean I have bit more work to do here before we visit the bank tonight, try and be back for midnight. Ooh and could you pick me up a pizza on the way back I'm starving.'

Sean couldn't help laughing at the by now predictable request.

'I know Martin, you get hungry when you get excited, I will make sure I get you a large one. See you at midnight'. With that Sean hung up the phone and turned to stare lovingly down into Anna's eyes, as she stood against him with an arm round his waist.

'Once we complete our work tonight we will be leaving tomorrow for Prague and then Krakow. Then I'll be back so we can talk about you coming home with me.'

'I know Sean, but before you leave tonight there is something I have been wanting to do for three months and now you're here it's an opportunity that's too good to miss.'.

Reaching her hands behind Sean's neck she pulled his head down towards hers and kissed him for the second time that night, this time with urgency and passion. Then taking his strong hand in hers, she lead him into the bedroom.

An hour later with a broad smile on his face Sean kissed a very contented Anna goodbye and left to make his way back to the hotel.

Chapter 26

By the time Sean got back to the hotel with a large pizza, Martin was sitting impatiently dressed all in black. Sean couldn't help but smile at the pint size 007 wannabe that he saw sitting on the bed.

Sean handed Martin the pizza and the parcel that he had acquired at Anna's apartment before asking him for an update.

'Whilst you were off reacquainting yourself with Anna, I've been busy. I have installed some remote keylogger software on the managers PCs in Prague and Krakow. There is no guarantee we will be so lucky next time, the chances of three lazy managers who don't want to have to remember and type passwords is wafer thin.

Plus, we don't want to raise suspicion by having another two branch managers ring the service desk about their user id being locked out. By the time we get to those other two branches we will have a record of every keystroke and password they have entered between now and our arrival.

I have confirmed that the same secondary security system has been installed on all three branch managers machines, so once we have their credentials it will be plain sailing. Right now you need to get changed we have work to do.'

After a quick shower Sean climbed into the darkest clothing that he had in his bag. A pair of black jeans, a blue tee shirt and a petrol blue bomber jacket. When he had packed for his "holiday" he hadn't given too much thought to what would be appropriate clothing to wear when breaking into a bank. After all it wasn't something that he would normally have to give too much consideration to.

They left the hotel shortly before one am in the morning, paying their bill and explaining that they had an early flight to catch, before walking to the branch. They both agreed that taking a taxi to a closed bank at that time of the morning might be a tad suspicious.

Arriving at their destination, the two erstwhile cat burglars donned balaclavas before using the scaffolding to gain access to the building site bordering the branch. They then found a ladder which they could use to descend into the bank yard.

Before putting the ladder in place Sean took his laptop out of his rucksack and connected into the banks systems before handing it to Martin. Martin used the proffered laptop to connect to both security systems, disabling the Alarm sensors and pausing the recording of the cameras on both systems.

Martin pointed out that if he simply unset the alarms this would raise an alert. They certainly didn't want Pavel turning up to check why the system had been unset, catching them in the act. The consequences of that could prove to be very unfortunate for them both.

With everything disabled Martin closed the laptop and put it back into Sean's rucksack, then they put the ladder in place and climbed down from the 2nd floor of the building site. Less than twenty steps took them across the yard to the armoured door and entry of the code that had been provided by Anna gave them immediate access to the back corridor of the bank.

At the end of the hall a door gave access to the rear of the bank, midway up the hall on the right they could see a door with a digital keypad, whilst on the left was another door with a normal lock.

The door on the right could only be the bulk cash management room, whilst the door on the left most likely gave access to Pavel's office.

While he had been waiting on Sean to return from Anna's, Martin had reviewed video footage from the hall camera. On the video playback he had observed a person who he presumed was Pavel, entering the room. After replaying the footage a number of times, Martin had been able to capture the code needed to open the door.

Within thirty seconds of gaining access to the bank the pair were in the room containing the PC and cash bags.

Martin sat down in front of the PC and took a portable hard drive out of his rucksack. Again, Martin had used camera footage to capture the login credentials for the PC and now logged in using the credentials that had been assigned to Pavel's assistant.

He then started a copy process which would copy the entire contents of the hard disk onto a portable drive.

Meanwhile Sean had been busy preparing for the installation of the high-definition spy camera and audio capture equipment. He had carefully removed a small number of ceiling tiles and connecting the power source for the equipment to the mains used to power the ceiling lights.

He also installed a small mains powered booster ariel, this would boost the signal for the mobile data dongle, which had been fitted with a prepaid sim card that Martin had bought in the airport. With everything connected to the mains there should be no issue with recording and streaming everything that happened in this room, out onto the internet based recording site that Martin had setup.

Once all equipment had been installed Sean neatly replaced the ceiling tiles exactly as they had been. Leaving Martin to verify that the installation had been successful, Sean made his way across to Pavel's office to prepare the way for the same equipment to be installed there, and to kick off a copy of the hard disk on the PC.

Sean had just finished preparing the power source, when he thought he heard the armoured door at the side of the building open and close. Probably Martin going out for a quick smoke he thought. But then he heard two voices, which were very obviously not Martin speaking in a language that he didn't understand. The first voice had a high nasal tone, whilst the second reverberated with a deep baritone.

'Shit' he thought 'Pavel and his side kick have obviously returned, he must have left something behind in the office'.

Looking around him Sean could see nowhere that he could hide if Pavel had indeed come back to pick up something from his office, nor did he have time to quietly reseat the ceiling tiles that he had taken down.

Pulling his Balaclava back over his face Sean grabbed a CO2 fire extinguisher from the wall and thus armed he went and stood against the wall beside the office door. Sean intended to shelter behind the door as it opened and once both individuals were in the office, use the heavy extinguisher to incapacitate the two individuals.

However, the next sound he heard wasn't the opening of the office door, rather he heard an audible sequence of beeps emanating from the digital keypad on the Cash handling room door opposite. Then he heard an ominous click, and he knew that the Cash handling door had been opened.

Sean quickly realised that Martin had been caught in a trap with nowhere to hide, and that both he and his partner in crime were soon going to be in some very deep shit. So taking a deep breath he gently opened the office door so he could get a glimpse of what was happening in the corridor.

Standing with his back to Sean, blocking the cash office door rose a veritable man mountain. Suddenly the high-pitched voice that he had heard earlier started up again and if anything, it went up an octave or two as instructions were shouted at someone within the room, someone who could only be Martin.

Sean saw man mountain in front of him put his right hand under his jacket before straightening his arm and pointing it into the cash room. Pavel had obviously found Martin and Sean now needed to do something to bring the situation under control. Opening the door wide and using the noise coming from the cash room to mask any sound that he made, Sean stepped into the corridor.

Sean's dad had often said to him "the bigger they are the harder they fall", standing where he stood now in the shadow of the biggest man he had ever seen, Sean had some doubts as to just how true those words of sage wisdom would prove to be in the current situation.

The monster standing in front of him must have been a good 4 inches taller than Sean's not insubstantial six foot two. From what

Sean could see his head attached directly to a set of massive shoulders that a London house builder could have squeezed a small maisonette onto. He really was an extremely big lad.

Sean had a strong sense of honour, but under the current circumstances he quickly decided that chivalry could very well get him killed. Given half a chance this guy would probably rip off his arms and beat him to a pulp with his own bloody limbs.

With all ill-considered thoughts of gallantry put firmly to bed and with a firm desire to keep all bodily parts firmly attached Sean did the only sensible thing, and swung the CO_2 fire extinguisher with every ounce of strength in his body.

The extinguisher connected with the back of the closely shaven head with a very satisfying clunk. Much to Sean's relief and amazement, the mountain crumbled like a sack of spuds to lie in a heap on the floor of the cash handling room.

Stepping over the prostrate mass blocking the door Sean bent down, picked up the Glock that had fallen from the unconscious man's right hand and pointed it at a very shocked and now very silent diminutive looking Pavel.

Neither Sean nor Martin spoke, in their silence they had a degree of anonymity, if they were to utter even a word Pavel would know they were not locals. Sean walked towards Pavel with the gun levelled and indicated that he should turn around. As he turned Sean raised the weapon and brought it down on the back of his head knocking him unconscious.

Next Sean motioned Martin to help him to drag the unconscious goliath into the cash handling room. He was a big man but the two of them easily dragged him across the polished tile floor.

Using a pocket knife Sean then cut some empty canvass cash bags that were sitting on top of the cash cage into strips which they then used to bind and gag both men.

They first tied their ankles together, before rolling them both onto their stomachs and tying their wrists together behind their backs. Finally, they tied both wrists and ankles together to further inhibit any chance of them getting free. Once both captives were safely bound, and gagged Sean searched Pavel, depriving him of an automatic pistol, his keys and a mobile phone. He then motioned with his head for Martin to follow him.

Once they were in Pavel's office Sean quietly asked Martin if he had finished in the Cash office. Martin confirmed that he had just been packing away his equipment when he had heard the outer door open and the voices in the corridor. He had tried to hide behind the cash cage where Pavel had found him.

'Well Martin as my old boss used to say, no plan survives first contact with the enemy. We are going to need to rethink our plans, but right now you need to finish up installing the surveillance gear in this office and then I need you to clone Pavel's phone.

While you are doing that, I'm going to transfer all of the cash bags from the cage into Pavel's car. When these two guys are found tomorrow all hell is going to break loose, we want to be as far away from here as we can possibly get, and we want it to look like a simple bank robbery.'

Leaving Martin to finish installing the cameras and audio equipment Sean went back to the Cash room and after three attempts found the right key on Pavel's key ring to unlock the cash cage. Sean had no trouble carrying all three bags that he found in the cage out to the car in a single trip. Hitting the boot release button on the car key, he dropped the bags into the welcoming boot of Pavel's car, along with the automatic that he had earlier taken from the unconscious Pavel.

Having placed all the money into the car he then used his pen knife to cut open each of the bags. Each bag had a label with a four-digit number which meant absolutely nothing to Sean.

The bags also appeared to have differing amounts of money in them made up of different denominations of notes. There were bundles of 50 Euro, 100 Euro and 500 Euro notes. From the bag which seemed to contain the most cash he removed several blocks of one hundred Euro notes.

'If you lie down with pigs you're going to get dirty' he thought. He knew it was dirty money, but he also knew they were probably going to need some of this dirty money to help clean out the sewer that they had uncovered at the bank.

Job done Sean went back in to check that Martin had finished his work, before retrieving the now cloned mobile and replacing it in the still unconscious Pavel's jacket. They then left the building and climbed into Pavel's five series.

Just as Sean leant round the steering wheel to hit the start button, the gate in front of them started to slide open. Both Sean and Martin ducked down in the darkened vehicle as a grey Audi A6 pulled into the yard and parked beside the side door.

Waiting until both occupants of the vehicle had disappeared inside the bank Sean hit the gate opening mechanism to reopen the yard gate. He then stepped out of the car and used his pocket knife slashed the two passenger side tires on the parked Audi, before stepping back into the five series and hitting the start button.

 'Pavel's phone rang while I was cloning it, looks like those guys may have been looking to speak to him', said Martin as Sean directed the car towards the open gate.

As they were pulling out of the yard Sean saw the occupants of the Audi burst through the side door. He knew that they weren't going to be able to put up any sort of chase. It didn't matter how fast their car might be on paper, with two of their wheels sitting on the rims they weren't going anywhere very far, or very fast.

Sean set the sat nav on the car to take them to Vienna airport and relaxing for the first time since he had left Anna's apartment he broke the nervous silence in the car.

'Buddy, After what has happened here tonight, its going to be too dangerous for us to go anywhere near any of the other two branches.'

Martin grunted in agreement.

'You'll have no argument from me on that Sean, when that big guy pointed his gun at me my whole life flashed before my eyes and I realised that there's a lot of things I would still like to do. Still being able to breath is way top of the list.'

Chapter 27

Sean had a strong feeling that the supposed robbery at the bank would not be reported to the local police. He felt sure that the four men who had been witness to the event would feel extremely uncomfortable talking to the forces of law and order. He also knew that the bank would not want the crime scene investigators sniffing round the room that had been used to launder large sums of dirty money, asking awkward questions.

That being the case Sean saw no reason to drive the wheels off the BMW and instead settled into a sedate cruise for the one-hour journey to the airport. Whilst Sean drove, Martin went online and booked two flights back to Dublin using Sean's Credit Card.

Once Martin had finished booking the flights Sean gave him the job of finding somewhere secure to park the car.

'We need somewhere close to, but not in the airport, there will be too many security cameras covering the airport car parks.'

After a couple of minutes of searching Martin found what he thought was the perfect location.

'It's an open-air carpark close to a mainline train station, we park the car and catch a train that will get us to the airport in less than ten minutes.'

Sean put the address for the car park into the sat nav, which indicated they were thirty-five minutes from their revised destination. Having completed his duties in relation to their travel arrangements Martin began reviewing footage from the cameras and audio recording equipment, which they had just installed.

Out of the corner of his eye, Sean could see Martin taking notes as he flicked between the various feeds on his laptop. Obviously, things were happening back at the bank, as by the time they reached the carpark at five am and Martin closed his laptop, he had four pages of scribbled notes.

The first train that would take them to the Airport didn't arrive until six am, so Sean asked Martin to give him a run down on what he had been able to glean from the footage that he had just been reviewing.

'Well Sean the two guys who arrived in the Audi were obviously Pavel's backup team and acted like ex military. They entered the cash room with weapons drawn immediately clearing the doorway, covering each other's blind spots.

When they saw Pavel and the big guy trussed up like two chickens, one of them stayed by the door covering the hallway and one went to check the status of the two men on the floor.

Both must have been awake, because as soon as they removed Pavel's gag he shouted something in foreign which I didn't understand and they both made straight for the outer door. They didn't even take time to untie their mates, Pavel must have told them we had only just left.

I couldn't see anything that happened out in the yard as we left, because the banks security cameras were still disabled. It obviously took them a few seconds to realise that you had disabled their vehicle because they didn't reappear back into the cash room for almost a minute.

Once they untied Pavel he left the cash office and reappeared on the camera in his own office. He made a call to John Covington, I'm sure he addressed the person on the other end of the call as Mr Covington.'

'Could you not listen in on the phone call with the cloned mobile', asked Sean.

'No I have been looking at recorded footage, besides you can only listen in on calls if both phones are using the same mobile mast and by the time he made that call, we were hot footing it towards Vienna. The good news is I will be able to see any texts or messages that are sent to, or sent from his phone wherever I am and I do have the number he called.

I could only hear one side of the conversation, but Pavel did most of the talking. Obviously John Covington doesn't speak the local lingo, because everything Pavel said was in English. From what I could make out Pavel seems to think that he had been lured back to the bank by someone disabling the security cameras in the cash handling room.'

Sean grunted and his face contorted into a frown.

'We made a mistake Martin, thinking that the cameras wouldn't be monitored after the building had been locked up. That mistake could have cost us our lives, and worse we might have gotten Anna involved.'

With the immediate threat of death passed, Martin was a little more upbeat in his assessment of the situation.

'Yes Sean hindsight is a wonderful thing, but in this case it has worked to our advantage. Pavel seems to think that we are from a rival criminal gang who were unable to break into the cash cage and so lured him back to the bank to get access to his keys. He seems to think that only for his backup turning up that he has his big friend would be knocking on the pearly gates right now.

We made a big impression, he called us a pair of silent assassins. He was extremely impressed with how easily the big one, which I assume is you, took out his mate Igor.'

Sean maintained a stony silence, still berating himself for making such a basic error. Martin on the other hand became more excited as he continued to speak.

'By the way from what Pavel said to John Covington, we have just over five million Euros in the boot. That's quite a haul, and probably will cement the view in their tiny criminal minds that it was a bank robbery pure and simple.

They won't be calling the police either to the bank or to report the car stolen. It might prove to be a difficult conversation if asked about the small change in the boot if the police were to stop the car.

Pavel is going to put some feelers out amongst local contacts to see if they can identify who would have the balls to steal from their organisation.'

Sean couldn't help but smile as he listened to his buoyant companion, and was thinking more positively when Martin finally took a breath.

'He's not going to have too much luck with that Martin. In five hours' time we'll be on a flight to Dublin and none of his local contacts are going to have a clue who, or where we are. The money is going to be a bit of a problem for the bank. That amount of missing cash will leave a bit of a hole that the banks auditors are likely to spot, so they are going to have to do something to sort it out.'

Sean then reached into the back seat of the car and retrieved his ruck sack. Taking one of the bundles of one hundred Euro notes out of his bag he split it in two giving half to Martin to put into his wallet and squeezed the other half into his own. He then took out another block of cash and handed it to Martin.

'Consider it travelling expenses, it's a form of natural justice that we use their dirty money to help bring them down'.

They then split the remaining spy cameras and audio equipment between both their rucksacks before getting out of the car.

Sean considered throwing the car keys away but decided against it and placed them carefully under the front passenger wheel arch on top of the wheel. They then both walked nonchalantly towards the train station that they could see in the distance.

When they arrived at the airport, they quickly checked in with their hand luggage and made their way through security. With security behind them, Sean voiced his surprise that the security staff had paid no attention to the surveillance equipment sitting in the trays with their laptops.

'If it looks electronic and doesn't look like it might go bang on the plane then they aren't interested' explained Martin. 'I come through airports all the time with stuff like this in my bag. The only reason we didn't fly in with it from Dublin was because we didn't have time to wait on it being delivered to the cottage. It just made more sense to have it delivered straight to your girlfriend's apartment.'

Walking through the shopping area, Martin found them a kiosk in one of the food outlets serving breakfast. Pulling out his laptop, Martin sat down and looked up at Sean with a mischievous grin on his face.

'Time to see how messrs Covington and Reid are getting on back in England. I'll have a large coffee and anything that combines meat with bread if you're buying?'

Sean set his rucksack down on the seat beside Martin and made his way to the breakfast counter. He ordered two large coffees and a selection of bread rolls, Austrian sausage, and cheese, which he was sure would meet with Martins not very exacting standards. As he returned to their table, he could see that Martin was focussed on events which were unfolding on his laptop screen.

He slid the food onto the table and sat down on the bench beside Martin. Martin took one of the earbuds that he had been using to listen to the audio feed and passed it to Sean, 'You need to listen to this, this is happening now.'

On the screen Sean could see that they were viewing John Covington's office, which currently had three occupants. As well as the chief executive, he could see that Trevor Reid and Alek Kulkas were sitting around John Covington's desk. Sean and Martin both listened as the conversation unfolded.

A very pompous and condescending John Covington did most of the talking.

'Alek this is just not on, you told us that there was no risk, to either us personally, or to the bank. Yet last night criminal elements, obviously aware of what you are doing broke, into our bank and stole five million Euros.'

Alek Kulkas's deep voice had a sharp edge to it as Sean and Martin watched him stiffen and glare at John Covington.

'John, you seem to forget that both you and Mr Reid are involved in what we are doing, and I should remind you that what we are doing isn't exactly legal. So could I suggest that you climb back down of that high horse you have just climbed onto.

We need to discuss what we need to do to protect both us and the operation from any adverse outcomes that might arise from last night's unfortunate incident.'

Martin glanced at Sean, popped a lump of sausage into his mouth and mumbled, 'Old Alek isn't going to let your boss forget that he's involved in this situation up to his neck. This footage is going to be gold dust when we expose them to the authorities.'

Sean wasn't overly concerned with Martin's bad table manners, nor the fact that Martin's partially masticated food was escaping into the environment. What he did care about was missing any of the conversation currently going on over five hundred miles away in London. So holding up his hand he turned to Martin saying 'shut up and listen'.

The chief executive gave no indication that he had any intention of getting out of the saddle alluded to by Alek and continued with his self-important tone.

'Well Alek the first thing that we need to do is resolve the issue that the missing money is going to create for the bank. Our finance team will be running a reconciliation on our bank accounts at the end of the month and we are going to be showing a shortfall of five million Euros in our clearing account. We are going to need to plug that hole before the reconciliation process takes place.

Trevor and I both feel that as you and your brother are creaming off the lions share from this little enterprise that you should replace the missing cash. If our auditors get wind of a missing few million or so in one of our bank accounts we would have to shut the entire operation down. I'm sure the people who you have made arrangements with would not be happy if their banking facilities were curtailed.'

Sean and Martin could see that Alek Kulkas had begun to lose patience with the situation.

'That is absolutely true John, but you forget that as Directors of this bank both your reputations need to remain beyond repute. If our arrangements were to come to light you might find yourselves taking an unwanted holiday in a very small room with steel bars for windows for quite some time.'

John Covington paused considering the not-so-subtle threat from Alek, before leaning across his desk and speaking quietly with a sneer on his face.

'Be that as it may Alek, security of this operation is down to you and Dimitri and you have failed, so you need to replace the missing cash and fast.'

Alek sighed in resignation.

'Very well John we shall do that, but a lot of our funds are tied up in property developments here in London and Florida. The security company that your sister Magda is heading up is costing us a lot of money.'

John Covington gave a contemptuous smile.

'She's my half sister and her addition to the board of your sordid little security enterprise gives it an air of respectability that it really doesn't deserve.'

As Sean and Martin watched enthralled, they saw Alek's knuckles whiten as he tightened his grip on the arms of his chair. He then leant forward, before speaking slowly in a cold deep voice that seemed to rumble with menace.

'Yes John, just like her addition to the board of your bank has given you the freedom to pursue the sordid little enterprise of lining your own pockets, with no interference from the board.

But let's not argue, we need to focus on resolving the situation that we find ourselves in. We need you to ensure that this month's transfer is done early so we have the funds available to make up the shortfall.'

It was a much more respectful John Covington who responded.

'OK Alek, I'm sure Trevor will be able to have his team initiate the bank transfer later today.'

Sean looked at Martin who stared back, whilst holding another piece of sausage millimetres away from being popped into the cement mixer that passed for his mouth.

'Well Martin, this really is turning into a family affair, Magda Harte is John Covington's sister. Obviously, they needed someone they could depend on as chair of the board and who better than the chief executive's sister.

I need to log in now and run the piece of SQL which is going to redirect those funds to Ceri's account in the Cayman's.

Also you need to message her and tell her what has happened and that the money is going to be arriving in the Caymans a few days early, so she can change her arrangements.

She needs to let us know as soon as she sees the money arrive in her Cayman account, as I will need to log in and do some work to muddy our tracks.'

Sean grabbed his laptop out of his rucksack and set about the process of updating and running the piece of SQL code that he had prepared a few days previously. Those who fail to prepare, prepare to fail he thought, before giving himself a small pat on the back for having the foresight to have the SQL already written.

Closing his laptop with an air of satisfaction Sean joined Martin in finishing breakfast before they both made their way to the boarding gate to board their flight back to Dublin.

Chapter 28

When Ceri awoke in her hotel room and checked her phone, she found a message from Martin explaining what had happened in Bratislava and the subsequent decision to return to Dublin.

She felt a thrill or excitement, or possibly trepidation, knowing that her primary Cayman account would receive the expected injection of funds that day. This made it all the more important that she get the shell company setup that morning with Jason Connor. She ordered breakfast delivered to the room and then set about getting herself dressed for her meeting.

At ten thirty she left the hotel and walked to Mr Connor's office, where she had to endure the obligatory banal conversation over a cup of coffee before the actual business could begin.

Jason turned out to be a pleasant enough conversationalist, a family man from what she could gather, fond of his wife, and very fond of his two young sons. Even so she felt her impatience grow, just wanting to get her business with Jason concluded.

Europe was around six hours ahead of the Cayman Islands, so if what Martin had said was correct, she could expect funds to be landing in the account no later than noon local time. That being the case she wanted to be at the bank early afternoon to pick up her Debit card and security device so she could commence distributing funds and move forward with the rest of their plan.

Eventually having run out of small talk and having drained the coffee pot, Jason started what turned out to be a relatively quick and painless process of creating the shell company.

Jason not unexpectedly was aware that Ceri had a Cayman Islands bank account. He was however quite surprised to find that she actually had four accounts, all of which had been opened the previous day. This wasn't going to be a problem, the shell company that Ceri would create through his services, would be the ideal vehicle for controlling these multiple accounts.

A very apologetic Jason asked Ceri for her ID, assuring her that it was a mere formality and her identity would be safe with him. Then, Jason enquired as to whether Ceri would require any nominee directors to appear on the company paperwork.

He assured her that whilst they would appear on the company paperwork they would have no real power, as for a small additional fee he would provide her with signed pre-printed undated resignation letters for all nominee directors.

'If you ever want to get rid of them you just sign and put in the date,' said Jason. 'And of course you can backdate the letter - in case you want them to have already resigned.'

Ceri provided Jason with the names and addresses of both John Covington and Trevor Reid, the details of which Sean had acquired from the HR system for Credit Finance Bank, during one of his many back door excursions into the banks systems.

Jason then asked Ceri if she had a preferred name for the company. 'Yes can we call it Covington Investments LLC'.

Finally, Jason apologetically brought up the small matter of payment for his services. Due to the number of bank accounts and nominee directors involved he explained it would cost around five thousand dollars to get the company setup and generate all the paperwork. There was also the small matter of the fee for his professional services this would amount to another four thousand dollars.

Ceri explained that her accounts would be funded that day and that once this had been completed, she would transfer the money to Jason's bank if he would kindly provide her with his account details.

Jason gratefully complied and assured her that as soon as he received the required funds, he would generate all the paper work required, and she would be able to pick up a copy the following day from his office.

By the time Ceri had finished with the business of setting up a new shell company, Sean and Martin had returned to Dublin and were once again ensconced in the cottage in Ashbourne on the outskirts of Dublin.

They had both laptops setup on the kitchen table and were studiously reviewing footage from the security cameras in both John Covington and Trevor Reid's offices. They just needed to be sure that they had all the security details that Ceri needed to clean out the accounts of Messrs Covington and Reid.

They intended to remain in the cottage until Ceri returned, and use the time available to monitor the situation and build up a body of video and audio evidence. With everything that had occurred the previous day in Bratislava that operation seemed to have been temporarily at least shut down. Their cameras might as well have been switched off for all the activity they were currently recording.

However, the banks own cameras in Prague and Krakow were providing really useful footage, recording multiple cash deliveries from unsavoury looking individuals. They already had some footage which was absolute gold dust, but with the additional footage they were recording they had no doubt they would be providing a completely bullet-proof platinum package to the authorities.

Using the video footage and the software which Martin had already installed on the branch managers PCs, they had been able to compromise the PCs in both cash offices. That had then given them the opportunity to extract files and data from both machines.

Ceri's activities in the Cayman Islands would be the icing on the cake, or from the perspective of John Covington and Trevor Reid, the crowning turd on top of the dung heap.

Chapter 29

At two PM local time, or eight PM Dublin time Ceri walked through the front doors of the bank intending to request a meeting with Mr Besoin the bank manager. Before she could make her request she caught sight of a beaming Julian Besoin striding across the marble floor of the bank towards her.

'Mrs Kulkas, it's a pleasure to welcome you back to our bank. Once again I would like to thank you on behalf of the bank for deciding to use our services. You can be assured at all times of our discretion and indeed our willingness to do all we can to facilitate you.

You are no doubt aware that the funds you were expecting have now arrived. If you would like to follow me to my office, we can deal with the formalities of issuing your security tablet and your debit card.'

Giving her his most radiant smile, that showed in Ceri's opinion a frightening number of gleaming white teeth, Julian turned on his heel and made for his office.

Ceri returned the smile, pleased that things were going a lot more smoothly than she had expected, She had envisaged having to wait whilst Julian played the I'm a very busy and important and busy bank manager game. She couldn't help but be astounded, that the rather officious individual who she had met yesterday, had turned into the fawning and deferential individual, currently falling over himself to be nice to her.

Once they both had seated themselves in Julian's office an impatient Ceri had to go through the motions of turning down the offer of a chilled glass of champagne, or a cup of coffee. Ceri just wanted to complete her business quickly, but Julian took her reticence to accept the offered refreshments as a challenge. He rhymed off a list of potential alcoholic and non-alcoholic alternatives before Ceri realised that she needed to play her part in the game and accepted a diet cola. Taking a placatory sip from her soft drink Ceri explained to Julian that she would prefer if they could conclude their business as swiftly as possible as she still had rather a lot of things to do that day.

'I quite understand Mrs Kulkas'

responded a very obsequious Julian.

'There is no doubt your husband has an extremely high regard for you, and I can quite understand that a man as wealthy as he will have a multitude of things that will require your attention.'

Julian then produced a security tablet from the top drawer of his desk, before lifting his telephone and requesting that the person on the other end of the line bring in Mrs Kulkas's debit card and a printout of the account details.

Whilst waiting on the debit card and requested paperwork, Julian explained how the banks security device worked. It would require entry of four things. Sort code, account number, the pin number which Ceri had chosen when opening her account, and the account balance to the nearest dollar or euro, depending on the denomination that had been chosen for the account. These were four things that only the account holder would have access to.

Ceri nodded indicating that she understood and slipped the device into her Chanel bag. Just as she had finished reclasping her bag the office door opened and a young lady in a well fitted short black skirt entered. She held a white envelop which she handed to Julian. 'Thank you Melissa' said Julian before reaching across the desk to hand the envelop the Ceri.

'Your account is fully active Mrs Kulkas, with all transfer options available to you. Your black debit card is also available for use. Before Melissa shows you out let me once again thank you for choosing to use our bank, we are indeed most grateful.'

Ceri, somewhat nonplussed by her welcome at the bank, nodded her thanks and slipped the envelop into her Chanel bag. Focussed on what she needed to do next she thought nothing more of it until she got back to her hotel room and opened the envelope, which she had been given in the bank. Inside she found two things. Her black debit card, a high-end metallic card, possibly aluminium which just oozed prestige, and a folded sheet of A4 paper.

When she unfolded the sheet, she suddenly understood Julian's reaction when she had arrived at the bank. It had obviously been a busy month in the three branches, because instead of the expected forty million Euro over eighty million euro were currently sitting in her new bank account.

After absorbing the enormity of what she, Sean and Martin had just done, Ceri sat down to make transfers. Firstly, to Jason Connor so that he could complete the setting up of the shell company, and then to her other three bank accounts. By the time she had finished she had a mere ten million Euros left in the original account.

Transfers complete she then made appointments for the other banks, so that she could pick up security devices, debits cards and paperwork. She wasn't sure if the enthusiastic welcome she had received from Julian would be replicated at the other institutions, after all she smiled as she thought to herself 'they were all receiving a lot less than eighty million Euro'.

Using her new debit card Ceri booked herself a flight to Geneva. To further muddy the waters, and further complicate the job of following the money trail she intended to open other accounts on Iryna's behalf, in the European capital of private banking.

She then used her encrypted telephone to ring Martin. She needed the details for John Covington and Trevor Reid's accounts so she could move on with the next phase of screwing the bad guys. She hoped that Martin and Sean would have the details that she required.

It had just turned nine pm in Dublin when Martin's mobile began to ring, he answered immediately putting the phone onto speaker, hardly able to contain his boyish excitement.

'Hello Ceri, have you been having as an exciting time as me and Sean. You should have seen superman here as he took out the biggest lump of humanity I have ever seen.

What has been going on at your end. More importantly has the money arrived in the Cayman Islands yet?'

A more business-like Ceri explained in great detail everything that she had done whilst in the Caymans. But even she couldn't help but be dramatic when she mentioned the amount of money that they had just appropriated. She heard a loud 'God almighty' as Martin expressed his surprise.

Sean was a bit more circumspect.

'It doesn't really matter if its forty million, eighty million or one hundred million, the results for us if caught are going to be the same. These people deal in human misery, they carry weapons and will have no qualms about using them on us.

Right now we need to make sure we cover our tracks and hope that when they realise they have lost another eighty million that they focus on possible criminal opponents.

They already think they have been the victim of a physical robbery perpetrated by an opposing organisation, we want them to continue to look inwards at their contemporaries and not in our direction.'

Ceri with an upbeat lilt in her voice, refused to allow captain sensible to spoil the moment .

'Well boys I think when they untangle the money trail I am laying they will start looking internally at their own organisation. It will look like members of their own financial mafia have tried to screw them over.

Right now I still need some details from you guys, so I can finish the job. I need the sort code, account number, pin number and the current account balance for John Covington and Trevor Reid's Cayman accounts.

Once I have cleaned out their accounts I'm heading to Switzerland, Iryna is aspiring to have a private swiss bank account or two.'

The excitable Martin wasted no time responding to his friend of many years.

'I can send you the sort code, account numbers and pin codes now, give me five minutes and I'll get the account balances for you.'

'Ok, I will wait on you sending me the details and once I have carried out the transfers, I will ring you guys back to see what we do next.'

As Martin turned to the task in hand, Sean set to doing a little work of his own. He logged back into the banks systems and reset the bank details that had been used to redirect the funds. He then deleted the bank file that had been used to carry out the bank transfers and removed all traces of the SQL used to make the updates. He knew they would eventually figure out where the money had gone, but he didn't see any point in making it easy for them.

It took Martin a little bit longer than his estimated five minutes to find the additional details that Ceri wanted, but within fifteen minutes she had everything she needed.

Five minutes later with a satisfied smile on her face Ceri had logged out of both accounts having downloaded a detailed statement from each showing all the funds transferred from Credit Finance bank.

After carefully considering what Sean had said, she had decided not to clear the accounts. She had a new plan starting to form in her head, it would be better if the money was seen to disappear at a more appropriate time. There had been over 12 million Euro in each of the accounts, smiling to herself she though 'that was going to add another very tidy sum to Iryna's already considerable wealth'.

Ringing Sean and Martin back she explained her decision in relation to not clearing out the accounts, summarising the plan that was starting to take shape in her head.

'Based on the normal percentage split of the bank transfers John Covington and Trevor Reid are expecting two million euro each.

The Kulkas brothers are expecting around twenty million, five million of which they are expecting to send back to the bank to fill the void created by your little excursion in Bratislava.

That leaves fifty million euro which is not going to arrive in the bank accounts of the organisations that they have been laundering the money for.'

Once they discover that they have lost over eighty million euro they are going to realise that their operation in the bank has been compromised.

We need them to put two and two together and decide that the robbery in Bratislava was cover for a carefully planned IT breach.'

Sean could see exactly where Ceri's mind was going with this.

'So what you're saying Ceri, is that we need them to think that the bank has been targeted by an eastern European criminal organisation. We don't want to make them think anything different at this stage, so we leave the money in the Cayman accounts untouched for now.'

'Exactly Sean, At some stage tomorrow they are all going to realise that the money they have been expecting hasn't arrived. No doubt grumblings will filter through to the Kulkas brothers from dissatisfied customers, which should further increase the stress levels.'

Martin, who had been sitting quietly taking in the exchange between Ceri and Sean was eager to share his thoughts.

'The way I see it, is that our Financial Mafia are going to need to make amends to their customers. By make amends I mean provide them with the money that they were expecting, otherwise I wouldn't give much for their life expectancy.'

Happy that all three of them were on the same page Ceri got ready to end the call.

'OK guys I going to have to go now, I have bags to pack and a flight to catch to Geneva, we'll talk tomorrow.'

With that Ceri hung up leaving Sean and Martin with the skeleton of a plan that needed more flesh on its bones.

Chapter 30

After Ceri's call the two men sat at the kitchen table drinking tea, quietly considering how they could implement the planned deception. After five minutes of unproductive silence Sean decided that they should go back to basics and look at the resources they had at their disposal.

'OK Martin, we currently have Cameras and audio equipment in John Covington's office and Trevor Reid's office in bank headquarters. In Bratislava we have the same equipment in Pavel's office and the bulk cash handling office.

Our access to the secondary security system in Bratislava has been blocked, and no doubt they have replaced the PCs in both locations as they would quite rightly suspect they have been compromised.

We still have an open trapdoor into the banks systems, but from what we can see from our cameras in London all email communication between Messers Covington and Reid and the Kulkas brothers is through private email accounts on personal laptops.'

Sean could see a smile forming on Martin's broad face and a mischievous twinkle appeared in his eyes.

'Well Sean their attempt to hide their illicit emails presents us with an opportunity. Those machines are not on the banks corporate network and I would suspect the same situation to exist for Alek and Dimitri. That means they won't be privy to the cyber protections that even the most basic corporate network would provide.

We don't need to worry about multiple layers of firewalls, intrusion detection and prevention systems or any fancy heuristic analysis engines. We will just need to bypass the basic security systems that will be on their laptops.'

Sean could hear the rising excitement in Martin's voice and wanted to hear more.

'OK Martin, this is your area of expertise what do you suggest.'

Martin smiled.

'I would suggest that we indulge ourselves in a spot of spear phishing, using Bratislava as the bait.'

Martin explained that he wanted to use spear phishing emails in order to install malware on all the target laptops, which if successful would allow them to both take control of and monitor all activity on the targeted devices.

The plan conformed to the KISS principle, of keep it simple stupid, Sean gave Martin an encouraging slap on the back, happy to go with his simple, but effective plan. With the plan agreed Martin set about fashioning an email in which he spoofed the sender address, so that the emails looked like they had come from Pavel Chenko 's private email address.

In viewing the camera and listening to the audio in Pavel's office they had seen Pavel request a password reset on his user account and had then heard him request a security scan on his computer once he had gotten logged in.

They decided that the thing most likely to gain the desired reaction would be an email identifying a systems breach, that would definitely put the cat amongst the pigeons.

The text of the email that would look like it had come from Pavel, would confirm that his corporate PC had been compromised during the robbery and had been removed from the network. This partially answered a question that had been asked in a previous email exchange, that had been copied to all parties.

However, the email would have a payload hidden within it, which once the email was opened would install both a remote access tool and a keylogger on the target machines. The keylogger would intercept and store all keystrokes, allowing things like user credentials and passwords to be captured.

The remote access tool on the other hand would allow Sean and Martin to view real time activity on the target screens and if required seize control of the target device and lock down and encrypt the contents of the laptops, to prevent them being used.

By eleven PM the email with its illicit payload had been generated and sent to the four targets. To generate a sense of urgency and encourage the four recipients to respond in the required manner, Martin also used Pavel Chenko's cloned mobile phone to send a text to all four individuals.

This text told the quartet that something had been found in the branch in Bratislava and to expect an email to confirm what had been found.

Martin smiled at Sean as the texts were sent.

'Sometimes a little positive reinforcement can help smooth the wheels, and if they are expecting an email from Pavel, they are more likely to open it without thinking.'

A pensive Sean nodded in agreement.

'Yes Martin, the use of deception to manipulate individuals into providing us with the access we require, is Social Engineering 101. Sometimes I think that your job as an ethical hacker wasn't always that ethical. To be honest I am struggling a bit with the ethics of what we are doing.'

Martin wasn't the sensitive type, but even he could see that Sean was dealing with an inner turmoil. Putting a comforting hand gently on his big companion's shoulder he spoke quietly in a reassuring tone.

'On occasion Sean I found yourself doing things that I would rather not have been doing, but in this modern world in which we live, an overactive conscience doesn't tend to pay the bills, and good guys don't always win.

I haven't always been proud of what I have done in the past, but we all break the rules sometimes, I'm sure you don't always stick to seventy on the motorway in that fancy car of your's.

I sooth my conscience by thinking that there are shades of light and dark, shades of good and bad. What these guys are doing is very much at the black end of the scale. They are laundering money for drug traffickers, people smugglers and very possibly arms dealers.

They have threatened the life of a person who I consider a close friend, they are very bad people. So if we have to shift a little into the grey zone to help bring them down, then I don't think we should beat ourselves up over it. '

Martin smiled trying to lighten the mood, 'like I say its shades of good and bad, we are going to fuck up the lives of some awfully bad people, by choosing to be a little less good than we would normally be, it is a good thing that we are doing.'

Sean nodded in silent acknowledgement, but when he spoke it was obvious that he wasn't totally convinced.

'I know, but I have spent my career both in the RAF, and over the last five years in the bank, doing my best to stop the things that we are doing happening. It just feels wrong that I have turned everything I have learned on its head and am using all the knowledge and experience that I have in a way which would have been totally unacceptable to me just a week ago. I feel like I have broken a trust.'

Martin wanted to take Sean by the shoulders and shake some sense into him. Instead he banged the table with his fist and angrily explained the reality of the situation to Sean in the most assertive way possible.

'Listen Sean, John Covington and Trevor Reid are the people who have broken a trust. They have broken the trust of the genuine customers who use the bank. They have broken the trust of the staff who look to them for leadership and direction. They have broken the trust of the people who appointed them to the board.

What we are doing is nothing in comparison. We are trying to put right a wrong that is being perpetrated by greedy men who are abusing their position. Winston Churchill once said. "It's a fine thing to be honest, but its also very important to be right." What we are doing is right, even if we both agree that we are being less honest than we would like to be.

Now stop being a big fucking pussy and lets get things back on track.'

Sean grinned, and gave his short companion a grunt eliciting friendly slap between the shoulder blades.

'Yeah, Martin I know you're right, honesty was something my parents instilled in me as a boy and it's just hard to go against it. But my dad, also told me "all it takes for evil to prevail is for good men to do nothing". So, I'm in this to the end with you guys whatever my personal feeling might be, sometimes you have to cross the line to stop a greater evil.'

Martin hoped Sean had now got his head on straight, because the last thing they needed at this stage was Sean's conscience getting in the way. A team was only as good as its weakest member and Martin didn't want Sean's misplaced sense of honesty getting in the way of nailing the bad guys. Closing his laptop Martin got up and grabbed two glasses from the kitchen cupboard, before extracting a bottle of duty free whiskey from his laptop bag.

He poured two generous glasses of the dark peaty liquid setting one down in front of Sean. The two men spent the rest of the evening swapping stories and comparing the scars that life had inflicted upon them. At two am as they both walked tentatively up the stairs holding firmly onto the bannister they were both ready to put the world to rights.

Chapter 31

The next morning at 8am things really started to kick off, one alert after another pinged up on Martins laptop as John Covington, Trevor Reid, Alek Kulkas and Dimitri Kulkas all opened the phishing email.

Martin and Sean with red rimmed eyes, mouths like the bottom of a budgie cage and heads that felt like they were home to a small man with a pneumatic drill, were able to remotely connect to all four laptops. They sat stoically, squinting painfully at the screens, as they waited the relief that would surely be provided by the paracetamol they had ingested on dragging themselves out of bed. With their heads in their hands they waited on the financial drama to unfold as John Covington and friends waited on the expected influx of funds into their respective bank accounts.

The remote access tool that had been successfully installed gave them an extra camera angle and additional audio that they could use to view proceedings. They watched through the laptop cameras as John Covington, Trevor Reid, Alek Kulkas and then Dimitri Kulkas logged into their online banking systems. They took great delight in the look of consternation that appeared on all four faces, as they realised that the funds hadn't arrived.

They already had everything they needed for Ceri to cleanout John Covington and Trevor Reid's Cayman accounts. Now they also had the user credentials for the Kulkas brothers accounts. Once the paracetamol kicked in, Martin was like a kid in a sweet shop when he saw that both Alek and Dimitri Kulkas had carelessly installed the software token that the bank had provided to prevent fraud on their PCs.

'That soft token provides a six digit use once code every 60 seconds that is designed to stop unauthorised access to the bank accounts that it is protecting. These dickheads have installed it on the same device that they uses to access their bank accounts. I don't know whether they're lazy or stupid, but either way they have just opened the door wide open for us to redistribute their wealth to a more worthy cause.'

Whilst Alek Kulkas had pleaded poverty to John Covington when requesting that that months transfer be executed earlier, there had been over forty million Euro's sitting in the various Kulkas brothers accounts. Sean and Martin could see from the list of transactions on screen that there had been sums of 20 million plus received over the previous three months, with large sums being sent to two other bank accounts.

As they watched Alek logged out of the first banking system and into what appeared to be, the two other bank accounts using different soft security tokens all of which had been installed on his laptop. These accounts contained another twenty million Euro.

'I've decided' said Martin, 'he's both lazy and stupid. He has just handed us the keys to all the money in all of those bank accounts. Just so he could make life easy for himself he has totally obliterated any security that using a soft key would have provided him with.

If he had even just installed those softkeys on his mobile phone, a different device we would have had a very difficult job doing what we are now going to do. The only challenge is going to be getting access to the laptop whilst its turned on and he isn't sitting in front of it.'

Having seen the amount of money which the Kulkas brothers were receiving each month, there could be no doubt in any ones mind that the Kulkas brothers are definitely the senior partners in this enterprise. To Sean and Martin it seemed only fair that the brothers receive their fair share of the shit that they were planning to generate.

Satisfied that they had everything they needed to carry out a major re-distribution of wealth when the time came, they continued to watch John Covington and Trevor Reid on camera. They watched as John Covington rang Trevor Reid and then Alek Kulkas from his personal mobile and got them on a conference call. They listened as all three men confirmed that none of them had received the expected funds transfer.

An agitated John Covington summarised the situation as he saw it.

'We know that a robbery took place in Bratislava which cost us five million euro, this shortfall in the banks accounts still remains to be filled.

We also know from Pavel's email that an information security breach occurred in the Bratislava branch.

It would also appear that something has happened to yesterday's funds transfer.

It is looking highly likely that the theft of the cash had been planned as a distraction to cover for the information security compromise that Pavel has advised us of.

That security compromise has been used to steal our money, and no doubt the funds of all the organisations which were benefitting from the service we were providing.

Does anyone disagree with anything I have just said?'

Neither Trevor nor Alek felt inclined to disagree. Alek however, felt it necessary to point out that if all transfers had been stolen, they were all going to have to deal with some irate customers. People who didn't tend to settle financial disagreements through mediation, and gentlemanly discussion.

The conversation continued for some time, but no matter how much they talked about it, the same conclusion was always reached. They would all need to go to Bratislava, there was nothing any of them could do whilst sitting in London. Alek was adamant that they needed to meet their clients face to face and try and calm the situation. They had to provide some form of explanation and do their best to pour oil on what could be very troubled waters.

Alek might as well have handed John Covington a freshly produced dog turd. His face contorted with disgust at the thought of breathing the same air as such reprehensible individuals. Individuals who he quite happily facilitated in their criminal activities, just so long as he didn't have to associate with them. If the look on his face didn't suffice, his imperious snarl left Alek Kulkas in no doubt of what he thought about the suggestion.

'Alek you know Trevor and I can't be seen to meet with such people.'

There was a sharp intake of breath as Alek sought to control his temper before he spoke in a very measured and unemotional way.

'John, if the situation is as we think, you either meet these people at a time of our choosing, our you may find that they come to your home and nail your hands to that large oak table you are so proud of, whilst they torture you and my sister.'

There was a shocked silence from both directors as Alek continued to speak.

'This is my world John, and you will need to listen to me when I tell you how we need to deal with these people. I will contact Pavel and tell him to expect all four of us this evening.

Pavel can arrange our accommodation and pick us up from the airport. I will also tell him to make contact with all our business associates and explain that we have had to temporarily suspend the service we offer, but that we would like to meet with them. We could do without any further drama and need to contain the situation.'

As the conference call ended, they watched as John Covington and Trevor Reid slumped forward at their desks and placed their heads into their beautifully manicured hands. It looked to both Sean and Martin that they weren't looking forward to the meetings that Alek had planned and getting those hands dirty.

Whilst Sean and Martin had been busy witnessing the ensuing carnage in London, Ceri had been busy in Geneva. She had visited three very private Swiss banks that had been recommended to her by Jason Connor in the Cayman Islands.

Using her passport in the name of Iryna Kulkas and copies of the paperwork provided by the banks in Cayman as further proof of ID she had been able to successfully open three private Swiss bank accounts. At her request, the banks had emailed the details of the accounts to Jason back on Grand Cayman so that he could associate the accounts with the shell company which had been created.

She had then booked herself an evening flight to Dublin before heading to the airport and using her laptop to transfer funds from the accounts in the Cayman Islands to the new accounts in Switzerland.

During the day, the cloned phone sitting on the table between Sean and Martin had vibrated a few times as Pavel had sent texts to Alek Kulkas. Each text built a worrying picture for the partners in crime as one organisation after another queried why they hadn't received their money. The final text from Alek, confirmed that their plane was about to take off and they would be arriving in Bratislava at 7pm that evening.

At 6pm Sean left the cottage to drive the short distance to the airport and pick-up Ceri. She looked a bit dishevelled having had little time for anything other than travel and work in the previous 24 hours but had a smile on her face, when she plonked herself into the car and sat back with a contented sigh.

When they got back to the cottage, they sat down to what Martin considered a substantial evening meal of sausage rolls, baked beans, and buttered toast. From Martin's point of view all major food groups were catered for, with protein, carbs, dairy, and vegetables all being present. Ceri wryly explained that baked beans were not a vegetable, but an adamant Martin insisted that baked beans represented two of your five a day when the tomatoes in the tomato sauce were considered.

As they ate Ceri explained that now that she had obscured the money trail using multiple accounts in the Cayman Islands and

Switzerland, she now wanted to completely obscure the trail by moving the funds into a crypto currency. Whilst she had been waiting in Geneva airport, she had used her time industriously and registered with one of the crypto currency exchanges in London. It had been really straight forward, and they now had a new digital wallet which currently has nothing in it.

She explained that in order to fund the new account and purchase crypto currency, she would need to complete a verification process and for that she would need help from Sean and Martin.

'I need to do three things to verify my new account. I need to scan my fake passport, scan a bank statement, and take a selfie of myself holding the passport and a piece of paper showing my account reference number.

Before I do that, I need one of you to modify my fake passport to replace my photo with a photo or Iryna. I then need you to photoshop the selfie and replace my face with that of Iryna.

In the UK there is no such things as private banking. So when this money eventually gets traced to the Crypto exchange I don't want my face to be on the pictures that the police are going to find when they make their request for evidence.'

Martin was rubbing his hands together in excited anticipation.

'That's a piece of cake Ceri, I'll grab a couple of pictures from her social media page and do the necessary, I might have to doctor them a little to make them passport quality, but it shouldn't take more than 10 minutes.'

As Martin turned to his laptop, ready to undertake his latest assignment, Sean interrupted.

'Hold on Martin, as a director's wife Iryna will have been given her own ID card by the bank to get her in and out of the building. Her ID photo which will already be a passport photo will be stored digitally on the banks access control system. I'll grab that photo whilst you grab a suitable photo to be used to doctor the selfie.'

As Martin predicted within ten minutes, they had updated the fake passport with the new picture of the real Iryna. Scanned and uploaded the newly revised passport and doctored and uploaded the required selfie. Finally Ceri uploaded one of her swiss bank statements to complete the verification process.

One receiving confirmation that the process had completed successfully, Ceri threw the fake passport into the fire that was blazing in the grate.

'No point keeping anything that could point back to us, if we don't need it. Now I need to start the process of funding my crypto currency account so I can start the final phase of hiding where the funds have gone.'

Ceri explained that once all the funds had been converted to digital currency. The funds would be transferred to an offline wallet held on an encrypted thumb drive. Once the crypto wallet was taken offline the money trail would go stone cold. Subsequently, if they needed to transfer any of the funds to anywhere in the world this could be done very simply with the aid of an internet connection and a wallet address to send the money to.

Sean couldn't help but be quietly impressed by Ceri's planning, but didn't understand why they needed to be so thorough about hiding the money.

'So, once we have hidden the money what do we plan to do with it, its dirty money and we can't keep it. '

'No, we can't keep it Sean, neither can we give it back to the people who it originally came from.'

'We could give it to charity ', said Martin hesitantly.

'No', said 'Ceri we are going to give it to the National Crime Agency along with all the other evidence we have gathered up. Its part of their remit to recover funds from criminal gangs. Whoever has the digital wallet owns the coins associated with it. So I would presume after a successful prosecution her majesty's treasury is going to end up with quite a windfall which will hopefully be put to good use. So we need to focus on doing our best to maximise the funds that we will pass to the National Crime Agency.

It goes without saying that we also want to maximise the stress that these assholes feel. When they see all the money they have gathered through their criminal behaviour slip through their grasping fingers.'

Chapter 32

Sean glanced at his watch, 'Its 8pm, lets see if they have arrived at the branch in Bratislava yet. It will be interesting to hear what they have to say'.

Martin opened up the screen on his laptop showing the bulk cash room, while Sean brought up the display for Pavel's office.

On the screen showing Pavel's office they saw the door open and could see six individuals filing into the room. There was no mistaking the brute that Sean had taken down with the fire extinguisher, his sheer bulk and the dressing visible on the back of his head clearly identified him. Even the normally towering figure of Trevor Reid seemed dwarfed in his presence. John Covington and Alek Kulkas were next to enter, followed by Dimitri Kulkas and finally, the diminutive figure of Pavel.

Alek Kulkas began the interrogation, 'OK Pavel, can you explain to us how you know your computer had been compromised.'

'The morning after the robbery I tried to login to my computer using my usual password and after three attempts I got locked out and had to ring the service desk to unlock me. When I tried again the same thing happened. When I rang the service desk the second time, I asked them to change the password.

This time I got logged in and could change my password. That was when I realised that someone must have logged in on my computer, and changed my password.

I asked one of the IT service team to have someone scan my computer. They confirmed that they found keylogging malware on my machine. That must be how they were able to gain access to my computer and disable the security cameras.'

'So that's when you emailed us to tell us about the compromise?' asked Dimitri.

Pavel sounded hesitant, but wasn't going to disagree with one of his bosses.

'Yes, I must have, it has been very stressful and confusing, but yes I must have.'

'So how on earth did they get the malware onto your machine in the first place and how did they know to target your machine?' asked an angry John Covington.

Pavel just looked meekly back at him and shrugged his narrow shoulders.

John Covington glared impatiently at Pavel, he expected answers and he obviously wasn't going to get any from that direction. He also knew that none of the other men in the room would be any better at providing the answers that they needed.

Seeing the angry confusion on his brother in laws face Dimitri Kulkas cleared his throat and waited until all eyes had turned in his direction before speaking.

With a voice that sounded like he gargled with broken glass he spoke directly to John Covington. He spoke with the calm confidence of a man used to getting his way.

'John The bank has state of the art security systems which your own security people and third-party consultants have all been crawling over for the last week. We need you to authorise one of the banks security team to look at Pavel's machine and tell us what could have happened.'

The normally self-assured chief executive nodded meekly and slipped his bank supplied mobile phone out of his inside jacket pocket. He searched through his contacts, before selecting a number and initiating a call.

'Hello, Richard, your service desk will no doubt have made you aware of the situation we have here in Bratislava. It's a situation we take very seriously as it could have serious financial implications for the bank.

We need one of your guys out here as soon as possible to help us identify what has been going on.'

Richard must have been talking, as they could see John Covington listening intently before giving a final response.

'OK if you think he is the best person for the job get him on a plane tomorrow first thing, we will expect him by lunch time.' He then hung up and placed his mobile back in his inside pocket.

'I wonder which poor sucker they're going to send over', said Sean to Ceri.

Just as Alek opened his mouth to speak, John Covington's Mobile started to ring. He took it out of his pocket glanced at the screen.

'Hello Richard, I presume you have a problem?', again he listened while Richard spoke, before saying,' I don't care if he's on leave and his phone is turned off, find him and get him on a plane to Bratislava.'

Ceri looked at Sean, 'It's only a guess, but I think the poor sucker they are talking about just might be you.'

Sean slowly got up from the table and walked up the stairs to his bedroom, where he retrieved his work mobile from his suitcase, before turning it on and walking back down the stairs.

He had only just got back to the kitchen when it started to ring, and he could see from the display that it was Richard Head. He ran his finger over the screen to accept the call, 'Hello Richard, what can I do for you?'

'Sean, we have a situation in Bratislava that needs a forensic cyber investigator, and you are the only one in the bank qualified to do it.'

'Richard I'm on leave and I'm over here in Ireland visiting my mum, can it wait?'

'No Mr Covington is adamant that we get you to Bratislava by lunch time tomorrow. I've checked and I can get you on a flight from Dublin at 10am tomorrow morning, there is nothing available from Belfast.'

'Give me 5 minutes and I'll ring you back, my mum and I had plans for tomorrow and I'm going to have to break the news to her, she doesn't get to see me that often.'

'Listen Sean I'm really sorry about this, please give her my apologises but the bank really needs your help.'

'OK Richard will ring you back in five'.

As he hung up, he turned to Ceri and Martin with a slight feeling of panic gripping his chest.

'What if Pavel or his big friend recognise me when I arrive on site at the bank? '

'That's very unlikely Sean, the last time we bumped into them we had woolly faces and we never spoke. As for the big guy he literally never saw what hit him, so how are they going to recognise you.'

There was a lot of truth in what Martin had said, they had worn balaclavas and hadn't spoken a word in front of Pavel or his big companion. He suspected John, Trevor and the Kulkas brothers were already considering whether their money had been stolen by a competing organised crime group. This turn of events could put him in the best position to convince the gruesome foursome that they are absolutely right. This was an opportunity not a problem.'

Sean looked at Ceri and Martin with a smile on his face, 'Perhaps we can turn this situation to our advantage. If we could convince them that they have been targeted by another gang we can keep them focussed in the wrong direction, while we finish what we've started.'

Martin suddenly looked very smug. Sitting back in his chair with a broad smile on his face he looked at both Sean and Ceri before sharing his good news.

When Sean had left him alone in Pavel's office, he had installed one or two pieces of malware on Pavel's machine. It had been a precaution, just in case they ever needed to get back onto Pavel's machine. The good news was that the software he had installed were the same tools that were used by a Russian Cyber gang called the cobalt group.

Sean's smile mirrored Martin's. When he carried out his forensic analysis of Pavel's machine, he would find evidence that a Russian Cyber gang have targeted the bank. As he considered the situation more thoroughly, Sean did have some slight concerns. How for example could he explain the fact that cobalt group had been able to bypass bank security.

Martin, not being the one walking into the lion's den and ever the optimist didn't see any need for Sean to be worried. He was certain that the four amigos would see Sean as the seventh cavalry riding to the rescue. He was their chosen man, so whatever he told them, they would believe.

Ceri who had been diligently watching the screens for any activity whilst Sean and Martin had been in conversation, brought their attention back to the here and now.

'Guys, looks like the company they were expecting has arrived.'

Sean and Martin both turned to the laptop screens in time to see three well-nourished individuals in expensive black suits walk through the door into Pavel's office. Apart from the expensive suits they certainly didn't look like the usual high profile bank client. The tattooed hands, heavy gold chains around their necks and expensive signate rings suggested they led a rather more colourful life.

A heavy set, balding individual in the centre of the trio immediately set the tone of the meeting. In a thick eastern European accent he stated, 'Your bank owes me 24 million Euro. I have entrusted you with my money, a job for which I pay you handsomely, where is my money?'

It was a statement echoed by both his companions. They were concerned about smaller sums but sums that were still counted in the millions.

Alek Kulkas raised his hands in a placatory manner, trying to calm the tension in the room.

'Gregor we have had a small issue with the bank transfer, its is nothing more than that. Like you we also haven't received the funds that were due to us.'

'Alek the fact that you haven't received you cut for laundering my money is of no concern to me, I want what I am due. It has been suggested to me that the bank security has been compromised and you have lost my money.'

Alek glanced at Pavel, who had taken a sudden interest in his own feet, before continuing, 'we believe that there has been a small issue with the process we use for transferring the money and we have a technical expert from the bank arriving tomorrow to investigate.'

Gregor paused and scanned the four men standing in front of him and his companions. John Covington and Trevor Reid were obviously nervous, their eyes darting around the room, they were in a situation they could never have imagined for themselves. Alek did his best to maintain a diplomatic calm, whilst his older brother Dimitri was stood impassively, showing neither fear nor concern.

Taking in the demeanour of the men standing in front of him, Gregor made his decision and growled.

'The bank has proven to be a useful tool for managing the money from our more illicit enterprises so we will give you a little more time. I would suggest your expert completes the investigation quickly, we will be expecting our money to arrive in the next two days.'

A nervous John Covington, slightly emboldened by what he saw as Gregor's willingness to negotiate, made the mistake of speaking.

'You can be assured Mr Solonik, the bank will do everything it can to expedite the transfer of your funds once the investigation has been completed. It may however take us a little longer than two days.'

Gregor Solonik glared at John Covington, took two steps forward and grabbed his shirt front in a huge meaty paw. Sean, Martin and Ceri could see the CEO recoil with the force for Gregor's words and no doubt the stench of his breath, as the gang boss practically spat out his words.

'Mr Covington if you cannot provide me with the service I require, then you are of no use to me. Things that prove to be useless in my world, don't tend to have a great life expectancy. I trust I have made myself clear.'

With that Gregor Solonik, and his two companions turned and left Pavel's office, before being escorted out through the side entrance of the bank.

As soon as the trio left, a trembling John Covington turned to Trevor Reid and spoke in a barely audible whisper. 'How much money do we owe each of them and how can we pay them?'

Sean and his companions listened attentively as a nervous Trevor Reid responded to his boss.

'John, we aren't completely sure at the moment, the bank file used for the transfer is unavailable. However, based on the total receipts for the month I have estimated that we owe Gregor just over 24 million Euro, with the other the other two being owed 12 million and 14 million Euro. So in total we need to find around 50 million Euro.'

This most certainly was not the news that John Covington had been hoping for and his dam of self-control burst as he started yelling at the tall figure of the finance director.

'Good god Trevor how are we going to find that sort of money just lying around. We obviously can't use any of the banks money, we already have a hole of 5 million Euro which we are going to have to explain to the Auditors. If they find another 50 million missing, we will have people from the regulator crawling all over the bank.'

Dimitri who up until that point had remained silent spoke slowly and patiently as he would have to an over excited child.

'John, I think we need to combine our resources to resolve this problem. The bank needs to remain above suspicion. If as you say the regulators should take an interest in the bank then the service we provide will have to end and that will present us with a completely different set of problems.

Not only will a source of income dry up for us all, but Gregor and has compatriots may be very unhappy when we close the door on what for them is a perfect way to launder money from their criminal enterprises.'

John Covington took a deep breath to calm himself before responding.

'So, what exactly are you suggesting Dimitri.'

Dimitri continued to speak in the same calm unexcited tone.

'What I am suggesting John is that all four of us combine the funds that we have acquired over the last 9 months of operation and resolve this temporary funding situation. By my estimation you and Trevor should have salted away around 12 million Euro each, Alek and I will make up the rest.'

The solution offered by Dimitri wasn't to John Covington's liking, from his perspective Dimitri was trying to take advantage of the situation and leave him carrying more than his fair share of the burden. It was a petulant rather than fearful CEO who responded to Dimitri's suggestion.

'Dimitri, Trevor and I may well have received 12 million Euro, but we have a lifestyle to maintain, so I for one have significantly less than that available. Besides, you and Alek should have received well over 100 million by my calculations so you should be funding the bulk of this.'

Dimitri's facial muscles tensed in obvious annoyance before he chided John Covington for obviously not understanding the situation.

'John, as Alek will have previously explained to you a lot of the money we received has been invested in property, so we certainly don't have that amount of funds readily available. We could perhaps get access to 32 million'

Martin sniggered as he watched the drama unfold.

'So much for honour amongst thieves', they are all lying about how much they have access to, I saw at least 60 million in those three accounts that Alek checked this morning.'

Ceri had a more combative attitude to what she saw unfolding in front of them. These were the men who had driven her from her job and her home, and men like had left her brother in a wheelchair.

'It doesn't matter how much they have access to Martin, once Sean has dotted the I's and crossed the t's on our cover story, tomorrow we will be cleaning out all their bank accounts. These assholes are all going to suffer for what they are doing.

If they're shitting themselves now after their conversation with Gregor Solonik. This time tomorrow they are going to be having terminal diarrhoea when they realise they have no money to pay him and his friends.'

'They are going to be caught in a massive poonami,' laughed Martin.

'Couldn't happen to a nicer shower of shite agreed Sean,' with a wicked smile.

Ceri found Sean and Martin's good humour infectious and smiled as she whispered.

'Gregor practically measured them up for a pair of concrete shoes and lined them up for a swim in the Danube if they didn't produce the money fast, and we are going to make sure they can't.

Let's leave them to their negotiations whilst we plan how to get access to the funds in the Kulkas bank accounts.'

During the next two hours, many ideas where raised and discarded, before they came up with a plan that everyone agreed with. It was a simple plan, and It wasn't without risk, but things worth doing seldom are, as Sean pointed out.

The first phase of the plan would involve hijacking the email accounts for all four targets. This would allow any verification emails sent as a result of subsequent changes or requests on their online banking systems to be deleted before they could be seen.

With access to the email accounts tied up, they would then change the contact details on the online banking systems that they were targeting. This would ensure that subsequent emails and texts relating to the withdrawal transactions that were going to be performed would never be received by the John Covington and his partners in crime.

They would never know their money had been taken until they actually logged into their online banking portals, and by that point it would be too late.

With the plan agreed, Sean contacted Anna explaining that he would be coming to Bratislava the next day at the behest of John Covington. He filled her in on everything that had happened in the few brief days since they had last been together, before asking if she would be willing to help.

When Sean laid out the plan that had been agreed and explained what part she would need to play, she agreed without any hesitation.

Chapter 33

The next morning Sean drove to Dublin airport with Martin. Ceri had booked Martin a ticket to Vienna using one of her Iryna Kulkas debit cards. Sean had received his digital boarding cards from Richard the previous evening for a direct flight to Bratislava.

Ceri had also booked and paid for a room in a good quality hotel less than three miles from the airport, which Martin planned to use as his base of operations. From his hotel room he would be on hand to execute the coup de main and takeover of the two Kulkas brother's PCs once Sean gave him the go ahead.

Ceri would remain safe in the cottage in Ireland and initiate the transfer of all funds to her crypto currency account and conversion into Bitcoin. All remarkably simple, but as Sean reminded them the best plans were always the most straight forward.

Once through security Sean and Martin had a quick coffee before bidding each other good luck and heading for their separate gates. Sean with a car magazine under his arm and Martin with a carrier bag full of chocolate, Crisps, and other savoury snacks. 'I know', laughed Sean when he had seen Martin walking out of the airport shop, 'you get hungry when you get excited'.

When he landed at Bratislava airport Sean had been met in airport arrivals by a member of bank staff holding up a white placard with his name on it. He had then been whisked straight to the branch with only a five-minute detour to allow Sean to check into the hotel that Richard Head had booked for him.

His driver had dropped him outside the front door of the bank and instructed him to report to the information desk at the front of the branch. Sean did as instructed, and was immediately asked to follow the pretty blond girl who had been manning the reception desk.

'Is Anna Szabo here today?' he asked.

The pretty blond girl without turning her head said 'No I believe she is not at work today, on holiday, I think you would say. Are you the Sean that she sometimes talks about from back in England?'

'Yes, that would be me, I'm the idiot who let her leave me and come back to Bratislava.'

The girl stopped, turned, and smiled, 'perhaps someday she will come back to you, I think she likes you a lot. I'm her friend Adela by the way. When we go out for drinks at the end of the week, she ignores the attention of all the men and when we talk about men she can only talk about you.'

'That's good to know.' said Sean with a grateful smile.

'Perhaps if she comes back, you won't be an asshole this time', said Adela with a bright angelic smile as she pointed Sean towards a door with a bilingual label, one of which said, "meeting room".

Slovakian women are definitely very direct, thought Sean, they leave you in no doubt about what they are thinking.

As he opened the door Sean didn't have much time to ponder the finer attributes of the fairer sex, Slovakian or otherwise. He walked straight into Pavel, who had been on his way out of the room. The short figure of Pavel took a step back in surprise and Sean thought a look of fear appeared in his eyes as he looked up at the impressive 6 foot 2 figure that Sean presented standing in the doorway.

The condescending tones of John Covington emanating from the depths of the room, broke the suspense.

'Aah Sean so glad you could make it, we have a situation here that Richard is adamant only you can advise us on.'

Sean did his best to sound deferential.

'Good afternoon Mr Covington I'm glad to be of service to the bank. Richard I'm afraid was very sketchy with what he told me, just that you need my skills as a forensic analyst.'

Still standing in front of Sean, Pavel said, 'Have we met before? there is something about you that seems familiar.'

'Can't say we have, not unless you've been to head office.'

An impatient John Covington interrupted the pair.

'Pavel if you would let Sean into the room perhaps he and I could discuss why he is here. Sean will come to your office shortly so he can start his investigation.'

Pavel nodded in servile acknowledgment of his dismissal, and Sean stepped to one side as once again Pavel tried to leave the room. This time he met with more success and skuttled off down the corridor towards his office.

'I hope this hasn't proved to be too awkward for you coming here today Sean', continued John Covington as he gestured towards a chair sitting in front of the long meeting table where he currently sat.

'No Mr Covington, my mother is a very understanding woman, and told me that my work should always come first.'

'That's good to know, but I wasn't referring to your mother. I understand that you were in a relationship with the assistant branch manager here, which ended badly. These wounds sometimes take some time to heal.'

Sean couldn't keep his annoyance from showing and was a little sharper than he wanted to be when he responded. Unfortunately, he also gave away a little bit more information than he would have liked to.

'If you don't mind me saying Mr Covington, that is my personal business and has no bearing on the work that you want me to do here. Anna and I parted but we have remained friends, so I have no concerns about coming to her place of work. In fact, I had hoped to bump into her today just so I could say hello and see how she has been getting on. Regrettably, it would appear that she is on leave. Now would you like to tell me what I am here for.'

John Covington loved to be in control, as far as he was concerned Sean's apparent feelings for Anna had just given him the means to control the current situation.

'It's good that you Anna are still on good terms, as the situation that we find ourselves in could cause a great deal of awkwardness for the bank and in particular this branch.

I feel more comfortable telling you what I'm about to tell you, knowing you have a vested personal interest in ensuring this situation is resolved sensitively.

I am sure you will already have guessed that what I say to you now is strictly confidential. If you do a good job in helping the bank to resolve the situation you can be sure that you will have protected the lives and livelihoods of all those working here in Bratislava.'

Sean's face hardened, he didn't dare show even a flicker of the emotions that he currently felt. His head buzzed with anger and he was amazed that fountains of blood were not bursting from both his ears. He just wanted to lean across the table and put his large strong hands around John Covington's throat and squeeze. 'What a pompous sanctimonious prick,' he thought, 'It's not the bank your concerned about, its your own crooked ass that you're trying to save and you're threatening Anna to do it.'

Taking the lack of response from Sean as an indication of understanding, John Covington continued to speak. All through his life he had been motivated by the pursuit of power and money and like many such men, he couldn't fathom how anyone could be motivated by anything else.

So, looking at Sean through the lens of his own greedy, grasping life he added, 'of course the bank will be very grateful for your assistance I would envisage provision of a very attractive bonus. Also, as you know we currently have a vacancy for a Chief Information Security Officer. I'm sure if you put your name forward the board would look very positively on your application.'

'Thank you, sir,' grunted Sean through gritted teeth, 'you can be assured I will do my very best to protect the bank. Now if you would like to tell me specifically why I'm here then I can get on with doing my job.'

As he waited for John Covington to respond, Sean glanced around the room, taking in the fact that there were four open laptops sitting on the table. One sitting in front of his chief executive and the others distributed evenly around the large table. From the reflection in the glass cabinets that lined the rear wall of the room he could see that all four screen savers were currently active.

Sean's scan of the room had not gone unnoticed by the smug John Covington.

'Yes Sean, you will have noticed that I am not alone. Trevor Reid, and two others including Alek Kulkas, who you worked with during the incident involving Ms Gillis are here with me. That should probably give you a clue as to why you are here.'

Sean to his credit made a passable attempt at feigning shocked surprise.

'Is this a continuation of that investigation? Do you believe that Ceri Gillis has gained access to the bank's systems in this branch?'

The CEO tried to be dismissive in his response, but the tension than Sean had witnessed on screen was reasserting itself.

'Not exactly, no, we believe that there has been a data breach focussed on this branch, carried out by a local criminal organisation.'

Sean knew he needed to be totally convincing when he identified the issue at the branch. That being the case he knew it wouldn't do his case any harm to question current preconceptions. After all he was the expert that they had called in and he wanted to be seen to be doing a completely professional job. Even if that job was going to be a stitch up.

'You do realise Mr Covington that the internet allows criminals to attack systems from virtually anywhere in the world. They don't have to be in close proximity to a location to launch an attack.'

The impatient response that he got from the bank executive made it obvious that at least one person had already made up his mind.

'Yes Sean we understand that, however there are a number of things which suggest to us that this is a more localised threat.'

John Covington then explained about the robbery where a small amount of cash had been stolen from the branch and how it transpired that this had been used to cover up a larger theft of a few million euros using fraudulent bank transfer. It was believed that this had been facilitated by a compromised PC in the manager's office.

Sean sat listening, he knew that 5 million Euros wasn't a small amount a cash, after all he had taken it, it was enough to fill a small suitcase. He also knew that 80 million Euros could not, even in John Covington's wildest imaginings be described as a few million. For many smaller financial institutions, a theft of that order would be catastrophic. Yet John Covington the chief executive of the bank, a man whose honesty should be beyond reproach spat out the lies and half-truths with an ease that Sean found breath taking.

'The man has his head so far up his own arse, every time he takes a shit, he must have to clean his teeth', thought Sean.

Sean gave not a hint of his inner thoughts, switching easily into IT security professional mode.

'Thank you Mr Covington, I think the best place to begin is for me to start a scan of the local network, just to be sure that as you say the breach is confined to a single PC.

While that is running, I would like access to the machine that has been identified as having been compromised.

That way I can investigate what might have caused the breach.

Where can I setup my laptop so I can initiate the scan?'

'You can work at Pavel's desk, and I will have him bring the infected PC to his office for you to analyse.'

John Covington then used his mobile to call Pavel and ordered that he come and show Sean to his office.

Pavel arrived within a minute and John Covington instructed him to provide Sean with everything he needed. Sean followed Pavel out of the meeting room and back to the office that he had been in no more than three days previously, albeit as an uninvited guest under totally different circumstances.

Once he had his laptop setup Sean asked Pavel if he could have someone bring him his old PC, the one that was believed to be compromised. A sullen Pavel indicated that he would get it from the bulk cash office, where it was currently being stored.

As Pavel left the office Sean stood up and followed him, watching as Pavel crossed the corridor and keyed in the security code. As Pavel stepped into the room the door started to close and Sean's good manners got the better of him. He stepped into the doorway and held the door open with his shoulder. Meanwhile Pavel had picked up the PC from the floor and turned to retrace his steps. As he turned and say Sean standing in the doorway a startled yelp escaped and his eyes widened in obvious panic.

'Sorry for startling you Pavel, but thought I'd give you a helping hand'.

'I didn't need any help', came the sullen reply, as Pavel put his head down and pushed past Sean, who had stepped back and now held the door open with his extended arm.

 Once Pavel exited the bulk cash office, Sean turned and opened the door to Pavel's office giving Pavel easy entry so that he could deposit the PC on Sean's temporary desk. With the PC in place Sean connected a mouse keyboard and monitor up to the unit before turning it on. Pavel was still obviously agitated, so in order to try and restore some calm to the situation, Sean explained what he intended to do.

'I will have to manually scan this machine as it can't be put back on the network. It will probably take me an hour or two.'

Pavel wasn't going to be easy to placate, he sat at his desk glaring at Sean, making no attempt to disguise his displeasure at Sean's presence in his office.

Sean knew he was pushing his luck, but he needed Pavel out of the way for a few minutes so politely asked the if Pavel could possibly furnish him with a cup of coffee and possibly a Danish pastry, explaining that he'd had an early start that morning.

Much to Sean's surprise Pavel got up from his desk and left the office without a word. As soon as he left Sean took out his encrypted mobile and rang Martin.

'OK Martin John Covington, Trevor Reid, Alek Kulkas and I believe Dimitri Kulkas, are all here. All their laptops are currently switched on and showing a screen saver. The only person currently in the room is John Covington so Alek and Dimitri's machines are currently unattended you could do the transfers now.'

Martin confirmed that he had full control of the four laptops and could see everything directly in front of the cameras on the machines, the built-in microphones were doing a great job at picking up all sounds in the room. Even so Martin was cautious, he didn't want to take any chances that someone in the room might see him at work. If John Covington were standing silently out of view of the cameras, the possibility existed that he might be able to see Martin making his unauthorised withdrawals.

Martin insisted they stick to the plan they had agreed the previous night and Sean must get all four men together with him in Pavel's office. That way Martin would have the freedom to work on all the laptops without any fear of discovery. Martin had checked the feed from the previous evening and knew that Alek, Dimitri, John and Trevor didn't intend to do any funds transfers until Sean had completed his work. That being the case they didn't need to rush into anything and make a mistake.

A suitable chastened Sean confirmed that he would message Martin as agreed, once he was about to start presenting his findings to their target audience.

Chapter 34

With Pavel out of the office and his phone call with Martin finished, Sean sat down at Pavel's machine before logging in with administrative privileges.

As he moved the keyboard a yellow post-it note came unstuck from beneath it. When he picked it up Sean couldn't help smiling. Pavel obviously had an awfully bad memory because he had written all the passwords for the banks systems and his own CCTV system on the one note. 'Very secure sticking it to the bottom of his keyboard, that's the last place someone is going to look', thought Sean.

Martin had spent some time reviewing the data on the two disks that had been copied during their night time incursion. He had identified several things which were going to be very useful to Sean in making his analysis more real and believable.

Martin had discovered by reviewing his browser history that Pavel had two weaknesses, online porn, and online gambling. Sean had been surprised by Martin's findings, not because he had any strong views on either activity, more because the banks security systems should have prevented access to both things.

When they look more closely at the security configuration on the cloned hard disk an explanation became apparent. The PC had been setup to traverse the internet by connecting directly through the external firewall. All other layers of security that had been put in place to protect the banks systems and data had been bypassed.

As something completely contrary to bank policy this would have required a change control to be issued to allow a PC with that sort of configuration to be placed on the banks network. In other words, someone in authority would have had to sign off on this deviation from the norm.

Sean had logged into the change control module on the banks service desk system to search for such a change request. He had found seven, two for each of the eastern European branches with the final one being for Pavel's replacement PC. All the changes had been requested by John Covington, signed off by Richard Head and then been actioned by one of the banks IT service team.

None of the changes had been put through the banks change board, on which Sean sat as a member. They had been put through as emergency changes not requiring ratification by the change board.

Sean was aghast at the stupidity that had been displayed in both requesting and approving such a change. Bypassing layers of security that had been put in place to secure the banks systems and data was akin to leaving you front door unlocked and a big sign in your front garden saying "please steal my stuff".

Martin pointed out that the reason for the bypass was unlikely to be a kindly boss facilitating Pavel's online habits. He had found both a dark web browser and a dark web messaging app, both tools used by criminal elements to communicate over the web. The change had in all likelihood be made to allow Pavel to communicate with the criminal elements who were using the bank to launder their money.

The highly secure and monitored environment that would normally have been in force on a bank computer, would have been an insurmountable obstacle, to such tools. Obviously, the powers that be within the bank were doing their best to ensure the smooth running of the more illicit side of their business.

Sean had been incensed by the reckless abandon with which people who should have known better had put the bank at risk. On the other hand, this obvious breach in security protocol gave him a great foundation on which to build his story of nefarious intrigue and criminal activity directed against the two directors and the Kulkas brothers.

Having logged into Pavel's computer, he removed the thumb drive that Martin had provided him with from his pocket. He inserted the drive into a usb socket on the front of the PC, before running a batch file to copy the malware to the correct locations on the hard drive. Whilst waiting on the copy to finish he felt the encrypted phone buzzing in his pocket, taking it out he was surprised to see that Martin was ringing him.

As soon as he hit the answer button he heard Martin's excited voice.

'Sean good news is Anna is here with me, bad news is we have a problem. Pavel is currently standing in front of John Covington telling him that he thinks you were involved in the robbery.'

Sean took a deep breath, before speaking.

'How on earth can he think that, he never saw my face, or heard me speak.'

Martin agreed, but pointed out that according to what Pavel had just told John Covington. He had seen Sean's eyes and now he had apparently just seen Sean standing in the doorway to the cash office, just like the guy on the night of the robbery. Pavel had also told John Covington that Sean's build was similar to one of two people who had been captured on CCTV walking backwards and forwards in front of the bank on the evening before the robbery.

Sean cursed under his breath, this wasn't part of the plan, then settling himself he asked Martin a question, the answer to which would decide his next move.

'Does Covington believe him?'

Martin spoke hesitantly.

'Not exactly, he's sceptical, but he is talking on the phone right now with Richard Head asking for the passport number that he used to book your flights.

This could get very awkward Sean, I'm not exactly in a position to get to you quickly if you need help, sitting here in Vienna. You need to get your ass out of there toute suite before the shit hits the fan.'

Sean had made his decision.

'No I think it'll be fine Martin, I just need to make sure I bury Pavel under a mountain of suspicion, and make it look like he's involved. That way it will appear he's panicking about my investigation and was trying to deflect blame.'

Martin's tone became more strident.

'Sean, he has asked for your passport number, he is probably going to get the same guys who tried to track Ceri's travel to track yours.'

Sean spoke calmly he didn't want Martin's concern to worry Anna.

'Martin don't panic we need to focus on giving them a more obvious target, If I do a disappearing act Pavel's suspicions are going to become a concrete certainty. I need to balls this out and make sure they see Pavel as the bad guy, or we will all be in trouble.

We've been lucky so far and we need to ride that luck just a little further. If Pavel succeeds in his attempt to point the finger of suspicion in my direction, it won't take them long to join the dots and realise that you and Ceri are my partners in crime. Even worse they know about my relationship with Anna, and she would be in serious danger.

Believe me if I run now, we will need to disappear and we will always be looking over our shoulders. I for one don't want to spend the rest of my life hiding in a hole waiting on people like Gregor Solonik to find me and I would never forgive myself if Anna got hurt.

Now put me on speaker and stop worrying about the passport, they will find nothing believe me, I'm absolutely certain of that. What we do need to do though, is make some adjustments to the plan we came up with last night.'

'Yes Sean I know', sighed Martin, 'no plan survives first contact with the enemy. To be honest I'm more concerned with us surviving than the bloody plan, what do you want to do?'

Sean checked that Anna had heard the conversation he had just had with Martin.

A playful sounding Anna responded.

'Yes Sean, I got the gist of it, that asshole Pavel has recognised your broad shoulders and beautiful blue eyes and is trying to cause problems.'

Sean laughed, before his voice took on a more serious timbre.

'A very succinct summary baby, yes, so we need to discredit him, and his theory and we are going to need your help to do this. Are you still happy to help? I would understand if you wanted to back out now, things could get dangerous.'

Anna seemed totally unperturbed.

'Sean like you have told Martin, they know about you and me and whatever I do they will think I have been involved. I couldn't back out now even if I wanted to, you're the man I love and I will do everything I can to help you no matter what.'

'Thanks baby, I love you too and I'm going to do my best to make sure you and I have a long life to enjoy together.'

Martin was starting to feel slightly awkward stuck in between the two love birds and jumped in to direct things back to the business in hand.

'OK Romeo and Juliette could we get on with the plan please, times a wasting and we have a lot to do.'

'OK Martin like I've said we need to make some minor adjustments to the plan, so this is what I think we should do.'

Sean explained to Martin and Anna what needed to be done then hung up and went back to complete the work that he had already started on Pavel's machine.

Job done he logged out of the PC, relocked the screen and sat back down in front of his own laptop and kicked off a local network vulnerability scan. Five minutes later Pavel re-entered the office, after talking with John Covington it appeared he had made a visit to a well-known coffee chain. He had two large coffees and what looked like a danish pastry wrapped in plastic.

'Thanks Pavel you're a star' said Sean with a smile. My Scan is still running so good time for a coffee break.

Pavel went over to his desk logged into the banks security system so he could find the video that he wanted to show John Covington, sipping his coffee as worked. After half an hour of trawling through the security footage he found what he had been searching for and forwarded the best image he could find of the two suspicious individuals to the Kulkas brothers and the two directors currently sitting in the meeting room.

Sean meanwhile appeared focussed on Pavel's old machine and every now and again he would make a noise signifying that he had found something interesting. Each time a noise emanated from his direction, he could see Pavel out of the side of his eye, look up in an enquiring fashion, obviously wondering what new revelation Sean had discovered.

Sean for his part studiously ignored the obviously uncomfortable Pavel as he trawled through the disk on his old Machine. He found very few surprises, in fact he found nothing that he wasn't already aware of, apart from one thing. Someone had made an attempt to remove the dark web tools that they had found when studying the copied disk for this PC. The executables were gone, but they had neglected to remove the install files, quite an amateur job of trying to hide evidence in his opinion.

At around 4:30pm felt the encrypted phone buzz in his pocket, the first part of plan B had just been completed. Sean immediately stood up, strode over the Pavel's desk and without warning lent down and removed the network cable from the back of the PC.

'What the hell are you doing!' yelled a surprised Pavel, 'I was working here.'

Sean's tone was brisk and business like and brooked no argument.

'I need to speak to John Covington right now, I have identified something that he needs to be aware of immediately.'

As a very irate Pavel left the office, Sean keyed in a message on his phone to Martin informing him that he had just started his presentation. Keeping the phone by his side he waited. Two minutes later Pavel and the four targets for their digital payback, came walking through the door, that's when he hit send.

'OK shit is going to hit the fan now for someone, just hope its not going to be me', he thought as he prepared himself for the performance ahead.

Chapter 35

Sean took on a serious demeanour, as he prepared to lead his audience down a very carefully prepared garden path.

'Gentlemen thank you for coming so quickly. Mr Covington was most insistent that I find an answer to the problems that the bank has experienced over the last week.'

Sean glanced at Dimitri enquiringly, then looked at John Covington, who taking the obvious cue, introduced Sean to Dimitri. No second name was provided, but Sean already knew who he was and only an idiot would think that the family resemblance with Alek wouldn't be noticed.

'Gentlemen, I have good news and bad news, the bad news is that the bank has indeed suffered a breach. The good news is that from what I can see it has been confined to two machines.'

An obviously impatient John Covington interrupted Sean.

'Two machines, what two machines?'

Sean on the other hand couldn't have been more patient, as he calmly continued with his prepared story.

'The two machines that I have identified as having been subject to a breach are both Pavel's. My network security scanner identified Pavel's machine as having been compromised just before I requested your presence.

 I have disconnected it from the network, so the problem has been contained for now. It is my view that Pavel's machine has been used to stage the incursion that you told me about earlier Mr Covington.'

Pavel stepped forward with a look of disgust on his face. 'We know my machine was used; you have spent the last 4 hours confirming what we have already told you.'

John Covington didn't look impressed as he put up his hand to silence Pavel and smiled mirthlessly at Sean.

'Yes Sean, what you have told us is not an earth-shattering revelation, frankly I am disappointed.'

Sean paused, he wanted the significance of what he was going to say next to be fully understood by everyone in the room. He then spoke calmly, as if speaking to an over excited child.

'I think Mr Covington that you have missed the point. I said both of Pavel's machines have been compromised. The one that was in place on the night of the robbery and his replacement machine.'

An indignant Alek was the first to pick up what Sean had just said.

'How on earth could that have happened, how could there have been a second security breach without the banks security systems raising an alarm.'

Sean could see the cogs start to click into place in John Covington's head. His look of puzzlement turned to anger as he pointed an accusing finger in Sean's direction.

'Yes Sean, how could the systems that you have helped architect and design have failed to miss it, this is a totally unacceptable state of affairs.'

Sean was totally unphased and his response was almost surgical as he cut John Covington off at the knees.

'I totally agree sir, there has been a complete failure, but the failure has been a failure to adhere to the strict security policies and procedures that are in place at the bank.

Both of Pavel's machines have been configured to completely bypass all of the normal security systems used by the bank.'

Choosing his next words very carefully Sean looked John Covington in the eye before adding.

'I have no idea who would have approved such a deviation from normal practice, nor do I have an explanation why this would have been done. I can only assume that this has been done to hide some nefarious activity.'

Sean saw a flicker of dawning realisation appear in John Covington's eyes, before he continued with his concise review of the situation.

'While I can't explain why this was done, I can tell you what the outcome of this deviation from policy has been. On both of Pavel's machines I have found a number of pieces of malware.

The selection of Malware found would suggest that the bank has been targeted by the Cobalt Group, a Russian Cyber-criminal gang who specialise in attacking financial institutions.

It is my understanding that they have mounted successful attacks on the First Commercial Bank in Taiwan and the Government Saving Bank in Thailand. They are also known to have run several spear-phishing campaigns targeting Russian banks.

How exactly they were able to install these tools on Pavel's machine I can't be 100% sure, however the browsing history on Pavel's old machine does suggest a number of possibilities.'

Sean looked directly at the unfortunate Pavel.

'The browsing history on Pavel's machine would indicate that sites of an adult nature and sites used for gambling have been visited on numerous occasions. Many of these sites are notorious for containing malware and spyware.

There is also evidence that a dark web chat app had been installed on Pavel's old machine, such tools are normally used by criminal organisations to secure communications with other criminal contacts

Whether it be intentional, or whether it be through sheer stupidity the reason for the breach is standing in this room with us now.'

'Yes Mr Burke, you are right the reason is in this room, the reason is you', yelled a red-faced Pavel.

'We have spent enough time listening to your stories. I know you were one of the two people who robbed the bank. You have planted this evidence to try and make me look bad, but my employer knows my loyalty is beyond reproach.'

Sean's deep voice didn't raise a single octave as he calmly, but firmly put the spotlight of suspicion on the now sweating Pavel.

'Pavel the evidence on your computer does not lie, nor does the scanner that I have used to scan the network. Your machines are the source of the network breach.'

Pavel became more and more agitated and in the direction his voice was going, soon only dogs were going to be able to hear him as he screamed almost incoherently at Sean.

'We know you were in Bratislava last week, and you were in my office, you planted this evidence. We have tracked your passport and we have pictures which prove you were here!'

Alek Kulkas who had been quietly watching the exchange, gently placed his hand on the shoulder of the screaming man. Pavel startled by the unexpected contact, swung round in panic, his rant forgotten.

Alek spoke quietly, but his voice was no less threatening for its lack of volume.

'Actually, Pavel we don't know that, the pictures that you seem to think shows Sean in Bratislava, do show someone of a similar build to Sean, but we cannot see a face. In fact, the picture looks like two tourists in baseball caps.

As for your assertion about his passport, the only time that Sean's passport has been used in the last two weeks has been to travel to Ireland and then this morning to fly to Bratislava.'

Pavel could sense that he was losing the battle and, in his desperation, resorted to an unsubstantiated if correct supposition.

'He must have flown in through another airport, he was here, and he knocked out Igor with the fire extinguisher, I'm telling you it was him.'

Alek Kulkas was staring coldly at the whimpering Pavel. Sean couldn't help but think that what he was witnessing, was akin to someone realising they were about to be eaten by a great white shark.

Alek's voice was cold and thoughtful as he spoke again.

'Pavel you are not listening Sean's passport has been used only twice, once to go to Ireland and once to fly here.

It would appear for some reason that you are incredibly determined to put the blame on someone for the difficulties that we currently find ourselves in.

Why is that Pavel?

And perhaps you could explain to us how Gregor Solonik was aware of some of the issues that we have been having?

When we spoke with him last night it was obvious that he knew more than he should.

Perhaps you have a divided loyalty Pavel?'

Sean turned to John Covington with an enquiring look on his face before innocently asking the obvious question.

'Excuse me Mr Covington, but how does Alek know that my passport has been only used twice and why would that even be of interest to you.'

John Covington was not usually a man who felt he needed to apologise, but his words to Sean were as conciliatory as he had ever spoken.

'I really must apologise Sean, but Pavel had a wild theory that you had some involvement in some of the issues we have been having. Alek put your passport number through a security check which proved you to be totally innocent of Pavel's allegations. It is starting to look like he was concerned with what you might find and how that might look for him.'

Sean's response was dripping with disgust and anger.

'The only reason I have any involvement in this situation Mr Covington is because you asked me to cut short my holiday with my mother and come here.'

Sean was sure his old drama teacher would have been proud of him if she could only see him now, giving the performance of his life. Then again, he thought, when your life depends on it, that's probably the time to give such a performance.

A rattled Pavel realising that he had exhausted all options with Alek and seeing Sean was gaining traction with John Covington, pleaded with the chief executive.

'Mr Covington, you know that my loyalty to you is complete, I have done everything I can to protect our enterprise. This man is not who he pretends to be he is an imposter.'

His pleas fell on deaf ears, John Covington had already drawn his own conclusions and the chill in his voice told Pavel exactly what those conclusions were.

'Pavel Sean is exactly who he says he is, he has worked for the bank for more than 5 years protecting the banks systems, and if he tells me there are things on your computer that shouldn't be then I believe him.

The question we now must answer is as Sean has rightly stated, did they get there through your stupidity, or were you complicit in their installation.'

Pavel was standing just in front of the other four men staring at Sean shaking with fear and anger. For reasons he couldn't understand, he felt the spotlight of suspicion was shining brightly in his direction.

Just as he was sure things couldn't get any worse there was an audible ping from his mobile phone. In a fog of panic and anxiety he reached into his pocket and on automatic pilot held the phone in front of him to view the message.

'Looks like Martin has finished the next phase of the plan', thought Sean. He suspected that Martin must have been watching proceeding on the covert camera because the text arrival couldn't have been any better timed.

Sean didn't need to be able to see the screen or even read Russian to know what the message on Pavel's mobile said. Alek on the other hand could do both and could see that the message in Russian said, 'Get out now it has been done.'

'What has been done? why must you get out now?', yelled Alek Kulkas as he made a grab for Pavel's phone.

That was the last straw for the already agitated Pavel. He didn't understand how, but his survival instinct told him he was in deep shit. He spun out of reach of the grasping hands of Alek Kulkas, who found himself impeded by the bulk of Trevor Reid and made a break for the door.

Alek pushed past John Covington and Trevor Reid in a vain attempt to catch up with the much lighter and faster Pavel. As the two directors were jostled out of the way by the surprisingly nimble Alek, Sean saw a look of consternation cross their normally superior faces. Sean felt certain the smug look they normally wore, would be taking a long holiday once they realised what exactly the cryptic text on Pavel's phone meant.

Chapter 36

Two minutes later a panting Alek returned to the office.

'He got away, I wasn't able to catch him, but I have directed some of my team to go to his apartment just in case he tries to go there. Right now, we need to go to the meeting room and do what we can to resolve the situation with Gregor Solonik and the others.'

Sean could only imagine how they were currently feeling. As far as they were concerned their money had been taken by a Russian cyber gang aided by one of their trusted lieutenants. To further rub salt in the gaping wound caused by the lose of millions of euros, they were now going to have to repay the money out of their own ill-gotten gains.

Sean struggled hard to keep the smile from his face as he thought about what they were going to think when they returned to the meeting room to begin their funds transfer.

As the four men left the room, Sean set about slowly packing up his equipment, and waited on their inevitable return.

As Sean placed the last item of equipment into his laptop bag and zipped it up, Alek Kulkas burst through the door.

'Sean we have a problem and we need your help!'

Sean followed an obviously agitated Alek back to the meeting room, where he found Trevor Reid, John Covington and Dimitri, pacing back and forth casting nervous glances at the laptops in front of them.

From what Sean could see all four laptop screens were showing the same image. The image indicated that their machines had been encrypted and there was a demand for payment of 1000 Bitcoin. Each laptop also displayed a timer currently sitting at just over 5 hours and 30 minutes. This was counting down the hours and minutes to when the machines would no longer be able to be unencrypted.

'Sean what does this mean?' asked a panicking John Covington.

Sean raised an eyebrow in feigned surprise.

'It looks like you have all been subject to a ransomware attack. Some of the malware that I found on Pavel's machine can be used to mount such attacks.'

Sean paused to assess the different emotions playing across the faces of the four men. John Covington and Trevor Reid were horrified, an enraged Alek Kulkas strode round the office uttering what could only be angry expletives in Ukrainian. Dimitri Kulkas was the only one who seemed totally unperturbed by the current situation.

Keen to push the theory that Pavel was the key to their current misfortunes, Sean asked a question to which he already knew the answer.

'Did any of you receive any recent emails from Pavel?'.

Sean wasn't surprised when they all confirmed that they had received recent emails from Pavel, including an urgent one received just that day containing the supposed picture of Sean and an accomplice. Sean's quietly spoken and obviously considered response was no great comfort to the men standing in front of him.

'That's a classic ransomware tactic, send an email requiring urgent attention so the targets will open the email without thinking. Opening the email, clicking on a link or a file, or in this case an image will then result in the malware being installed.'

Keen to emphasise Pavel's betrayal and raise their anxiety levels even further, Sean twisted the knife just a little bit more.

'Looks like whoever Pavel was working with has used him to get access to your machines, with the purpose of installing the ransomware that we now see.'

Sean could see that they were obviously in turmoil. As far as they were concerned a trusted member of their team had helped another crime group to steal over 80 million euro and had now impeded their efforts to repay an impatient Gregor Solonik and friends. Sean struggled manfully to keep his face rigid, so that the smile currently straining to take over his face was kept in check.

Sean knew the current upset they felt would be nothing compared to the mayhem which was going to ensue once they realised their illicit bank accounts had also been cleaned out. Dimitri Kulkas seemed to be the only one of the quartet currently capable of coherent thought. Taking Sean's stoic silence and rigid jawline as a sign of calm competence, he quietly asked the question that no one else was currently capable of asking.

'Sean, what can you do to fix this, we all need to get access to our machines now, we have something we need to do.'

'As with any such attack Dimitri, there are two things that you can do. The first thing is to pay the ransom they are demanding, which at the current Bitcoin exchange rate is extortionate.

Even then you are taking a chance that the criminals you are dealing with are going to be honest and will give you the encryption key needed to get your machines back.

The second thing is what I would recommend and that is wipe your laptops and restore them from a backup.'

Dimitri's voice was still calm, but the frown lines that had appeared on his forehead and around his eyes betrayed his growing concern.

'Sean, we don't have the time to do that, we have business that we need to conclude tonight. Surely there is something you can do Sean, you're an expert in Cyber security, there must be another option.'

In response Sean took another opportunity to give the quartet a mental kicking.

'No, I'm sorry Dimitri, but the only other option you have to resolve this quickly is to find Pavel and hope that he can persuade his partners in crime to give you the encryption key to decrypt your machines.'

Dimitri wasn't pleased, he had spent his life having his every whim and demand catered for. The words "No" and "Sorry" were words usually only heard whilst enjoying the application of electrodes to the testicles of someone who had displeased him. His voice had a hard edge when he spoke to his younger brother.

'Alek we need to speak to Pavel, have your men find him and quickly.'

Sean's usefulness had come to an end as the Dimitri waved his arm vaguely in the direction of the door and coldly dismissed him.

'Sean you may leave now we have things that we need to discuss which do not concern you.'

Sean brindled, he didn't work for Dimitri, he worked for the bank. He knew he should just leave but chose to ignore Dimitri's edict and instead turned and addressed the disconsolate figure of John Covington.

'Mr Covington, if you have no further need for me tonight, I will be on my way. I intend to return to Dublin tomorrow, but I will check in with you here in the morning just in case I can be of any further assistance.'

Without another word Sean turned and left the room, the door closed firmly behind him. Slinging his rucksack over his shoulder Sean wondered out of the building and made his way to Anna's apartment where he fully expected to find both Anna and Martin.

When Sean arrived at the apartment, he knocked gently on the door, which was opened by a beaming Anna. She flung her slim strong arms around his neck and kissed him full on the mouth.

Anna had just finished preparing an evening meal and the smell of the cooking mingled with the smell of her perfume reminded him of their time together back in England. When she disengaged her lips from his she whispered, 'your plan is working my love', before coming close for another kiss.

Martin was sitting at the kitchen table with his laptop turned on listening to the Sound of four incredibly angry men. Martin had total control of the four laptops that were still sitting in the meeting room and had been making the most of the built-in cameras and microphones to monitor events back at the bank.

'Hi Sean looks like the change in plan is working, they have found Pavel's car parked at his apartment and have forced the boot open and have found the stolen cash. They are crazy angry at him and believe that he was preparing to leave with his cash bonus after screwing them over today.

I have messaged Ceri and she has confirmed receipt of the sixty million Euro that I managed to extract from the Kulkas accounts. She is now working through turning all the money we have taken into digital currency. She thinks she will have completed her work by the end of tonight.'

Sean couldn't help but be amazed at just how smoothly things had gone and smiled at Anna as she started to put the meal she had prepared on the table. Just as the pot of Goulash was placed in the middle of the table a ringing telephone could be heard through Martin's laptop speaker.

They heard Alek's voice answer the phone, 'Hello have you found him?'. They couldn't hear the reply, but from the flurry of swear words that were spewing from Alek's mouth they were sure the news he had received hadn't gone down well.

As they watched Martin's laptop screen, they saw Alek sit down in front of his currently useless machine, throw his hands behind his head and lean back in his chair.

'We are screwed, they found Pavel, or rather Pavel found them at his apartment. When they tried to detain him, he panicked and pulled out his gun and started shooting. He wounded two of my men before they were able to disable him.'

Sean voice betrayed his concern, as he looked at Martin and Anna, 'why the hell did the stupid idiot go back to his apartment. This could get messy for us if they question him, and he sticks to his story.'

Sean's concern soon turned to confusion; he could see from the screen in front of them that Alek Kulkas didn't look happy. A perception apparently shared by someone in the room with Alek.

'What's the problem?', the voice of John Covington asked.

'We have him, so get the little bastard here, so we can get these machines sorted.'

Alek's response was cold and very much to the point.

'The problem is they disabled him by shooting him in the head. I'm afraid we are going to get no answers from Pavel.'

The calm façade that Dimitri had been maintaining broke with a resounding crack. His words were fizzing with anger.

'What part of "we need to speak to Pavel" did the imbeciles you employ not understand. Short of finding someone who can commune with the dead we have lost our last hope of resolving this situation tonight.'

There was a shocked silence in Anna's kitchen as Martin, Sean and Anna looked at each other. Pavel had been as Anna called him an asshole, involved up to his eyes in money laundering. The slippery rat had even tried to shaft Sean, and had the favour returned with interest, but they hadn't thought he would end up dead.

Sean was first to recover from the shock. 'Martin is Pavel's mobile still turned on?'

'Yes and its located as we know near his apartment.'

'OK send another text to Pavel's mobile.'

'Why the poor little bastard is dead?'

'I know, but let's take the opportunity to put a further cramp in Alek's style. Anna can you send a message saying, meet us at the train station so we can transfer the cash from your car. We will get you out of Bratislava.'

Within 30 seconds of the text being sent they once again heard Alek's phone ring. They saw Alek lean forward in his chair as he spoke for a few seconds to the person on the other end of the call. He then hung up and turned in his seat to speak to his red-faced brother. John Covington and Trevor Reid were obviously neither use nor ornament, totally out of their depth in the current situation.

'Pavel's friends have sent him a message; they want to meet at the train station. I have told the team to put Pavel in the boot with the money and to head for the station.

Stephan will drive Pavel's car with another man hiding in the back seat. The rest of the team will shadow him in their own vehicles, we might still be able to retrieve the missing money and unlock our laptops.'

Dimitri's clipped response to his brother seethed with barely suppressed anger.

'No guns, no noise, no mess, no dead bodies, we need a conversation, not another funeral. Do they understand that?'

Alek nodded in confirmation, whilst John Covington and Trevor Reid sat disconsolately staring at their laptops, unable to contribute in any way to the unfolding drama they now found themselves a part of. They both looked like broken men, men who realised that they now had absolutely no control over what was currently happening. It was no doubt a strange and uncomfortable feeling for two men who were top of the tree in the finance organisation that they ran as their own personal money-making fiefdom.

Sean grinned, 'OK Anna now we need you to ring the local police on Martin's burner phone tell them you have witnessed a shooting at Pavel's address.

Tell them that you witnessed them putting the body into the boot of a car and give Pavel's registration.

I need you to sound emotional and scared.'

Anna made the call and Sean had to admit, she had given an Oscar winning performance. After giving her story, she screamed and shouted, 'they have seen me, I must run', before hanging up and turning off the phone.

Martin then removed the SIM, replacing it with another from the stash that he had bought at the airport during their previous trip to Bratislava.

Satisfied with how things were currently progressing Sean helped Anna to lay out the evening meal so they could all take a well-earned break. Events were going to unfold for the unfortunate quartet currently sitting in the banks meeting room, which neither he nor they had any further control over.

Chapter 37

An hour later with the evening meal finished, Sean helped Anna to clean up. Martin still sat in front of his laptop, eyes dropping on the four increasingly tense men who were still in the meeting room at the bank.

They had consumed a considerable amount of coffee and were obviously very agitated as they awaited the return of Alek's men. Hopefully, this time they would have someone with them who had a heartbeat, someone who could release their machines from the impending digital Armageddon that continued to slowly count down on their screens.

With everything currently under control at the bank they decided to check in with Ceri.

'Hello boys', came the cheery greeting, when Ceri answered her phone. 'Hello boys and girl', 'corrected Martin, 'we have Anna with us here too, in fact we are in Anna's apartment.'

Ceri was surprised at Martin's light-hearted revelation. It had been her understanding that Martin would meet up with Anna and take her to Pavel's abandoned car. Anna would then drive the car to London so that the incriminating cash could be planted in John Covington and Trevor Reid's offices. The cash would then be found when the bank was raided by the National Crime Agency.

Martin explained to Ceri that they had changed the plan, in reaction to Pavel identifying Sean as one of the two people who had robbed the bank and stolen his car. They had flipped the accusation, and Sean had done a sterling job convincing John

Covington, Trevor Reid and the Kulkas brothers that Pavel was in fact a member of the gang who robbed the bank.

Martin sounded incredibly pleased with himself when he described how his strategically deployed text had pushed the under-pressure Pavel to run. He was barely able to contain his excitement; when he told how they had been able to blame emails sent by Pavel for installing ransomware on the target laptops.

The final figurative and literal nail in Pavel's coffin had been Anna leaving the car load of cash at Pavel's apartment. This had been accepted by the criminal foursome as the final confirmation that Pavel had been part of the conspiracy to steal their money.

After listening to Martin's story, Ceri couldn't help but sound impressed.

'Sounds like you guys did a top job of pushing the Pavel story, but what happens when they catch him and put him through the ringer. He's going to revert to his Sean theory again.'

Martin quickly dismissed Ceri's concern.

'Well, he didn't have much concrete evidence to back up his theory and the only thing which I was worried about drew a blank for them.

I must admit to being worried when they said they were doing a trace on Sean's passport, but that trace confirmed Sean's innocence in their eyes.'

Martin's final revelation left Ceri in no doubt that Pavel was no longer of any concern. There was a shocked silence at the other end of the line when Martin revealed that Pavel wouldn't be answering any more questions, or in fact doing much of anything after being shot in the head.

To break the silence Martin turned to Sean and asked, 'So why were you so sure that their trace on your passport would draw a blank?'

'That's quite simple Martin, I was born in Northern Ireland and as such I am entitled to have both a UK and an Irish passport. I used my Irish passport when we flew to Vienna and gave Richard Head my UK passport details when he booked my flight for this morning.'

'You're a regular secret agent', laughed Martin.

'The names Burke, Sean Burke,' responded Sean with a strained laugh.

Ceri struggling to absorb the information that someone had just died as a direct result of what they were doing, realised that Sean and Martin were hiding their own discomfort at the situation behind fake laughter. Typical men she thought, they think it's a weakness to show any sign of their true feelings.

Once things had quietened down Ceri updated Sean, Martin, and Anna on her progress. She had successfully transferred all funds from John Covington and Trevor Reid's accounts to her accounts in the Cayman Islands.

She was sure the 60 million euro acquired by Martin from the Kulkas brothers, would certainly have put a smile on her favourite bank manager Julian's face when it had also arrived in her account. Though she doubted the smile would last long when he realised that she had moved all the money to her accounts in Switzerland.

Finally, she explained that she was in the process of moving the 140 odd million they had accumulated into her digital exchange account. She hoped that by the end of that night an amount of money that would normally take a forklift truck to move, would be on a thumb drive that would fit into a pocket in her skinny jeans.

'Well, that should make the job of getting the money into the hands of the authorities much easier', said Sean.

Sean then confirmed that he and Martin were still working on putting together a montage of all the best video and audio clips, to go with Ceri's collection of bank and shell company paperwork. They intended to finish that work when they returned to Dublin the next day.

As Sean stopped speaking, Alek's phone started to ring. There followed a brief exchange, before Alek said one-word, which Sean was sure would have made his mother blush if she could speak Ukrainian, before he hung up the phone.

He turned to John Covington, Trevor Reid and his brother and snapped, 'we need to leave, we need to leave now. Stephan and his companion have been arrested at the train station with Pavel's body and a lot of cash in the boot of Pavel's car.

A heavily armed special response unit turned up and surrounded the car. The rest of the team could do nothing, so they are on their way back here.

We need to get to the airport and get back to London, Gregor Solonik is not a man known for his patience and it would be best to put some distance between him and us.'

Dimitri nodded in agreement.

'Yes, we can speak to Gregor when we are safely back in London. Hopefully, he will be understanding and will accept a further small delay in the return of his money.

What of your men, will they talk?'

Alek dismissed his brother's concern, his men's loyalty was not in question, even though recent events might indicate otherwise. Regardless of Pavel Alek was certain that Stephan and his companion would not talk. However, with the combination of Pavel's car, the cash in the boot and whatever ID Pavel still had on him, Alek knew it wouldn't take the police long to make the connection with the bank.

Dimitri agreed that it was highly likely thar the police were soon going to be crawling all over the branch. That in conjunction with the other issues they had just experienced would mean at least a temporary suspension of the money laundering operation in Bratislava.

It was obvious that the two bank directors were now passengers in the unfolding drama, they sat dumb struck in front of their laptops. The last words that the listeners heard, were the two Kulkas brothers agreeing that they would offer Gregor Solonik and his friends a discounted service through the branches in Prague and Krakow.'

As Alek and Dimitri finished speaking, they shut their laptops and one by one the connections that Martin had open to the machines in the meeting room were lost.

It certainly looked like things had just taken a turn for the worse for John Covington and his confederates. They were now in the process of hot footing it to the airport to avoid possible police detention and the money laundering operation in Bratislava was in tatters.

Sean was sure when they got back to London and realised that they have no money to pay off their debts, they were going to welcome a vigorous hug from the long arms of the law. Leaving Ceri to get on with Digitising the funds, Sean terminated the conference call and he and Martin went back to bringing together their digital evidence folder.

That night work virtually completed, Martin was too tired to do anything other than wrap himself in a blanket and bed down on Anna's sofa. An equally exhausted Sean and Anna made their way to Anna's bedroom to share the large double bed. They didn't make love; they simply lay in each other arms enjoying the simple intimacy of being together and talked quietly about their future together.

'We just need to get through tomorrow babe and then you can fill out a request for a transfer back to London. The only problem we are going to have then, is persuading my dog Otto that three in a bedroom is one too many.'

'I'm sure Otto will understand if I talk to him nicely,' laughed Anna.

Kissing each other one last time, they closed their eyes and drifted off into a deep contented sleep in each other's arms. Getting some welcome rest before the busy day that lay ahead.

Chapter 38

The following morning a bleary eyed Martin left the apartment at 6am and headed for the train station. It had been agreed the previous night that he should return to Dublin via Vienna. There was nothing to be gained by taking a chance on he and Sean being seen together in Bratislava airport.

Besides Sean felt that there was a possibility that his trip back to Dublin could be subject to delay. He intended to call into the bank the next morning and if given the opportunity lay a bread crumb trail for the local forces of law and order in relation to the untimely demise of Pavel.

That morning when they awoke Sean and Anna had discussed how they should deal with the expected police presence at the branch. They had agreed that Anna should tell the police about Pavel's corporate customers and how he managed the cash office but say nothing else.

Sean had been more than happy for the opportunity to spend a little more time with Anna but to maintain his cover story they both agreed that it be best that he have breakfast in his hotel, so had headed there after he and Anna had finalised their plans.

After eating breakfast, during which he had done his best to be noticed by as many staff as possible, Sean went upstairs and had a quick shower. He dressed, ruffled the bed so that it appeared it had been slept in then went downstairs to pay his bill and checkout.

When he got to the bank at 9:30 there were two police cars parked in the street outside the front door and Sean had to show his bank

ID to gain entry. Obviously, the police had now linked the incident at the train station the previous evening to the bank.

Sean stepped through the door into the foyer, only to be immediately confronted by a uniformed police officer saying something in Slovakian. Even after spending three years living with Anna Sean couldn't speak much of the language, but he did know enough to say, 'I don't understand, do you speak English?'.

The police officer shook his head and called to one of his colleagues, who Sean hoped had a better grasp of English than he had of Slovakian. As they waited on the other officer striding towards them Sean felt a tug on his sleeve.

Sean turned to see Adela, Anna's friend who had introduced herself to him yesterday. 'Hello Sean, welcome back'.

'What's going on Adela? Why are the police here?', Sean asked innocently.

Adela explained that the bank manager Pavel, who Sean had been working with the previous day had been found dead. The police had also found a large sum of cash which they suspected had come from the bank with the body.

'My God Adela that is horrible, does Mr Covington know about this? is he here? I only called in this morning to see him.'

'No Mr Covington seems to have left yesterday evening, but Anna is here if you would like to say hello', said a smiling Adela.

'I would like that Adela, but I'm not sure how practical that would be with all this going on'. As Sean turned with a sweeping gesture to indicate the branch full of police, he realised that he had become an object of interest for two of those officers.

The second officer, who had just arrived was in plain clothes and spoke perfect English. He introduced himself as detective sergeant Johan Kovak working for the financial division of the national police force. He verified Sean's identity before starting to question him.

'I understand from what I heard your colleague say that you were working with the deceased yesterday?'

'To be precise I shared his office, the chief executive of the bank had asked me to come to the branch to investigate a possible security incident.'

At the words security incident detective Sergeant Kovac's ears pricked up. 'So, the bank was aware that money had been taken?'.

'No, not that type of incident, I am a cyber security specialist, my job is to prevent, or investigate unauthorised access to the banks IT systems. I had been asked to look at a potential breach of our systems which had allowed someone to steal money electronically.'

'So, the bank believed that something had been stolen?'

'I believe that is the case, although the chief executive never confirmed exactly how much might have been stolen, he just asked me to investigate how it could have happened.'

'So, are you back here to continue with your investigation?'

'No, I concluded my investigation yesterday and presented my findings to the chief executive, the finance director,a Mr Alek

Kulkas, and a fourth individual who I believe is called Dimitri Kulkas.'

'Can you tell me the conclusion that you presented yesterday?'

'I'm not sure that I can, the chief executive had been at pains to point out the highly confidential nature of my work here, I would need to ask his permission.'

'Mr Burke we are investigating the murder of someone who you were working with yesterday, as well as the discovery of a large sum of cash that may have come from the bank. If there is anything you can tell us which might help us, you are duty bound to do so.'

'Well officer Kovac, what I can tell you is that the source of the breach was Pavel Chenko's computer. After I confirmed that a heated argument started, and Alek Kulkas tried to grab Pavel.'

'So, this Alek Kulkas attacked Pavel?'

'No, he didn't exactly attack him, he tried to grab him and take his phone because of something he had seen on it and when Pavel ran out of the room he followed him.'

'So did he catch Pavel?'

'No, after two minutes he returned saying that Pavel had been too quick and had gotten away. I never saw Pavel again after that.'

'Can you remember anything else Mr Burke?'

'There is one final thing, I remember Alek Kulkas saying that he was going to send some of his team to Pavel's apartment to see if they could catch up with him there.'

'OK, so just to be clear, you heard this Alek Kulkas say that he was sending men to find Pavel at his apartment?'

'Yes, I am sure that is what he said.'

'Where is this Mr Kulkas now?'

'I thought that he would be here with Mr Covington our chief executive. I just called in this morning on the way to the airport to check if I could be of any further assistance.

After Pavel left all four of their machines were subject to a Ransomware attack demanding the equivalent to one million Euros. The attack appeared to have originated from Pavel's email address.'

The story which Sean was allowing to trickle out slowly had detective Sergeant Kovac hanging on every word. Sean could see that the police officer thought he had hit the jackpot.

'I'm very sorry Mr Burke, but I just want to be clear. Are you saying that yesterday afternoon Pavel Chenko was identified as the source of an IT security breach within the bank. Had an argument with senior members of the bank, which turned physical, and then tried to extort several million euros?

On top of that, one of these senior people, Alek Kulkas discussed sending people to Pavel's apartment. Do you not think that this would appear to be in any way suspicious?'

Sean made a show of considering what office Kovac had just said before agreeing that it certainly seemed suspicious. Especially given that the four people involved in the argument with Pavel seem to have left the country.

Detective Sergeant Kovac then enquired as to whether Sean had any idea of when the four men had left the bank the previous night. Conscious that he couldn't be seen to know all the finer detail, Sean suggested that Anna the assistant manager would be able to give him access to the banks CCTV and access control system.

Sean firmly believed that both systems should allow the police to gauge when they left. On a roll and apparently now in a mood to do everything possible to help the forces of law and order Sean also let slip that he was aware of another CCTV system used to cover activity in the rear of bank.

Sean made it clear that he felt it his civic duty under the circumstances to get officer Kovac access to that system also. After all someone had died and the more information the police had the better.

Sean buzzed with excitement. Not only were the four protagonists in the shit with Gregor Solonik and his associates, but he suspected the Slovakian police would soon have a keen interest in their activities.

As Sean's mind wondered down the happy path of victory, Officer Kovac gestured for one of his colleagues to come over. The more junior officer with a grasp of English every bit as good as detective sergeant Kovacs started to take Sean's statement.

Sean was keen to finish what he had started with Officer Kovac but was also conscious that he still had a lot to do and explained that he had a flight back to Dublin in four hours. Officer Kovac was at pains to put the font of knowledge that had dropped serendipitously into his lap at ease. So reassured Sean that he would be on his way in an hour or so, once the statement had been signed and access to all CCTV systems had been organised.

Sean gave his statement and spent the next hour whilst waiting on it being typed up, working with Anna in her office. Together they had helped the police to extract useful CCTV images from the previous evening.

Sean had also had the time to provide one of detective sergeant Kovac's fellow officers with access to Pavel's private CCTV system. Leaving him to trawl through the images from the previous afternoon and evening. He was sitting quietly having a coffee with Anna when a beaming officer Kovac walked into the office carrying several sheets of typed paper.

'We are very grateful for the CCTV footage which you have given us access to. The images from the system in Pavel's office were most enlightening. We were able to see the chase that you described, and the return of the man who we assume is Alek Kulkas. Would it be possible for you to give me five minutes just so you can verify his identity?'

Sean happily obliged and followed the obviously excited officer as he spun on his heel and bounced out of the office. As they walked towards Pavel's office, officer Kovac took the opportunity to update Sean on what they had found.

'My colleague took the liberty of reviewing footage from several days. He has identified a number of individuals entering the bank through the rear door, who shall we say, would be people of interest. We are wondering if these are the special corporate customers that the assistant manager has told us Pavel dealt with.

Did you hear any mention of a man called Gregor Solonik at any time?'

Sean paused giving the impression of being in deep thought, 'I believe that name was used during the argument, I think I remember Alek Kulkas using the name and questioning Pavel's loyalty.'

'Thank you, Mr Burke, now if you can confirm the identity of Alek Kulkas on the CCTV image we have and sign your statement you can be on your way to the airport.'

'I am happy that I could be of assistance officer Kovac, perhaps you could provide me with your card, just in case I remember anything else. I can contact you by telephone or email, you never know what I might remember.'

Leaving Pavel's office having confirmed Alek Kulkas's identity and signed his statement, Sean placed officer Kovacs card carefully in his wallet.

Sean smiled; it had indeed been a very useful morning. The information he, Martin and Ceri had been preparing would no doubt result in an investigation in the UK by the National Crime agency.

What he had just told detective sergeant Kovac and the footage he would provide him with anonymously could well result in an additional investigation by Interpol. The people in the bank who had broken the trust placed in them and the Kulkas brothers couldn't even begin to imagine the tsunami of shit about to envelop them.

Before leaving the bank and heading to the airport, Sean said his last farewell to Anna, enfolding her in his arms and kissing her passionately in the privacy of her office. 'I'll be back for you once this has all been resolved in the meantime just know that I love you.'

'I love you too Sean, please be careful and don't take any chances, I don't want to lose you again.'

As Sean walked out of the bank, he waved at officer Kovac who nodded in acknowledgement, before turning to direct the efforts of his team in their quest for further evidence.

Chapter 39

While Sean had been doing his best in the branch in Bratislava to further incriminate them, John Covington, Trevor Reid and the Kulkas brothers had been having a very unpleasant phone call with Gregor Solonik.

When they returned to London, Richard Head had successfully restored the machines for John Covington and Trevor Reid, from backups that they had taken several days prior to their trip to Bratislava. Alek and Dimitri using one of their own team, had been able to do the same.

However, no amount of restores were going to replace the money that they all now found had disappeared from their bank accounts. They had been sick to their stomachs when they realised that they no longer had the means to repay Gregor Solonik and his compatriots in crime.

Gregor had been less than sympathetic when they had explained the situation, and they had been left in no doubt that he didn't care that it been a Russian Cyber gang who had stolen his money. Gregor had been amazingly calm and his voice barely raised above a sibilant whisper as he reminded them of their financial responsibilities. In short he wanted his money back and if the money was not forthcoming, then they and their families would suffer a bloody retribution.

Even offering Gregor use of the Prague and Krakow branches to launder his money at no cost didn't calm the situation. If anything, it had turned Gregor into an angry bellowing bull, who ended the conversation ranting incoherently down the phone in Ukrainian. Even if they couldn't understand the words, John Covington and

Trevor Reid were left in no doubt about the sentiment behind his thunderous rage.

With the conference call over the four men sat in Silence in John Covington's office contemplating their next steps. The silence was broken by Trevor Reid's mobile ringing. Trevor answered grateful for the momentary distraction from the perilous situation that he now found himself in.

'Hello Steven, do you have news for me on the bank transfer file?'

There was silence as Trevor listened intently to what he was being told. He made a few brief scribbled note as he listened, then he hung up the phone and looked at John Covington in puzzled silence. A frightened, petulant and as a consequence impatient John Covington was in no mood to be kept waiting.

'Well Trevor don't keep us in suspense, I'm not sure if my blood pressure can take any more excitement, what do your guys have to say?'

'The missing money was transferred to an account in the Cayman Islands in this bank.' He pushed the scrap of paper across the table so John Covington could see what he had written. Getting no response apart from a blank stare from the chief executive, Trevor spoke slowly.

'The bank account that all our funds were transferred to is with our bank in the Caymans. It's the same account that was used to empty our own personal accounts.'

John Covington could only stare at his finance director in shock.

How the hell did that happen?'

'That's a very good question John. Steven asked the IT team that exact question, and apparently the audit records on the system indicate that you changed the bank details against the accounts for Gregor Solonik and the other gentlemen that we have been providing a service for.'

John Covington sat back in his chair in shock as three pairs of eyes turned in his direction.

'That's absolute nonsense, why would I have done that?'

'According to Steven, they have been able to identify the owner of the recipient bank. They restored the bank file that had been lost and the name against the outgoing transfers is Iryna Kulkas. Your wife…'

John Covington's face reddened at the implication of what Trevor had just said, he spluttered an indignant response to his finance director.

'Now hold on are you trying to say that I stole the money and that my wife is somehow involved, that is absolute bollox Trevor. I have every bit as much to lose as anyone sitting here as a result of this situation. That doesn't make any sense.'

Dimitri Kulkas who had been sitting quietly listening to the exchange spoke softly, but with authority.

'Gentlemen I think as you English say we have been led up the garden path. It is obvious that someone with a deep knowledge of the banks IT systems has set this up. I do not believe that my sister and John would do this.

Perhaps Ms Gillis who we have so carelessly ignored has taken advantage of our inattention and is now enjoying the benefit of our hard-earned cash.

Might I suggest John that you contact your bank in the Cayman Islands and speak to your bank manager. I am sure he will be only too willing to help, when you explain how his bank has been implicated in the fraudulent appropriation of millions of euros.'

John Covington retrieved his mobile from his jacket pocket, selected the personal contact details for Julian Besoin at the Grand Cayman Investment Bank and dialled.

'Julian hello, John Covington here; I have a situation that I need your help with. It would appear that money has been taken without permission from the accounts of Trevor Reid and myself.'

A fuzzy headed Julian, who had just been awoken from his night's sleep was in no mood to accept that any such situation had occurred.

'I can assure you John that the security at our bank would not allow this to happen.'

John Covington was equally adamant in his response.

'Julian, I have the account details for the account that the money was transferred to. It's in the name of Iryna Kulkas, and I can assure you I did not authorise the transfer.'

There was silence as Julian Besoin absorbed what he had just been told before he started to speak again just a little hesitantly.

'That name is familiar I have to admit, she opened an account with us last week, she was apparently helping her husband to restructure his finances.'

'Julian Iryna Kulkas is my wife's maiden name, and I can assure you she was here in London all of last week. This person whoever she is, has stolen money not only from your bank, but also from mine.

We need to work together to resolve this issue, before both our banks suffer reputational damage for allowing such a theft to happen. Could you describe what this woman looked like?'

'John it is highly irregular, I will review what you have told me and come back to you once I have been to the bank.'

With the call with Julian terminated, Dimitri gave his analysis of the situation.

'Whoever has stolen this money has tried to be too clever by half. Not only have they tried to implicate you John in an obvious way, but they have also made the mistake of trying to implicate our sister.

That also raises questions over whether the situation with Pavel might not have been as it appeared. We already knew of his relationship with Gregor Solonik and it suited us to over look it. So why did we suddenly decide that he suddenly couldn't be trusted?'

John Covington couldn't hide his impatience with Dimitri's nonsensical questions, and he practically spat out his answer .

'That's obvious Dimitri, because Sean showed us evidence of Pavel's involvement, evidence that Pavel couldn't deny.'

Dimitri's spoke slowly his words dripping with sarcasm.

'Yes John, just like the irrefutable evidence that you changed the bank account details to send all our money to a new account that had been opened for Iryna.'

Dimitri paused, the implications of what he had just said hitting home.

'Were we perhaps too swift to accuse Pavel, and is there any possibility that Pavel was correct about Sean Burke after all?

Was Pavel sacrificed in order to protect Mr Burke?'

John Covington's was a man on the verge of panic who was seeing his whole world about to come apart at the seams and couldn't bring himself to believe it was happening. His voice was a miserable whisper.

'Alek had his passport number checked Dimitri and he couldn't have been in Bratislava when Pavel said he was there.'

Dimitri ignored the pathetic soon to be former chief executive and snarled at his brother.

'Alek might I suggest that you have another check carried out, and perhaps this time could we be more thorough. Do a name search and carry out a check on his bank cards.

If Ms Gillis is involved in this, she had some help from within the bank, and right now Mr Sean Burke might well have been the person to help her. A human trojan horse, a man on the inside, someone who we trusted, someone who may have betrayed our trust.'

As Dimitri finished speaking the ring tone on John Covington's mobile phone kicked in, John accepted the call and put the mobile onto speaker. 'Hello Julian, what information do you have for us?'

'Mr Covington, I can confirm that there were five transfers into Iryna Kulkas's account yesterday. One from your account, one from Trevor Reid's account and three from international accounts totalling approximately 84 million euros. There was also a large transfer of over 80 million euros the previous day.'

All four men looked at each other, they all knew that they had lied to each other about how much money had been in their accounts. But were all too excited that they had traced the money to voice it.

John's voice was strident as he made his demand.

'Julian you must freeze that account, the funds transferred need to be returned to the accounts from which they were sent.'

Julian's no nonsense reply didn't do anything to sooth John Covington's jangling nerves.

'I'm sorry Mr Covington, but that will not be possible.'

An angry John Covington seethed at what he saw as Julian's complete disregard for a totally reasonable request.

'Julian don't give us any of that client privilege crap, that money was stolen and needs to be returned to its rightful owners.'

Julian's response was diplomatic and very much to the point.

'That is not what I meant Mr Covington, the Iryna Kulkas account is now empty. All money was transferred out of it over the last two days to other accounts in the Cayman Islands in the name of Iryna Kulkas. Accounts to which I don't have any access.

I have no doubt if what you say is true, that those accounts also will have been emptied in order to hide the stolen funds.

What I can give you is a copy of the identification document that she used to open the account with our bank. I will email it to you now, but I am afraid there is nothing more I can do to help you.'

A deflated John Covington hung up his mobile without so much as a thanks and turned to look at his similarly troubled brothers in crime.

Only Dimitri spoke.

'Alek have that check on Sean Burke carried out now. If we find that he is not as innocent as you thought, then he is our only definite connection to Ceri Gillis and our money. Where is he now?'

'He told me yesterday evening that he was flying back to Dublin today to continue his holiday with his mother. I will have HR dig out his mother's address, I'm sure she will be on his file as next of kin.

He also had a relationship with the assistant manager in our Bratislava branch and from speaking with him yesterday they are still very much friends.'

'Excellent John, once you have the mothers address, we will have some of our men stake out Dublin airport and his mother's home and await his return.

We will also have some of our colleagues in Bratislava call on his girlfriend. Now can you check your email so we can see what this person pretending to be our sister looks like.'

John Covington went to his recovered laptop and clicked on the email that had just appeared at the top of his inbox. The picture that appeared was very definitely not Iryna Kulkas but bore a striking resemblance to Ceri Gillis. As John Covington looked up from reviewing the picture his three companions were staring at him expectantly.

'It's Ceri Gillis, that bitch has taken our money, and put us all in danger.'

The fact that the tables had been turned was totally lost on them. They had opened Pandora's box and were now suffering the consequences. But as far as they were concerned it was all someone else's fault and someone else was going to be made to pay.

Chapter 40

Not that Ceri and Martin who had been watching the entire episode felt much like gloating. From feeling totally secure only an hour previously, they now felt very vulnerable.

Martin reacted first, he picked up his encrypted mobile and dialled Sean's number, hoping that he hadn't already boarded his flight. To his relief Sean answered immediately.

'Sean, we have a problem.'

Martin explained to Sean what he and Ceri had just observed.

'You need to get Anna and find another route for you both back to Ireland. They are going to be waiting on you at Dublin airport and they are planning a visit to Anna's, just in case you might be there.'

Sean immediately hung up the phone and rang Anna. He kept his voice calm even though his heart was in his throat.

'Anna are you still in the branch?'

'Yes, the police are still here asking questions and I can't lock up until they leave.'

'Do you have your National identity card with you?'

'Of course, I never go anywhere without it.'

'Give your keys to your friend Adele, and meet me at the train station, get a taxi, don't walk and don't delay, make whatever excuse you have to, but leave now. I'll explain everything when we meet. Do you understand? leave right now.'

With Anna affirming that she was leaving right then, Sean hung up his mobile and made his way back through airport security and made his way to the taxi rank.

20 minutes later, after getting out of the taxi at Hlavna station in the centre of Bratislava. He found Anna wondering around the concourse of the station, she wasn't hard to spot still wearing her bank uniform.

That's the first thing we have to sort he thought. He walked up to Anna and tapped her gently on the shoulder. Anna spun round a smile lighting up her face on seeing Sean before speaking in a concerned voice.

'Sean, what's this all about, shouldn't you be on plane back to Dublin?'

'Well that was the plan, but real life has just gotten in the way of that.' He then told her everything that Martin had told him and waited for the fireworks to start flying. But instead, she calmly said, 'so what do you think we should do now.'

Sean felt relief at how well Anna took the news and couldn't help being slightly flirtatious in his response.

'Well the first thing we do is get you out of those clothes.'

Anna smiled coquettishly, before responding with a laugh.

'Sean there is a time and place for everything, and this is neither the time nor place for that.'

Sean laughed back, 'no we need to get you different clothes.'

Fishing in his ruck sack Sean peeled a few notes off the bundle of 100 euro notes that he had kept from his previous visit to Bratislava and handed them to Anna.

'Get yourself some jeans and things in those shops and bin the uniform. I'm going to get us a couple of tickets to Vienna, then I'm going to phone Ceri and Martin. I'll meet you back here in 20 minutes.'

As Anna walked towards the shops that edged the concourse Sean made his way to the ticket Kiosk where he bought two singles to Vienna, then he rang Martin.

'Martin I am with Anna, we are heading to Vienna shortly by train. Once we get there, I am going to get us back to London by train and the channel tunnel, its probably going to take us the rest of today and tomorrow.

If they are tracking my passport as you say they should be waiting patiently on me at Dublin airport. I had checked in and had been about to board just before you rang me. It'll be a bit of a surprise when I don't turn up.

It might be a good idea if you guys got yourselves back from Ireland if that's where they currently have their beady eyes focussed. We will meet up with you in London.'

There was a hint of concern in Martin's voice when he acknowledged Sean's plans.

'You be careful big man; Ceri and I will find a safe place for us all in London. Take it easy and we will see you soon.'

Five minutes later, Anna came walking across the concourse looking very trim, in a well fitted pair of Jeans, light blue blouse and a short green jacket. Smiling she linked her arm into the crook of Sean's elbow and looking up at him said, 'lets go.'

The train journey to Vienna was uneventful, but Sean was tense, he wasn't far enough away from Bratislava for him to relax just yet. The journey from Vienna to London was a much more relaxed affair. The journey took them through Austria, Germany and France. They stopped in Salzburg where Sean couldn't help bursting into a rather tuneless rendition of "The hills are alive with the sound of music", much to Anna's amusement.

They chatted endlessly as the train journey took them through, Munich, Stuttgart and then Paris. As the train was pulling out of Gare Du Nord Sean had an almost overpowering impulse to get down on one knee and propose. However good sense prevailed, and he decided that perhaps a more romantic trip which actually involved a stay in Paris and an actual ring might be a better time to ask that particular question.

Eventually more than 22 hours after leaving Vienna their train pulled into Saint Pancras station, at just after six thirty in the evening. Sean rang Martin who provided him with the address of an apartment in Chelsea that Ceri had borrowed from one of her well-heeled friends.

Sean and Anna took a tube and arrived at the apartment just under an hour after arriving in London. Ceri had prepared something what smelt like chilli , but looked suspiciously like something Otto had expelled from his bowel after a particularly bad stomach upset.

Nonetheless, hungry after their long journey, Sean and Anna gratefully accepted the food offered, though Sean wasn't so grateful for the heart burn it subsequently produced. Much to his great surprise Ceri and Anna got on like a house on fire over dinner. He was amazed at how they found so many things to talk about, hardly even needing time to take a breath.

The girls were obviously busy, so he and Martin reluctantly cleared the table and set about doing the dishes. Leaving the girls to chat and pour themselves another glass of wine. Dishes sorted, Sean and Martin sat back down at the table. After all things had taken an unexpected turn and they needed a council of war to consider how to proceed.

After apologizing to the girls for breaking up their party Martin and Sean both set their laptops up on the kitchen table, there was still a lot of work to be done. Whilst the crime busting quartet were discussing the package of evidence that they were going to be sending to the National Crime Agency, John Covington, Trevor Reid and the Kulkas brothers were in the middle of a heated conference call.

The additional trace that they had initiated on Sean, had indeed shown up a person of that name, traveling on an Irish passport flying into Vienna the morning that the bank had been robbed. The additional checks on his bank card had shown various purchases, including an overnight stay in a Bratislava hotel on the same day that he flew into Vienna.

Whilst the trace was being carried out, John Covington had asked Richard Head to have a chat with Sean's colleagues on the security team. What he had reported back had left no doubt that Sean was indeed involved.

Some of Sean's team had called around to Sean's house on the previous Saturday, hoping to take the hard drinking Irish man out for a night's craic. Sean hadn't been there, but they had bumped into his neighbour who was minding his dog. She had told them that Sean had left that day, to go to Bratislava to try and patch things up with Anna. The same Anna who according to their men in Bratislava had left the bank early the previous day and had now disappeared.

Sure that they had found the evidence that they needed to tie Sean to their current misfortune they waited with impatience on Sean's arrival into Dublin airport. When the flight from Bratislava that Sean had checked in on had arrived with no sign of their target, things started to get a little bit anxious for the four men who were now firmly in the sights of Gregor Solonik.

Hoping that Sean had simply been missed in the crowd at the airport, attention had then turned to Sean's mother's home, but 24 hours later there had still been no sign of their person of interest. That however had all changed an hour earlier when they had been contacted and informed that monitoring that had been placed on Sean's passports showed that his UK passport had been checked at Saint Pancras station in London.

Right now an argument raged over what they needed to do next. They all agreed that Sean must be aware that they had discovered his deception. Why else did he abandon a perfectly good flight to Dublin and take a long train journey back to London.

What wasn't so obvious was his current location, was he at home, or was he staying somewhere else. Eventually they agreed that the only thing they could do, was to send a team to Sean's home to either find him or find evidence of where he might be.

Chapter 41

Sean, Martin, Ceri and Anna had been busily reviewing the results of their endeavours. Ceri had made great progress in digitising all of the money that had been taken from the various bank accounts. She had also been busy creating an archive filled with bank statements and shell company documentation. This would be a damming body of evidence that could be used by the National Crime Agency in their pursuit of the financial mafia running the credit finance bank.

Sean's analysis of the data that had been extracted from the bank's systems , details of all suspicious accounts and of the electronic smurfing process that had been used to create then was in yet another archive. This archive also held a spreadsheet and text file, which Martin had extracted from the disk copy of the Bratislava Cash Room PC. This spreadsheet held a ledger showing the deposits made by various individuals. Martin had realised that the 4 digit codes used to identify the owners of the lodgements were the same codes that he had noticed on the cash bags they had borrowed during their first visit to Bratislava.

After a little digging, he had discovered another encrypted file, which had tied up the codes to specific names. Names which included Gregor Solonik. Finally, Martin had done a magnificent job of creating a video and audio montage of all suspicious activity that they had managed to record. This included material captured through their own covert cameras as well as the video and audio devices on the four laptops that they had compromised. The last fraught telephone call with Gregor Solonik had also managed to make it into Martin's greatest hits selection.

Martin compressed each of the archives in preparation for sending from an anonymous email address. They were sure that the National Crime Agency, and the bank's regulators were going to be very interested in the copious amount of incriminating information that was being provided.

Just as Martin was about to send the archives Sean's mobile starting pinging an alert. Sean removed the mobile from his pocket and glanced at the screen, the ghost of a smile visible at the corners of his mouth.

'I was wondering how long they were going to take to get around to this. Looks like Alek's boys are paying me a visit.'

Opening the surveillance App on his laptop, Sean cycled through the footage from the hidden cameras that he had installed on Martin's advice. He saw three armed men, one of them obviously Olek, ransacking his home.

Borrowing the burner phone from Martin he made a 999 call to the police. In a panicked voice he told the police that he had seen three armed men enter a house, and it sounded like they were attacking the inhabitant. He gave his home address and before hanging up shouted hysterically, 'Hurry I think they are killing him.'

'The flag that my mate Andy put on my address should ensure a quick response, we'll be a lot safer if a few more of the Kulkas's armed goons are taken off the street.

There is one last thing we need to do Martin, once you have emailed those archives. Can you put the footage that we recorded from inside Pavel's office and the footage that we recorded from the laptops the night Pavel died in a fresh archive?'

'Sure can, but why?'

'There is a detective Kovac in Bratislava who's email address is on this card, that would be only too pleased to receive some anonymous footage to back up some theories that he developed yesterday', Sean answered with a smile.

'Well Ceri, I think between us, we've done enough to put John, Trevor and the Kulkas brothers away for a long time, not so sure about Dimitri though.'

'Aye Sean, but what about Richard Head and Magda Harte , there is little if anything in what we've gathered to incriminate them.'

'I think Richard was just a dupe, John Covington brought him as someone who would ask no questions and do exactly what he was told. I'm not sure that he knew what exactly was going on. What I am sure of is that he will lose his job at the bank when I complete my investigation into the incident in Bratislava and hand what's left of the board my report.

I think Magda Harte was just a sister being used by her brother to control the board and make sure things weren't questioned in a meaningful way. A board chaired by a sibling is not going to properly hold a chief executive to account. Once the Financial Conduct Authority review our archives, she won't be sitting in her big seat for much longer.

As for Dimitri, he is not an honest man, but I think he is a smart man who has been only too happy to take a back seat whilst his younger brother does all the running. I have a feeling that he will be able to wriggle his way out of any legal shenanigans by putting the blame for everything on Alek.

However, I'm not so sure that he is going to find things too comfortable with Gregor Solonik gunning for the family. He might find it safer to join his brother in prison, though that might depend on whether the institution in question is here or in Slovakia.'

Martin nodded in agreement, but appeared pensive , he obviously had something else on his mind.

'Now that I've emailed the evidence, what are we going to do about the money Ceri? We can't just email that to the national crime agency or the Financial conduct authority.'

Ceri appeared totally unconcerned.

'Don't worry Martin I have the 104 million in a digital wallet on an encrypted thumb drive and we can deliver it by courier to the NCA in the morning. We also have around two hundred thousand euros in cash which I would suggest that we keep to cover our expenses.'

A look of surprise crossed Sean's face.

'Hold on Ceri, you just said there was 104 million in the digital wallet that we are going to give to the NCA. I thought that with the Kulkas money we had around 164 million?'

'We do Sean, the evidence we have provided will allow the authorities to identify the 104 million we are giving them as proceeds of crime and will allow them to confiscate the money.

The sixty million we took from the Kulkas accounts isn't just so clear cut, which could result in the money being given back.

We know that the money we took from the Kulkas brothers was gained through criminal activity and we know they are bad people. Why should we take the chance that it will be given back to them?'

Sean interrupted her angrily, 'Just because we have been dealing with corrupt money grabbing assholes over the last few weeks doesn't mean we should be like them.'

Anna slid her arm round Sean's waist and placed her other hand on his now clenched fist. 'Sean is right we would be no better than them if we simply take that money.'

Ceri took four thumb drives out of her pocket, 'I think you misunderstand what I am trying to say. I have created an offline digital wallet for each of us with the equivalent of one million euro in each. The fourth contains 57 million Euro.

We will be making an anonymous donation to the anti-slavery charity that my brother works for. We can't give the money back to the people who it was taken from, but we can do the next best thing.

As for your own personal thumb drive, you can each decide what you do with yours, but I'll be keeping mine.'

Sean reluctantly lifted the thumb drive that had been placed in front of him and looked at Anna.

'For now, we wait and see what comes of the seeds we have planted tonight, as the saying goes, the wheels of justice grind slowly. let's hope it's not so slowly that the rats escape the trap. Then perhaps we will decide what we do with these.'

Having already pocketed his drive, Martin was sitting staring excitedly at Sean's laptop screen.

'Guys looks like the boys in blue have arrived at Sean's house.'

They all turned in time to hear a crash emanating from the speaker on the laptop as a policeman in body armour was getting medieval on Sean's front door with what they assumed was a battering ram. The three men that they could see on camera were panicking as they realised, they were about to have visitors. Visitors who were better armed than they were.

After a few seconds there was a bang and a blinding flash on the screen as a flash bang was thrown through the front door which now hung sadly off its hinges. Seconds later shouts of 'Armed Police' could be heard as the boys in blue, or rather the boys in black body armour entered the house.

Sean and his companions stood staring at the screen enthralled by what was currently happening in front of their eyes. They heard several shots, which sounded like they came from the interior of the house probably from a handgun. These were followed by the staccato burst of a heavier automatic weapon as the police returned fire. Then everything on the screen was bedlam as the house was invaded by what seemed like a horde of black suited men bearing automatic weapons.

They continued to watch as two struggling men were dragged out of the house in hand cuffs. The screen suddenly became very bright as someone turned on the lights, obviously the operation was over. They were starting to wonder what had happened to the other intruder when they saw two paramedics rush past one of the cameras.

Was it an injured police officer or the third man? they couldn't be sure. That was until they saw the two paramedics come back past the camera carrying a stretcher. The stretcher held Olek, obviously still alive, but he didn't look in great shape, with a large dressing tinged with red strapped to his chest.

That night at the end of the news it was confirmed that three men had been detained by an armed response team from Kent police. There had been a brief exchange of gunfire in which one of the men currently being detained had been seriously wounded. There was a brief piece of camera footage with the story in which Sean saw his neighbour Mary standing with Otto apparently speaking to a police officer.

Sean looked at Anna, 'I think we'll be paying a visit to the police station in Sevenoaks in the next few days. I'm sure the police are going to have a few questions for us.'

Chapter 42

Sometimes the wheels of justice do turn slowly, but not on this occasion. The car that had transported Olek and his companions to Sean's house had been registered against Odessa Capital Investments in London.

When the three were processed at the police station and their fingerprints taken it turned out that there were outstanding international warrants for them. They were wanted in Ukraine, Poland and Hungary for murder, conspiracy to murder, human trafficking, and financial crimes.

It also turned out that Olek was actually called Uri Kumarin and was a high-ranking member of a Ukrainian Mafia organisation. When these things were combined with the mass of information that had just been received by the National Crime Agency. Information which implicated both Dimitri and Alek Kulkas in an international money laundering conspiracy, as well as a murder in Bratislava. The normally clunky wheels of justice started to turn with well-oiled precision.

The next day John Covington and Trevor Reid were arrested at the headquarters of Credit Finance bank. They had all watched through the covert cameras that were still in operation in the two offices. It appeared to them that the two men almost looked relieved as the hand cuffs were put on their wrists and they were led away to the comfort and security of one of her Majesty's holiday camps.

Unfortunately, they didn't have such a ring side view of the arrest of Dimitri and Alek Kulkas. They had been taken into custody as they attempted to board a flight to Florida, no doubt hoping to put as much distance between themselves and Gregor Solonik as possible.

The news said, that they had been arrested under an international arrest warrant issued by Interpol for charges of conspiracy to murder and international money laundering.

Whilst the Kulkas brothers were being arrested at Heathrow a padded envelope containing an encrypted thumb drive with a digital wallet holding 104 million euro was delivered to the NCA offices

Shortly afterwards the encryption key for the drive was emailed to the NCA, from the same anonymous email address that had been used to deliver the initial packages of evidence.

That very same day both the Prague and Krakow branches of the Credit Finance Bank were raided by local police, who had been tipped off about suspected money laundering activities taking place in both branches. Camera footage provided to the authorities had shown large volumes of cash being delivered to both locations by known members of organised crime groups.

The next day the Financial Conduct Authority and the Prudential Regulation Authority had requested the presence of all remaining members of the board of Credit Finance bank to attend a meeting. During that meeting the regulators had instructed the bank to cease all further operations in eastern Europe. They also indicated that they had found the control operated by the board to be totally inadequate. As a result, they expected the chair of the board to resign immediately and for the vice chairman to step temporarily into that role.

The role was temporary as far as they were concerned. Issues had been highlighted within the management of the bank that could severely impact the public's perception of the banking system. To protect the national banking system the banks operation would be merged with that of a bank untainted by the stories that were currently appearing in the national and international media.

The regulators explained that they expected the board to whole heartedly embrace the merger. To do otherwise may well result in enforcement which could place a legal and financial burden upon all remaining Directors.

Sean and Anna returned to Sevenoaks the day after his house had been invaded. They had been met by a police officer as they walked up to the garden gate. Down at the station they explained about Sean's trip to Bratislava to review a security issue at the banks branch.

They also smiled lovingly at each other as they told the disinterested detective who was taking notes about how they had rekindled their love and about how Anna had agreed to come home with Sean. They explained that they had spent an evening with friends in London after taking a romantic train journey home to allow them to reconnect.

When asked why armed men would possibly have been at his house, Sean paused seemingly deep in thought before responding.

'Well it's obviously something to do with what happened in Bratislava. I uncovered a data breach which had resulted in the bank losing a lot of money. From what Detective Sergeant Kovac told me in Bratislava two men Dimitri and Alek Kulkas may well have been involved in the murder of one of our bank staff.

It was my intention to provide a report on the incident to the board of the bank. So perhaps these men were sent to stop that from happening.'

Sean then produced Detective Sergeant Kovac's card and suggested that the detective contact him for corroboration of what had just been said. Sean and Anna were asked to wait outside whilst the detective did just that. Ten minutes later the detective stepped into the corridor shook both their hands and told them they were both free to leave.

Back home again in Sevenoaks an overjoyed Mary threw her arms round Anna, welcoming her back, whilst a very excited Otto couldn't decide whether to lick Sean's face or pee on his shoes, so just did both.

The police had resecured Sean's door after completing their forensic investigation and provided him with a new set of keys. When he and Anna entered the house with Otto, it was a mess. It was like a small tornado had spent itself in emptying the contents of all cupboards and drawers all over the house.

Whilst Anna set about bringing some sense of normality back to the scene of devastation that surrounded them, Sean completed his report on the security breach in Bratislava. He included his observations on the breaches in policy and procedures that had been requested by John Covington and sanctioned and implemented by Richard Head. He then emailed this to all remaining members of the board.

As Sean expected, Richard Head quickly followed Magda Harte out of the door of the banks board room. But as has been the case from ancient times, the bearer of bad news isn't often received well, and Sean was no exception.

The acting chairman of the board emailed Sean his thanks and in the same email informed him that the bank would be terminating his employment. He would receive a year's salary and would be expected to sign a compromise agreement which included a non-disclosure clause preventing him from talking to the press about anything that had happened.

'So much for not shooting the messenger!' was Anna's angry response when she heard the news.

Sean was sanguine as he put a comforting arm around Anna's shoulders.

'Looks like neither of us have a job anymore Anna, let's look on the bright side we can use this time we have been given to get to know each other again and plan our wedding.'

The sensible and direct Anna that Sean knew and loved just couldn't stop itself from surfacing, it was obvious that Anna was concerned about their current employment situation.

'Sean but how can we get married, we have no jobs, how can we support ourselves?'

Sean gently grasped Anna by both shoulders and looked gently into her beautiful blue eyes and whispered gently.

'Anna I will be getting a year's Salary from the bank, you will have redundancy and let's not forget this.' Sean took the thumb drive out of his pocket.

Over the next week the news was filled with experts discussing the case. It was only when an official police briefing was held that Sean felt comfortable. Apparently there had been an ongoing investigation into an international money laundering operation. The investigation had involved undercover operatives who had gathered video and audio evidence, implicating high ranking bank officials and key members of a crime syndicate.

These individuals had now been arrested and were currently actively helping police with their enquiries.

Sean gave a sign of relief.

'Looks like we are off the hook, the police have taken the credit for all the information we provided them with.

So no matter what our villainous quartet might believe, Gregor Solonik and his compatriots will think that they have been taken down by a police operation.

An operation which now has active help from the Kulkas brothers. I think we should all be able to relax just a little now. Dimitri and Alek will most definitely not be on Gregor's Christmas list.'

That evening, as Sean and Anna sat on the couch holding hands and drinking a celebratory glass of wine they heard a knock at the front door. Sean walked down the hall accompanied by Otto, who obviously was interested to see who could be calling at that time of night. Sean opened the door to find Ceri and Martin both standing in his porch. Martin Carrying two pizza boxes and Ceri holding a bottle of Prosecco in each hand.

'Martin and I have a proposition for you, and we thought some food and drink might help with the conversation.'

Ceri confirmed that she too had been let go by the bank's board and had been into London that day to sign the compromise agreement drawn up by the bank's solicitor. Like Sean she was now free to do something else.

'The job that we started with the bank is not even half finished.'

Talking round a mouthful of pepperoni pizza Martin explained what Ceri meant.

'The data that we extracted from the two PCs in Bratislava and the keyloggers from Prague and Krakow have allowed me to piece together the details of 20 individuals. Criminals who were and still are benefitting from the suffering of others.

Between us we have the skills and the money to help set things right.'

Ceri looked at Sean.

'Martin and I both know your conscience was troubling you when you took that thumb drive.

What we're proposing is that we all put that money to good use and set up an IT security company that helps legitimate organisations against these criminals.

Not only that but we take it one step further and actively target individuals within these criminal organisations and take away the thing that gives them power, their money.

We already have the list of 20 people that Martin has come up with. My brother's charity and a few others like it could certainly use the money. What do you think Sean?'

Sean looked at Anna who smiled and gently nodded her head, before lifting one of the bottles of prosecco and filling all four glasses.

Lifting his glass Sean looked round the three people in the room. Anna the love of his life, the woman that he wanted to marry and have kids with. A woman who had trusted him completely when he had told her about what was going on in the bank.

Ceri a person who only three weeks ago he had detested with a passion, but someone who he now understood and had a grudging respect for.

And last but by no means least Martin. A short man with a big appetite, who looked out for his friends no matter what the danger was to him. Martin was a man who he had quickly grown to trust completely during the adventures that they had shared.

A smiling Sean raised his glass.

'Let's drink to our new enterprise "Total Trust security", and let's try and make our next job a little less exciting, my walls still have bullet holes from the last one.'

Printed in Great Britain
by Amazon